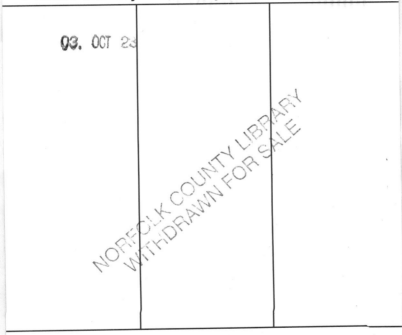

The Light of Day

GRAHAM SWIFT was born in 1949 and is the author of eight acclaimed novels and a collection of short stories; his most recent work is *Making an Elephant*, a book of essays, portraits, poetry and reflections on his life in writing. With *Waterland* he won the *Guardian* Fiction Prize (1983), and with *Last Orders* the Booker Prize (1996). Both novels have since been made into films. Graham Swift's work has appeared in over thirty languages.

GRAHAM SWIFT

THE LIGHT OF DAY

PICADOR

First published 2003 by Hamish Hamilton

First published in paperback 2004 by Penguin Books

First published by Picador 2011
an imprint of Pan Macmillan, a division of Macmillan Publishers Limited
Pan Macmillan, 20 New Wharf Road, London N1 9RR
Basingstoke and Oxford
Associated companies throughout the world
www.panmacmillan.com

ISBN 978-1-4472-0111-3

1 3 5 7 9 8 6 4 2

A CIP catalogue record for this book is available from
the British Library.

Typeset by SetSystems Ltd, Saffron Walden, Essex
Printed in the UK by CPI Mackays, Chatham ME5 8TD

For Candice

All's fair in love and war

1997

1

'SOMETHING'S COME OVER YOU.' That's what Rita said, over two years ago now, and now she knows it wasn't just a thing of the moment.

Something happens. We cross a line, we open a door we never knew was there. It might never have happened, we might never have known. Most of life, maybe, is only time served.

Morning traffic in Wimbledon Broadway. Exhausts steaming. I turn the key in the street door, my own breath coming in clouds.

'Something's come over you, George.'

But she knew even before I did. She's not in this job for nothing, she can pick up a scent. And soon she's going to leave me, any day now, I can tell. I can pick up a scent as well.

She's here before me of course. When isn't she? She doesn't sleep these days, she says. 'These days' have lasted years. Always awake with the dawn, so why not? Always something to be done. And I pitch up after her. Boss's privilege. Though it's not yet half-past eight, and last night I was out on a job till gone two. And today's a special day.

As I reach the top of the stairs I hear the click and hiss of an already warm kettle being switched on. The computer in her little compartment (we call it the 'reception area' but area's a generous word) is already up and running. It feels like she might have been here all night.

'Cold,' she says, with a shiver at the air I've brought in and a little nod to the outside world.

'But beautiful,' I say.

She'll have been here before the sun hit the streets.

'Coffee or tea?' she says, ignoring my smile – and that word – as if insisting I'll have had a rough start.

But I don't have a sleep problem, not now. Though maybe I should. I can grab it when I can, cat-nap, get by on little. An old trick of the trade. And Rita's sleep problem, if she's honest about it (and sometimes she is), isn't really a sleep problem either.

'An empty bed, George, that's all it is. If there was someone there . . .'

'Tea, I think, Reet. Nice and strong.'

She's wearing the pale pink top, soft wool, above a charcoal skirt. Round her neck a simple silver chain. The small twinkly stud earrings, a waft of scent. She always gets herself up well, Rita. We have to meet the public, after all.

But the pale pink is like a flag, her favourite colour. A very pale pink – more like white with a blush. I've seen her wearing it many times. I've seen her wearing a fluffy bathrobe of the same soft pink colour, loosely tied, tits nuzzling inside. Bringing in morning tea.

I go into my office, leaving the door open. The sun is streaming through my first-floor window, the low, blinding sun of a cold November morning, the sun Rita never gets in her compartment, except through the frosted glass of my door.

She follows me in with the tea, and a mug for herself, a bundle under her arm. There's always this morning conference – my office door open – even as I settle myself in, take off my coat, switch on my own computer, sit down. The sun's warm through the glass, even if outside the air's icy.

She puts down my tea, already sipping her own, eyeing me over the rim. She slips the bundle on to my desk, pulls round the other chair – the 'client's chair'. She steps through bars of bright light.

It's like a marriage really. We've both thought it. It's better than a lot of marriages (we know this). Rita – my assistant, my associate, my partner, or not-quite partner. Her job description has never exactly been set in stone. But I wouldn't dream of calling her my receptionist (though she is that too) or even my secretary.

'Be an angel, Reet.'

'I am an angel, George.'

Where would I be without her?

But she's going to leave me, I can tell. One morning like this one: she won't bring in a mug of her own and she won't put down the bundle of files, she'll keep it hugged tight to her, a shield, and she won't sit down. She'll say 'George' in a way that will make me have to look up, and after a bit I'll have to say, 'Sit down, Rita, for God's sake,' and she'll sit facing me like a client.

'It's been good knowing you, George. It's been good working with you, but . . .'

She knows what day it is. A Thursday, and Thursdays are special, but she knows the date, the day of the year. November 20th. Two years – if you count it from *that* day. Two years and it hasn't stopped. And if it hasn't stopped, it will go on for the years to come, however many they'll be. The time's gone when she could say (as she did once), 'How can you, George – with *her*?' Or when she could say, to herself: He must be mad, he must be off his head, but he'll come round, it'll stop, give it time. He'll come slinking back. And meanwhile what better guarantee, what better safeguard, really – that woman being where she is?

I think she's come to accept it – even to respect it. A fact, a feature. Mr Webb is always 'on an assignment' every alternate Thursday afternoon. I've even seen this look of sweet sad understanding in her eyes. That's why I think she's going to quit.

'Those are for Mrs Lucas – this afternoon. Five forty-five. Earliest she can do.' A quick glance. 'You'll be back?'

We both know what's in the envelope. Photographs. Photographs of a man and a woman in a hotel room. A little blurred but clear enough for recognition, at six-by-nine enlargement. 'Surveillance equipment' is reliable these days. We have to get the film processed specially – a private contract – and Rita collects, A man and a woman doing things with each other. But this sort of stuff hardly raises an eyebrow or even gets that much of a look from Rita and me. It sits there, like the morning mail, between us.

Our stock-in-trade. Can you see who's who? That's the vital thing.

'Yes, I'll be back by five-thirty.'

'And I'll just say' – she doesn't push the point too much – 'you'll be out of the office till then?'

'But I won't leave before ten. I can take calls till then.'

'Okay.'

'It's a beautiful day out there,' I say again. 'Cold, but beautiful.'

Another sideways look, more lingering this time. She might be saying, You poor bloody idiot.

The eyes are tired, made up immaculately, but tired. The sunlight streaming in is like a warm bath, but it isn't kind to the lines round her eyes. It catches a wisp of steam rising from her mug and puts a sparkle in her hair. She moves a bit closer to point out something. A silver bracelet at the end of the pink sleeve.

A long time now, since the last time. I'd asked her round to try some of my cooking (Rita may be an angel, but she's a hopeless cook). I might even have spelt it out to her: a meal, that was all. But that's the trouble with good cooking (if I say it myself). Not to mention red wine. It warms the heart, the cockles, as well as the stomach. Melts the resistance.

'Things on your mind, Reet?' The considerate boss.

'Not exactly, George. You?' She'd cupped her wine glass in both hands – her nails wine-red too. 'It's just not having anyone there. You know. Somebody by your side.'

2

SOMETHING HAPPENS. 'Something comes over us,' we
say.

'Mrs Nash, can I ask what your husband does?'

'He's a gynaecologist.'

And I didn't voice any of the thoughts I had, of course
not. Though one of them was that this was a new one –
I'd never known this before: a gynaecologist. Shouldn't
they make safe husbands? Wouldn't it be like a guarantee?
Since they're seeing other women all the time. You'd think
they see enough. But what does it feel like to be married
to one? A man who sees other women every day.

'I see,' I said.

But I think she read my thoughts. Women (Rita, for
example) read thoughts, faces, quicker than men. A working principle, a lesson of the trade. Maybe it's also a
gynaecological law.

I looked at her face – brown eyes – looking at mine
and had the exact thought: She's reading my face like a
book. But that's just an expression. I didn't read faces

like books (I didn't read many books), I read faces like faces.

Brown eyes. A special brown. Clever, I thought, and none too sure of me. My dumb 'I see's. This hideaway of mine, up narrow stairs, overlooking the Broadway. But not so clever, or so sure of herself – or why was she here?

Later, on one of my Thursdays, she'd said, 'He wasn't a gynaecologist when I met him – fool. He was just – a not very committed medical student.'

And she'd actually laughed, a small dry laugh. A laugh – it was possible. And I'd thought: This might be ordinary life, we might not be here.

Later still, she'd say, ' "Gynaecologist", it comes from the Greek. It literally means "womanizer". Ha. But he wasn't that. I mean, there was only *her*. I know.'

The truth is she's taught me to say things, to say all this, to put things down in words. It's been an education, really.

He was a gynaecologist and she was a lecturer in languages. English included, of course.

'I see.'

The sun came in at a low slant through my office window, just like it's doing today. Cold outside, warm slabs of sun indoors. It fell like a partition across the desk between us. It just touched her knees, making them look as if they couldn't hide.

She's not sure of me, I thought, she can read my thoughts – my gynaecological thoughts.

But if she could, if she did, she'd have read the one I felt, like a small pang, for her. That it must make it worse for her – the pain and the shame. All the tired old jokes and remarks popping up and pressing round to haunt her. Him a gynaecologist too . . .

She looked at me and smiled, for some reason. A smile as defenceless as her knees.

You cross a line.

3

THE FLORIST'S is only just starting its day. Trails of silvery bright drips across the floor. Here, on the other side of the Broadway, at ground level, the sun comes in from behind, through a back window, so the girl who's serving becomes for a moment a silhouette against a sheet of light.

If Rita's watching (it's just my guess), if she's gone to my office window to look out, she'll have seen me cross over and confirmed it to herself: he's getting the flowers. Though it's Rita who's the regular customer here, not me. I haven't seen this girl before. The first time it was like a blatant message: the flowers, in a brand-new vase, on my desk.

That's for nothing, George – now start something. A slight sway of the hip.

But she bought some for herself too – for 'reception' (a smaller vase) – and I saw she'd put it down in the books she was starting to set straight: 'Office Flowers'. A weekly item. Not for nothing: I was paying.

One of her many introductions – along with sorting out those books, along with her whole 'refurbishment plan'.

'Presentation, George. It makes sense. If they see a vase of flowers, it's reassuring. It's good for business.'

True. And no nasty smells. And no bad jokes. *You're* my presentation, Rita. When they see you . . . I didn't say it. All the same, it was true.

And why hadn't I thought of it myself? A simple touch. A vase of flowers. From Jackson's here, only just across the street. Not to mention the personal factor. Be kind to yourself. Eat well. Go easy. Buy yourself some flowers.

I used to be a cop. The police don't go in for flowers. But I had the example from long ago: my dad's shop, with the studio above. Right next door to a florist's. And Dad was always buying flowers.

The girl wipes her hands on her apron. The buckets are packed tight. Everything has the feeling of being just picked – as if there's a magic garden, just out the back, defying the November frost. A cold sweat on the grey metal.

All the little daily mysteries. How do flowers – lilies in midwinter – arrive in town? And the bigger mystery, which isn't such a mystery: how come flower shops still *exist*? In this day and age. This place, Jackson's, I'm always expecting it to go, the way shops suddenly vanish, but it hasn't. Whole shops full of flowers. How come it hasn't been scrapped long ago, this daft soft urge to go and buy *flowers*?

And he was actually called Rose – the florist next to my dad's. Charlie Rose. As if he'd never had a choice: a whole life in a name. But no choice in any case, according to him: 'You think of all the reasons why people buy

flowers, and you tell me if there's a better thing to sell.'
Charlie and Kate Rose (her name should have been Daisy
or Violet at least).

'And shall I tell you the biggest reason? What they're
really for. Conscience. That's what they're for.'

Why haven't we all become florists? And, yes, if I
could arrange it, this place wouldn't even be here, on this
side of the street, it would be below my office. What
presentation, what planning. They'd have to come up
almost right through a florist's.

Though what I have is special enough: a tanning
studio, a 'Tanning Centre'. Under my office – but I don't
think about it much – naked women stretch themselves
out. I've said to Rita, 'Why don't you give it a go? You
could pop down for an hour, pop back up. My treat.' But
she never has. It's full of young girls. I think she thinks at
her age it only shows up the lines.

'Why don't *you*?'

A tanning studio. Flowers, suntans in winter. We have
it easy, a place for every need.

The girl steps through the light again as if she's passing
through some screen. She's wearing one of those puffy
sleeveless jackets, over an apron, a polo-neck sweater. A
loose strand of hair. You can picture her breath steaming
not so long ago as she unloaded a van.

I don't have to dither. I go for the tried and true.
Anyway, I have my commission. I point to the red roses,
the flowers still thick half-buds, the outer petals, in the
shadows of the shop, sooty-dark.

'A dozen, please.'

The girl counts out the stems, holds them up for me
to approve. I nod. She smiles. You can't help the obvious

thought: a flower as well. I smile back. She turns into a silhouette again, then goes to the table in the corner and spreads out a sheet of wrapping-paper.

There's a cold draught from the back and a woman bustles in: the owner. She's wearing a thick coat, undone, the collar turned up, and boots that show an edge of fleecy lining. I know her, she knows me. She knows what I do. Could she even know what day it is today? Put two and two together?

A quick nodding smile. She's thinking of other things. A pair of scissors in her hands. Perhaps all she'll say to the girl, after I'm gone, is: 'He's a private detective, and he buys flowers.'

Roses, blood-red roses. The same as last year. What else could it be?

The girl hands me the bunch and I reach for my wallet. Half-past ten. It's a short drive. I get a sudden black bitter taste.

In my father's studio there'd always be – easily restocked – a big vase of flowers. A prop, if required, or just an encouragement, a prod. I can hear his routine (one of many):

'Look at the flowers . . . now look at the camera . . . but think of the flowers. Smile!'

4

Two years ago and a little more. October still, but a day like today, blue and clear and crisp. Rita opened my door and said, 'Mrs Nash.'

I was already on my feet, buttoning my jacket. Most of them have no comparisons to go on – it's their first time. It must feel like coming to a doctor. They expected something shabbier, seedier, more shaming. The tidy atmosphere, Rita's doing, surprises and reassures them. And the vase of flowers.

White chrysanthemums, I recall.

'Mrs Nash, please have a seat.'

I could be some high-street solicitor. A fountain-pen in my fingers. Doctor, solicitor – marriage-guidance coun-sellor. You have to be a bit of all three.

The usual look of plucked-up courage, swallowed-back hesitation, of being somewhere they'd rather not be.

'My husband is seeing another woman.'

There aren't so many ways of saying it – but you have to look as if you haven't heard it said in every possible way. They're all unique: the only one to have to come to the doctor with this rare complaint.

'I see. I'm sorry. Can I offer you some coffee – tea?'

A doctor – a specialist. You're already gauging the symptoms. At any moment now there could be tears, curses, fireworks, waterworks. They all come with a script, fully rehearsed, and at some point it all gets abandoned.

Something I never expected: that this would be the most demanding, the most absorbing, the most rewarding part of the job. Things you weren't taught in the Force.

She didn't want coffee or tea. But Rita, I knew, was outside, like a trained nurse with the emergency trolley, ears pricked, kettle primed, ready to rush in with the tray at a moment's notice.

And, as an extra fall-back, the bottle of Scotch in the little cabinet in the corner. Strictly for client use only. Though it's surprising how often they'll say, 'Aren't you going to have one too?'

'You know, or you think?'

'I know.'

No hesitation there. She had eyes that seemed to shift – under a slight frost – from black to brown, to ripple. Tortoiseshell. The hair was the same. Black, you'd say, but when the sunlight from the window caught it you saw it was deep brown.

Another thing I never expected – though it's obvious, you only have to think. Mostly women. Or say sixty per cent.

I said to Helen, my daughter, 'They're mostly women, Helen.'

She said, 'Is that a complaint?'

And some of them don't just come in with their lines rehearsed, they come in as if for a full-blown audition, as if they've spent the last two hours in front of a mirror. (Rita, for example.) Dressed to kill. Clouds of scent. They don't want you to think it's for *that* reason, that it's out of neglect. They've made the decision, but they've got their pride.

Doctor, solicitor, casting director . . .

But she wasn't one of the star turns – if she wasn't cheaply dressed. The black coat: pure cashmere. She'd done her face, I guessed, in the hasty, automatic way of women who don't need to slap it on like war paint. She didn't need to – though she might be going to war.

You think, of course, of the husband. You think: What could be going on here? You put yourself in the husband's shoes (that's what they know you'll do).

Early forties – forty-two, forty-three – and in good shape. The eyes with just their touch of frost. Clever quick eyes – the frost making them look stern. But you could imagine them melting.

A teacher, it turned out, a college lecturer. Used to running the show.

Teachers – even on day-release in the Force – always used to give me the willies.

Clever, and comfortably off: the coat. An easy ride through life, probably, till now. So the sternness was thin. One of those women who come with a little professional crispness and firmness, but you can still see in them the woman of half their age, the girl.

'I see. So you know who the woman is?'

She'd undone her coat but hadn't taken it off, and she was carrying a bag, a plain black soft-leather bag which she'd unhooked from her shoulder and let slip to the floor. The flaps of her coat fell open. A black skirt of some velvety material, a sandy-coloured top over a white blouse. The bar of sunshine between us caught her knees and gave them an almost tinselly sheen. They didn't seem like the usual knees of women that can project from a skirt with all kinds of angles and meaning. They were just knees caught in the light.

It was her knees, maybe.

'Yes. Her name is Kristina Lazic.'

'That sounds foreign.'

'She's from Croatia.'

'Could you spell—?'

I'd pulled my notebook towards me. There's a point where it helps to get brisk.

'And do you know where your husband and Miss Lazic – is it Miss? – meet?'

'It's Miss. Yes, I can give you the address. It's a flat in Fulham. A first-floor flat. We rent it for her – I mean, my husband rents it for her.'

'I see.'

'Before this – I mean before she lived in the flat – she used to live under our roof.'

'I see.'

I sensed her watching my pen move over my pad, as if I was being slow. It was Rita who bought me the pen (when she found out my birthday). 'It looks posh, George, it's got class. A fountain-pen, not these crappy old biros.'

A fountain-pen. Tortoiseshell. It was Rita who'd used the word.

'I see. And you'd like me to – keep your husband and Miss Lazic under observation? You'd like me to establish evidence?'

'No.'

'No?'

'No. You see, it's all over. It's all over. Kristina is going back to Croatia – in maybe three, four weeks. Do you follow the news? It's agreed. She's getting a plane. What I want you to do is follow them to the airport. Watch them. That's all.'

'Let me get this clear. It's "all over" – you mean it's all over between Miss Lazic and your husband?'

'Yes.'

'But you said "them" – "follow them". You mean your husband is going to take Miss Lazic to the airport?'

'Yes. To see her off. It's – a last concession. It's his last three weeks.'

'But – if it's all over, if she's leaving, why do you want me to follow them?'

The first real pause. The first slight quiver of the lips. She looked like someone owning up to something.

'To see if she really goes. To see if they really go to the airport. And, if they do, to see if she really gets the plane – I mean, by herself. If they don't just fly off together, somewhere. Any plane, anywhere. Will you do this for me? Will you follow them and watch them and tell me what happens?'

As if she was suddenly begging some friend.

'Of course.'

And I was thinking: jobs don't come easier. Money for old rope. I might have handed it over to Rita.

But I saw the glitter in her eyes. Melting frost. Sometimes they gush or explode. Sometimes there's just a wetness in the eyes. It can lead on to other things, but if it doesn't you have to pretend it isn't there.

All the time she'd been holding on to the strap of her

shoulder-bag, twisted round her fingers, like a pet on a lead.

'Of course I can, Mrs Nash, no problem. But I'll need details. The date and time of course, details of the flight – the intended flight. Are we talking about Heathrow? The address you mentioned, is that where they'll be driving from? In your husband's car? Will they be going in his car? What does he drive?'

The tears didn't spill, they didn't dry up.

'And I'll need photographs, of each of them, if you can supply them. For recognition purposes, you understand. Can I ask what your husband does?'

5

I CROSS BACK over the Broadway and make for the side-alley where I leave the car. If Rita's watching she'll have lost me now. Well, if she wanted, she could sneak out and shadow me all day, the office left on hold. If she did it carefully, how would I know? Under surveillance by my own staff – all one of them. It's what happens. You train them up . . .

The car, tucked in, by old arrangement (and annual rent), against the side wall of Leigh's yard, is like an ice-box, though it's only been standing a couple of hours. There's still an oval of unmelted frost on the roof.

I put the flowers on the back seat. The wrapping (silver and grey stripes) is almost superfluous, since I mean to take them out and lay them just by themselves and flat. There are those little perforated pots you can get, made for the purpose, I don't know where from. Florists maybe. And the cemetery must have water taps. But it's November, a cold snap: they aren't going to last long, either way. And the flowers themselves are almost superfluous. It's the thought that counts.

'Will you do it for me, George?'
'Yes, of course.'

I don't know how she gets through this day. This night. November 20th. Is the second year easier than the first? Is that how it works – it's time that serves you? Does it get any more possible to say (how can it?): That was someone else, another person, not me?

Like the photo of yourself as a kid, staring at you from another world, another planet. Was that me, really *me*? And the kid stares back as if he doesn't know you either, never seen you before in his life.

Time: it's really on your side?

I switch on the engine. The dark taste again. The old faded sign on the wall says 'Leigh's – Bathroom and Sanitary Ware'. Then I creep out from the shadow of the wall and turn into the glare of the sun in the alley, grabbing my shades from the dash.

'Yes, of course I'll go. And take flowers.'

And report back.

It's the first time this has happened (though it's only the second year) – this day and my visit coinciding. It won't happen again, maybe. Every two weeks (and it can't always be Thursdays). Two years now, and – we don't know – another eight, if we're lucky, maybe nine. Another five before we'll even know the chances. By then she'll be somewhere else, again. She'll have done the rounds. But now two years have gone, she knows, we know, we don't have to think about it any more: I'm here for the duration.

And wherever she goes . . .

The time's gone when she used to look at me coldly,

almost with hate. (She had to do it, I know, turn herself to ice.) You won't keep this up, George, you'll stop, just wait, just you see. The time's long gone when she first let the look change – if she didn't risk the words. Please come back. Please be here next time.

Now it's a different look still. It's just a look that passes between us, a look that could pass through a wall.

Where would I be without you, George?

In prison, I suppose.

Eight more years. Maybe. Five before we'll even have a clue.

A photo of Sarah when she was five years old. I wanted a picture, I don't know why it was important, of when she was small. She told me where I could find the albums, the loose photos, a whole collection of stuff, tokens, souvenirs, little things her parents had put away once. (Thank God, she said, they were both dead.) Treasures from another life.

'Burn it all, George. Fucking burn it all.'

But I didn't. I'm their secret curator now (I think she knows).

And there – would you believe it? – in a white embossed-card frame, behind a flap of gauze-paper, was a photo of Sarah aged (I'd say) five. And it was taken in my father's studio – his stamp on the back – in Chisle-hurst High Street, in nineteen fifty-something (she'd lived in Petts Wood then).

The things that wait and lie in store.

The sun feels warm through the windscreen, but the street's full of people hunched in coats, chins buried in scarves. I drive along the Broadway, past the station, towards the Hill. From Wimbledon's lower end (my end) to the snooty Village on the hill. Past Worple Road. Then at Woodside I turn right, and then left into St Mary's Road, and I'm into the leafy, looked-after, quiet zone of houses set back from the street, of lawns and drives and hedges and burglar alarms. Rooftops backed by trees.

I have to do it. I didn't say – nor did she. But I have to do it, today. Beecham Close. Number fourteen. Someone else lives there now. Another world, another planet. I could find out all about them, check them out. It's how I make my living, after all.

A zone, as you climb the hill, of verges and double garages and wrought iron and speed bumps and private nursery schools. But don't knock it. If you make your living how I do, then make it where they'll pay your fees, and where – with all they've got – they can still (you'd be surprised) do the strangest things.

And don't knock it anyway. This home-and-garden land, this never-never land where nothing much is ever meant to happen. These Wimbledons and Chislehursts. What else is civilization for?

6

Money for old rope. I might have passed the job to Rita.

'These are my terms, Mrs Nash.' I handed her the slip of paper. 'For a job like this I won't ask you to sign anything – and I won't assume I'm hired until I get precise instructions. The rule is – for obvious reasons – you contact me, I don't contact you.'

They blink, a little startled. They've already entered a conspiracy, a pact.

Sunlight streamed between us. The stickiness had left her eyes and she looked for a moment simply lost. But they all look like that, as if they'd come on purpose but now they seemed to be here by accident. A mistake, the wrong door – they'd meant the Tanning Centre. They came in as the injured party – now they'll leave in a sort of guilty daze.

That's why – unless they're a certain type – you always leave them the option, the margin. You allow for the call that might come the next morning, even the same day. A change of mind, a reconsideration. My services wouldn't be required after all. And sometimes, though I don't say it and I don't like to lose a fee, I think: that's the best decision you could make.

Rita might have come in and said, breezily: 'Mrs Nash – yesterday morning. We can cross her off the list.'

I said, 'You can send the photos – or bring them in if you prefer.'

She seemed to have got stuck to her chair. She still clutched the strap of her shoulder-bag, knuckles squeezed tight.

Someone some day should write a book about hand-bags, shoulder-bags. Maybe they have. About how women cling to them, as if they're their closest friend. When all else fails. The things you find inside them. (I've lost count of how many I've rifled through.)

Where she is now they can't have handbags. The straps.

And now, of course, I have that shoulder-bag – along with all the other things. In my safe keeping. And, yes, it's like a pet. I've stroked it, talked to it. Inside, all the contents of a precise day, two years ago. November 20th 1995. That slip of paper, with my terms, folded in four.

A treatise on handbags.

'You should write things, George, write them down for me.'

My teacher.

She clutched the strap, as if she were waiting for the bag to get up first.

'So—' I said. 'Unless there's anything else?'

Like the full story, the whole story. But they don't have to tell you that. You don't have to know.

I held out my hand, through the shaft of sunshine. She managed to stand.

Moments later I went to the window to see if I could catch her crossing the street – as if, just by looking, I might stop her stumbling into the path of some car. And there she was, marooned for a moment on the traffic island. The sun on her head. She crossed and turned left, past Jackson's florist's, clutching the strap of that shoulder-bag tight.

Rita came in and saw me looking. She was always doing her private assessments: my female clients (she was one once). But I'd never done this before – gone to the window to look. She'd have noted it, definitely. She's a good detective, doesn't miss a trick. Later that week she said, 'Something's come over you, George.'

I turned when she came in and, as if to explain myself, said, 'It's a beautiful day. A beautiful day out there.'

'For some,' she said.

She'd brought in a cup of coffee. She cocked her head innocently as if at a third party still in the room. 'Not for her, I suppose.'

The sun picks out bursts of frozen fire. Rowan berries, pyracanthas, Virginia creepers in flame. This safe-as-houses land where nothing is meant to disturb the peace.

Rita, a job for you.

Or no job at all. I might never have seen her again, never have learnt the full story (or become part of it), if it wasn't for my little private passion (and unsuspected talent). A private eye, a private belly. I cook. Even for myself, I cook.

The supermarket, that next evening: Friday. Coincidences happen. I only half believe in them. I'm a detective. We see what we're ready to see.

She was there. I came round the corner of the aisle. I took a pace back. She was holding a jar, reading the label, aimlessly it seemed, as if she was browsing in a book shop.

I watched, I stepped back. I didn't have to, but it's my natural mode, an occupational reflex. And there's something anyway about that moment that it's in your power to stretch. You see them, they don't see you. The strange urge to protect.

Ha – a store detective. (And that could have been me once.) As if she might have slipped that jar suddenly into her coat pocket. And why not, why not? Women in cashmere coats do the strangest things. They walk around in a dream, an aimless daze, they take up shoplifting. When the ugly moment comes they say it's because my husband doesn't love me any more.

Madam – would you step this way?

But I think I saw – peeping round the corner of the aisle – how it was for her. What do you do when your husband's seeing someone else? When life carries on, but around this new and not even secret fact. You go and stand by the Fine Foods section and stare, as if they're forbidden fruit, at the packets and jars.

I think I saw it. Cooking. It was something for her too, a bit of a thing, a passion. And once life had been, maybe, a kind of constant, regular feast. I saw it, never having lived it, exactly, myself. Dinner parties, pulling of corks. Windows lit up, through the trees.

But what do you do when it falls apart? You still have to eat. (And it's a well-known substitute.) You even still have to feed *him*. So you go on cooking. In fact, you cook even more keenly and ambitiously, because – who knows? – that's one feeble, pathetic way you might get him back.

'I bet,' they say to themselves (it wasn't a comfort open to Rita), 'I bet *she* can't cook like me . . .'

I stepped forward (you watch, you wait, you intercept). The clinching coincidence. She'd come to me, but she might have cried off. Now she'd be held to it.

Besides, you know that moment when a door opens. You enter someone else's life.

I said, 'It's not bad – the red-pepper *tapenade*.'

She jumped – as much as anything, I think, at that French word. Coming out of my mouth. (But I can speak French: *restaurant, rendezvous, parlez-vous*.)

We're all supposed to stay in our boxes – you don't meet your doctor in the street. And I was supposed to be Mr Invisible anyway, seeing but not seen.

'I shop,' I said. 'I cook too.'

She looked at me, still holding the jar – a bit like somebody holding a rock. But I must have had the right expression on my face, I must have struck a chord. A *cooking* detective: not so creepy after all. Maybe the whole idea hadn't been so mad . . .

And it was true. In recent years – I'd one day tell her the whole story – I'd learnt to cook. Discovered, in fact, a bit of a flair. I take trouble. I chop and mix. I look up recipes, I'm choosy about ingredients. I stop at the Fine Foods section, even when I'm shopping for basics.

And food counts, I'll bear that out. In times of trouble, eat well, don't skimp. Look after yourself. Don't live out of the microwave. Use love and care. Just because you're on your own.

I'll vouch for it, I've been there. Just because I was an ex-cop – twenty-four years fuelling up on canteen grub and whatever you could snatch on the hoof.

Even now when I'm out on a night's job, I don't do myself down. A thermos of good coffee – or my own tomato-and-basil soup (a tiny pinch of chilli). And Serrano ham with thinly sliced Emmental, on ciabatta, with a few leaves and a smear of Dijon, knocks spots off a cheese-and-pickle wad.

'Seriously,' I said, 'I'm not bad.'

I didn't know then about the kitchen with the copper pans and the oven hood. A kitchen to die for. I couldn't have guessed that even right then she was thinking of that welcome-home dinner.

'It's just me,' I said, 'but I cook.'

'So what's it tonight?'

A little line crossed her forehead, but it was a laughter frown. Her lips stayed slightly apart. Simple fun-poking.

'Mushroom risotto, with porcini and vermouth.'

'Vermouth?'

'Of course.'

Now – where she can only eat what she's given – we still talk about food. I run through every meal. It was a good sign, a good moment, when she said, like an uppity hotel guest, 'The food in here, George – it's awful.' And she still says: 'What's it tonight?'

Eat well. Eat well for me till I get out.

Those tables that still get laid for two after the other's gone.

But it matters, I'll vouch for that. The stomach is next to the heart. I've seen it, had it pointed out to me in autopsy rooms – and then, to be mean and to hard-school him, taken the green young constable I'm with to the nearest greasy spoon. Mud tea and egg-and-chips.

I reached up to the shelf and flipped a packet of dried porcini into my wire basket.

I suppose if we hadn't met the day before she might have thought I was one of those sad cases who hang around in supermarkets on the pick-up – looking at what they put in their baskets. (And I suppose that could have been me once too.)

I said, 'About the photographs. It's best if you could bring them – if you could find a moment. That way I could look at them and they need never leave your hands.'

I think she may have glanced round – as if spies might have been listening, behind the pasta shelves.

'You mean – you'd just look, and remember?'

'My job. File in the head. But you need a history – a history to go with the face. Then you remember the face.'

She looked away. She was still holding the jar – inside, a dark reddish sludge. If it weren't for me, she'd have put it back on the shelf.

'You really rate this?'

Trolleys were squeezing past. The Friday-evening, home-from-work rush. In supermarkets you can't really tell who's happy or miserable, who's toppling over the edge. There's a tunnelled expression. We all have to eat.

I looked at her trolley.

'Nearly done? Me too. You know, there's the Café Rio, the new place, just over the street. It's not so busy around now. If you've got – ten minutes. Yes, the *tapenade*'s pretty good.'

7

THE SUN FLASHES off the road where the frost has turned
to a black dew. I reach the corner of Beecham Close, as if
a magnet has pulled me. I didn't say I would, she didn't
say I should (and I won't tell her I did). Though it's hardly
a detour. It's even a short cut, avoiding the Village. Wimbledon Broadway to Putney Vale.

But now I'm almost there I have to pull up. I taste the
dark taste again, like a gush of oil in the throat. I have to
stop. It's even hard to look.

Two years and everything is quiet. Frozen. The simple
turn into a quiet street. A cul-de-sac with verges and chain-
links and houses screened by autumn trees. It could almost
be a private road. Private, keep out: not for you.

I stop by the kerb, some yards back from the corner,
engine idling. Two years on, and how are these things
managed? Is the date remembered? Ignored? Look – it's a
beautiful day.

In number fourteen they must be well settled in by
now. Their name was Robinson, I know. I never met
them, of course. The estate agent's job – the estate agent's

problem. A challenge, it's true. But the place had been unoccupied for months by then.

Sell all the stuff, George, get rid of it. As if she might have said: Leave me nothing.

Thank God I was a private detective experienced in tricky situations.

They must have known – the Robinsons. But why should they care? What was it to them? A kitchen to die for. At a bargain price. And now they might even have sold on, for a small killing, the new owners never knowing. Until a little bird tells them. The Nash Case – ring any bells?

And what then? The sudden urge to move again?

It's out of sight from here, back from the corner. And there's this gold-and-rust camouflage of trees. A stillness, a crystal light.

I can't do it. As if there's a cordon, striped tape, stretched across. The kind of cordon I might have lifted, years ago, and stepped casually under. A police matter, but I was the police. And of course there was a cordon *then*, and a policeman stepping under it, in charge of proceedings. Marsh, DI Marsh. The Nash Case.

When he found out who I was I saw the shift in his face. An interview room, a statement. I was principal witness, after all, and principal snag in an open-and-shut case. How strange to be there, in an interview room, on the other side of the table. The other side of the law.

The sights and sounds of a nick. The whiff of the cells.

When he found out who I was, he might have leaned on me pretty hard. If it wasn't for that little admission he let slip in return – the one thing for the other, it almost seemed. That he was retiring in four weeks, that this was his last real case. And they'd put him on it because it was a simple mopping-up. No complications – except me, so it seemed. He might have leaned on me pretty hard, and he did a bit. Grey shifting eyes. So that while he had me there on the spot, and sweating, on the other side of the table, it was as though he too was on the edge of some scary gap, and I was even the one holding out a hand and saying, Come on, you can do it, you can take the jump. Lean on me.

I could see in his face the question he never exactly asked – and that had become less simple anyway, just by meeting me.

What's it like? What's it like, not being a policeman?

The Nash Case. Who remembers it? Not every case that finds its way into police files makes the papers as well. It takes something. But even then, in a little while, it's forgotten. Even right here, maybe, they've forgotten. Especially here.

I can't do it. As if the car doesn't want to make the turn, wants to forget as well. I rev the engine. A cold sick feeling of betrayal. As if Sarah's still in that house, locked up in it – it's her real prison – and I'm leaving her.

But how can I approach that house without bringing back how I approached it, twice, that night? The black taste suddenly filling my mouth as I drove away then, the first time. And I knew what it meant. Or why should I have *gone back*, turned round and gone back?

I should have understood it sooner, tasted it sooner. I should have stopped him, overhauled him, right here maybe, at the entrance to his own street. Blocked his way. 'Mr Nash? Mr Robert Nash? I'm a police officer . . .'

Or I should have overtaken him long before. Got there *first*. 'Sarah – it's not Bob, it's me.'

I shouldn't have just followed him to the corner, watched, then turned away.

He wouldn't be where he is now. Nor would she.

8

CAFÉ RIO. A big stencilled mural on one wall: Sugarloaf
Mountain, parrots, palm trees, beach girls. It's what you
need in Wimbledon at the thin end of October. And they
play samba music, smoochy and soft.

Our cars waited for us in the supermarket car park.
We'd had to deal with our shopping first. I'd said, 'I'm
over there,' pointing to my car, near the far corner, 'I'll see
you in a moment.' She might have just driven away.

Late October. The clocks about to go back. Now more
things could happen in the dark.

I've got the job, I thought. I won't pass it on to Rita.

And she's got something too, I thought, and knows
it: more than the simple job she'll pay for. Not just a
private eye, a private ear. I fetched coffees. This might not
have happened, I might just have got her second-thoughts
call.

Doctors and patients aren't supposed to meet by
chance, but they do, and there's a loosening, an unwind-
ing, a Latin-American beat.

'So you want to know the story?' she said.

I hadn't said I did. I might have given the barest nod. But it helps if you're going to talk and you need someone to talk to, if that someone's a stranger, a neutral party, as close as you can get to talking to a wall.

And it helps if you aren't sitting face to face but side by side at one of those narrow front-window counters, watching the rest of life pass by. The traffic in Worple Road, the homeward rush. That's why all those places, rooms that are set up for the purpose – two chairs on either side of a desk – have got it all wrong. Doctors' surgeries. Not to mention police interview rooms with the tape humming on the table – the worst places, usually, for getting anyone to blab.

You couldn't stare them in the eye, that never worked. Get up, walk around, let them talk to your back. Better still: two stools at a bar, a couple of drinks and (if it only counted as evidence) you'd have them nailed in a jiffy.

I think Marsh thought (and he was right) that I was judging his technique.

Interview rooms. Grey walls, scuff marks. An ashtray nobody empties.

She sipped her cappuccino, looking straight ahead. That curve the cheek makes up to the hollow of the eye. I know when to pretend I'm not there.

'I'm a teacher,' she said. 'I lecture at Roehampton. French and Spanish . . .'

For a moment I saw her standing in front of the class – to tell them everything she was about to tell me. Today's lesson will be different, today's lesson will be special. I pictured myself at a desk in the front row.

Ten minutes . . . twenty, more perhaps. I hardly risked a word. A teacher of languages.

'It's all my own fault . . .' she said.

I go there now, of course. The place is still running, minus its newness. I sit, if I can, where we sat that time. And she's the one now who's made herself go invisible – so invisible you'd think she wasn't there.

I could speak to the air. Our few free moments together. They'd barely add up to a couple of hours. And if I'd never said, 'I cook too.'

I look at the palm trees on the wall, the beach girls. As if everywhere's a prison and we need to peer out at a different world. In Rio de Janeiro, maybe, there's a Café Wimbledon where they think of cool green lawns.

'It's all my own fault . . .'

And what I didn't know then, what she had no reason to say, was that at that very hour Bob and Kristina – Mr Nash and Miss Lazic – would have been together at a flat in Fulham. So Mrs Nash had no need to hurry home.

Afterwards we walked back to our cars. The homeward rush, though not in her case, or his. The supermarket still in full swing. We stood by her car, a silver Peugeot. Her husband had a black Saab. The car I'd have to follow.

She said, 'All right. I'll bring in the photos.'

So it was settled.

'Fine. Give me a call first.'

The tingle of conspiracy, undercover work – meeting in car parks. The excitement that, in spite of everything, begins to infect them. The thrill of the chase.

She unlocked her car. Then she said, as if she'd forgotten her manners – as if we'd met by accident at some gathering, some convention of language teachers, say (though what would I be doing there?): 'I've just talked about me. I don't know about you.'

Her face even looked a little guilty in the dark.

The car park was heaving. Trolleys careering, boots yawning, a scene of plunder.

'That's okay,' I said. 'You don't need to know.'

9

I DRIVE OFF QUICKLY, forgetting the speed bumps. The car bucks. The flowers almost fall off the back seat.

All her fault? Yes, in the sense that if she'd never let that girl under their roof . . . If she'd never tried to be more than her teacher . . . She should have seen it coming: the wife's fault for putting temptation under the husband's nose.

But was that supposed to be her first consideration? And was he supposed to have put up his hand and forbidden the whole thing, on the grounds that – you never know – he might just be tempted?

And anyway it wasn't like that. He wasn't a 'womanizer'. Only professionally. There wasn't a history. Just the history of them being a happy couple with good careers, a grown-up son who'd flown the nest, and (her own sad words): 'pretty well everything we could want . . .'

She poked her spoon in her cappuccino. The traffic slid by outside.

'And, anyway, when she first arrived, she looked – well, she looked like not much at all. You know what I mean? She looked like she didn't care how she looked . . .'

If you have everything, why go and risk it all? The good life. That house up there, through the trees, in burglar-alarm country. Why go asking for trouble? All her own bloody fault.

But for pity's sake. Or charity's. Since wasn't that the point? If you have everything, then shouldn't you be able to afford that? And to look out from your window at the world now and then? Why do people spend money on flowers?

'Do you follow the news . . . ?'

It wasn't really a question, and I didn't say anything. I sipped my coffee. I follow people, I follow scents, it's how I make my living. And where would I be if the well-off didn't go chasing trouble now and then, with their cheque books to wave in its face?

The black cashmere – to shop in. How much did a gynaecologist make?

And she'd thought the vermouth was wrong.

A teacher, she said. French and Spanish. A little freelance translation. A little English as well.

I sipped my coffee. I didn't say: Teachers – smart-arses, they always used to piss me off. But there must be something about them . . . I married one once.

She looked straight ahead at the window but I could see her reflection in the glass.

A teacher. A 'lecturer'. Twice a week, Tuesdays and Fridays (so it was where she'd just been), she took an English class, open to all-comers but aimed especially at foreign students. Brush up your English. And into that class had walked, one Tuesday afternoon, Kristina Lazic from Dubrovnik in Croatia.

I looked it up, I wasn't sure. You could say my field was domestic affairs.

Croatia then – Yugoslavia before (and in my out-of-date atlas). The 'former Yugoslavia': a familiar phrase.

'They won, you see. The Croats beat the Serbs.'

What did this have to do with a flat in Fulham?

And Dubrovnik, Dubrovnik in Yugoslavia, had once been, I knew this, in the holiday brochures. Hot old walls, blue sea. A tourist destination. The 'Dalmatian Coast'. And that's how it had been before she left – before Kristina had left – five years ago.

She'd won a studentship and come to London only months before the serious trouble began. It must have involved calculations, hard thinking. Conscience-searching. Eighteen years old: her big break. And then the world she'd left behind her had been smashed apart.

But not just that – worse than that.

'It's hard to imagine . . . You might as well know . . .'

First her brother, then both her parents had been killed. She'd got the news in two terrible, barely separated stages. The brother had become a soldier – but not for long. The parents had been unluckier still. They'd left for where they thought they'd be safer. A mistake. The wrong place, the wrong time. They weren't the only ones to be rounded up.

'Can you imagine . . . ?'

I cleared my throat, the way you do during a lecture. The samba music swayed on.

It put paid to her studies, of course. What was the point now? Though she was granted an extension to her studentship – and counselling – and, slowly, she'd begun to pick up the pieces, to make up for lost time. But even when she'd walked that Tuesday into Sarah's class she'd looked 'only half there – like some convalescent'.

So Sarah had taken her under her wing.

This would have been late in '93. Then the summer had drawn near when her studentship – and visa – would expire, when her only option would be to register as an asylum seeker.

'You know what that means?'

I nodded. My work takes me around. It means the bottom of the heap.

So there was Kristina Lazic, about to become an official refugee, and there were Sarah and Bob Nash, just the two of them in a smart house in Wimbledon, and even a room in it recently knocked together with another to make a 'guest suite', after the son had left to go and work in the States.

'He's in Seattle. Computers. He makes a mint. He doesn't know about any of this. I mean, about Bob and her. I hope he never will.'

She turned for a moment and looked me straight in the eye.

My eyes might have flicked away.

Charity: okay if you've got the money, if you've got the room. Okay for some. A luxury item. And was it such a fine piece of charity anyway, if what you got out of it was an unpaid help around the home and the bonus of feeling good? Look, we have everything – including our very own orphaned Croatian maid. Look at the good life we lead.

But for pity's sake. Have a heart. Can't a good deed be a good deed? And who can say when the urge to commit one won't suddenly steal over you? You never know. Someone walks into your life and you want to care for them specially, you want to protect them. You know you'll put yourself out for them, never mind all the other cases, the thousands of other cases. This is your case.

And that poor girl. Have a heart.

Kristina. A name like fragile glass.

Girl? She was almost twenty-two – a woman, even if she'd lost a chunk of her life. Poor? She'd landed on her feet. A damaged soul, a convalescent, a stunted flower. But, put down in new soil – I hadn't seen the photos yet – she'd bloomed.

10

I COME OUT on to Parkside. Opposite: the Common, a sea of glittering yellow leaves.

And what about him, the husband, Robert – Bob? Why does it still seem (to my crude, ignorant, private-investigator mind) like some bad kind of joke? Do gynaecologists marry? Can they have affairs? Can a woman love a gynaecologist? But she did, she did. And he wasn't a gynaecologist when they met – of course not. Just a student, like her, who said he'd drive her, one summer, in a purple Mini Cooper, to the South of France.

'I had the French, he had the car . . .'

And either a trip like that turns out to be a disaster – a disaster trapped in a purple bubble on wheels – or a lasting success. It was a success.

Wouldn't gynaecologists be, like diplomats, immune – protected? And how does it work for women: 'I'm a gynaecologist' – chill or thrill?

I'm a private investigator.

Clearly, he wasn't immune. A girl under his own roof. Though it was the first and only time, Sarah swore, she *knew*. So, when it happened, however it happened, it must have hit him like a train. Under his own roof, with a *refugee* for pity's sake. Surely, for that very reason . . .

And him a gynaecologist too.

It must have knocked him clean off his feet.

She would have moved in one Saturday, in September, three years ago. Become part of the household at number fourteen. Of course, she'd come before – to look, to be introduced. She'd have met Mr Nash. '*Bob* – please.'

How do they deal with it – the professional tag that comes with them – as they hold out a hand? Do they learn a special kind of smile – a bit apologetic, a bit boyish? Or do they go for the breezy and frank?

I'm a private eye. Call me Dick . . .

'He works at Charing Cross Hospital, in Fulham – and privately of course. He does a day at the Parkside. Just up the hill. It's handy.'

It looks out on Wimbledon Common.

All of it, anyway, on a trial basis. And maybe it wouldn't be for long – till things 'sorted themselves out'. She wasn't allowed to work, to take paid employment, but receiving charity wasn't against the law. And, yes, if it bothered her, then she could think of herself as their unpaid au pair. A sort of joke, of course, but, as it turned out, it was just how it was, in the beginning. She wanted to *do* things – she didn't have to, but she did. To clean and tidy, to fetch the shopping. To show she was grateful, to be their servant, to earn her keep. An initial cool, polite, obedient stage.

And cooking, I thought, did she cook? Surely not, if

that was Sarah's speciality. But then she would have helped, perhaps – been Sarah's under-chef. And yes (I guessed right) that's how they really got to know each other, preparing meals. There are worse ways. That's how the cool and awkward phase turned into something else. This girl about the place. A kitchen warmth. Good food, winter evenings. The smells that can creep from an oven and into the nostrils like kindness itself.

Did Sarah even learn a thing or two from her? What do they eat in Croatia? In those days, not much, I suppose. What do refugees normally get fed?

But, as it happens, there was a connection. There was a ghost there in that kitchen, at the side of this girl who was ready to act like a maid. There were three ghosts. But the brother, the soldier of just a few weeks – his name was Milos – had once worked in a restaurant, first in the kitchen, then as a waiter. Too handsome – Kristina had said – to be kept in the kitchen for long. One summer, before it all happened, in the tourist days. A waterfront restaurant in Dubrovnik. Having a high old time – cutting a swathe through all the foreign girls.

You never know what's in store.

But that first Saturday in September (Sarah would tell me later) was almost a disaster. It was almost the point where she'd had to say it had all been a terrible mistake.

All her own fault.

They'd picked her up – in the Saab – along with her few boxes and bags of things. It had all been arranged, discussed, agreed. But, to their surprise, she'd sat in the car not speaking, not even looking at them, as if she didn't know them, as if she was under arrest. At any moment, it seemed – when they stopped at lights, a junction – she might have made a sudden bolt.

And when they'd arrived she'd just sat rigidly at their kitchen table, while Bob carried her boxes silently up to her room. This was her home now, her place, but it was as though she was trying not to be there. She said things, mumbled things to herself, but they weren't in English, or any other language that Sarah could understand.

She just sat there, like a prisoner, in Beecham Close.

And then – 'Thank God' – the tears had come, in a gush, in a flood that went on for minutes, and Sarah had simply put her arms round her while she sobbed and moaned, and had known then that it would be all right, once the tears had stopped, they could make a start.

She'd never seen Kristina cry before. She'd seen the student with the frown and the dark eyes that were dark in some extra way, but she'd never seen her cry.

I can see it. You have to put yourself in the scene. The two of them in that kitchen. The girl sobbing and Sarah holding her, as if there was no question who needed protecting.

But him? What about him? What did he do with the two of them glued there together at the kitchen table? He'd carried up her boxes, like some servant. His feet had crunched on the gravel as he'd to-and-froed from the car.

He felt it too. A relief. It would be all right now, after the sobs. A lump in his own throat maybe – though, God knows, he'd heard enough women sobbing, in his job. Not such a mad idea, not such a bad idea, after all. A good idea. But right now – standing there empty-handed in the kitchen doorway – what should he do?

A gynaecologist. But this was a woman's thing.

He'd have made himself scarce, he'd have beat a wise retreat. September: a nip in the air. But he'd have gone outside, warm from lugging boxes, paced around, like a man whose wife is in labour. He'd have thought of other things. His son in Seattle, maybe, who didn't even know yet (would he have to?) that a Croatian refugee girl would be sleeping in his bed.

He'd have looked at the garden, at the trees, beyond, in other gardens, screening other houses all around. The first berries. Spiders' webs glinting. But even out there he might have heard the sobs, somehow tugging at his own chest, and as he paced he might even have peered through the kitchen window and met his wife's eyes (Kristina's head buried under her chin) staring steadily back at him.

I know what he'd have thought: a thought that had never occurred to him before then. The nape of Kristina's turned, shuddering neck. That he couldn't do it, could he? It wouldn't be permitted, would it? That simple, obvious and healing thing Sarah was doing. Put his arms around her.

11

SHE BROUGHT IN the photos the following Tuesday. It's true, it's better that way. The file in my head. The less such things have to pass in the mail between me and my clients the better. Suppose everything turned out just as she wished – but then he discovered that all along he'd been watched.

They cross a line, it's not a simple line. They're the injured party, but they're spying on their husband. Up to something too.

They enter a little web of deceit.

It's true, I didn't really need the photos. I had to follow a man and a woman in a car. It made me seem scrupulous. It meant she might call by my office again.

She knows all this by now: the days when I got her to visit me.

She came late in the afternoon, direct from her classes again. A Tuesday – Tuesday and Friday afternoons: English classes. And was this another afternoon when, right then, at the Fulham flat . . . ?

Almost five-thirty. Dark outside. The way people change on a second, a third meeting, as if the air around them changes as well. She must have been carrying those photos with her all day – her husband and her husband's lover tucked up inside that shoulder-bag.

If I'd been a fool I might have said to Rita: 'It's okay, off you go . . .'

She had something more than the photos: the date and the flight. (So I had the job.) There was a light in her eyes when she told me, a small brief flush. I saw how she might look – must have looked once often enough – when real happiness washed over her face. Her glance by the Fine Foods section: What's it tonight?

Maybe I had the thought: She looks like she's about to be released.

It was to be a Monday evening, in three weeks' time, Monday 20th November. The girl was to fly to Geneva to be officially cleared as a returning refugee. Then on to Zagreb.

How did this work? 'Officially cleared'? It had all been openly arranged? Her husband had shown her the ticket – as proof, as pledge? Or just said? It wasn't his ticket, of course. But then there might have been two – or none.

Geneva. That might mean anywhere.

But all these things she must have thought through herself. Why was she sitting there, why had she come again, if anything was sure?

I said, 'You've seen the ticket?'

'She's got it.'

I looked at her. There are ways of checking if some-one's on a passenger list.

'The flight exists. Seven-thirty – in the evening. And I've checked – she's on it. Just her.'

So, a detective too – a detective glow in her face. But

he might always book a ticket for himself meanwhile. And if you wanted – what's the word? – to abscond, elope, disappear, you might go to some pains to cover your tracks. Even buy an air ticket you never intended to use.

She'd thought of it all, all the possibilities. All the same, there was this brightness about her. This was really happening. A release? A verdict at any rate. The look of a bright, hard-working student waiting for a result. I felt for a moment as if I was her teacher now.

I thought of Helen, when she was young. How she hated me.

'And you've brought the photos?'

'Yes.' She unzipped the shoulder-bag. Her homework, ready for handing in.

She took out a stiff-backed envelope, pulled out the photos and put them on my desk, leaning forward in the same huddling way you might to show snaps of your kids.

How had she chosen? For 'recognition purposes'. The one of him – of Bob – showed a man in a holiday pose: a loose shirt, the sleeves rolled up, a pair of sunglasses tucked in a breast pocket, a pullover round his shoulders. A smile just breaking. A good-looking man in his mid-forties. What do gynaecologists look like? What are the tell-tale signs? He looked like some lean and handsome cricketer, a good eye, a straight bat. A flop of dark hair across his forehead, which you could picture him smoothing back.

What do you say? Some guff? Commend them on their choice of husband? I didn't have to ask: it was taken two summers ago – before Kristina had arrived.

The photo of Bob that appeared in the papers must have been from a professional file. For use in some medical brochure. Head and shoulders only. A picture of clean-cut reliability. A studio shot.

The photo of Kristina was the poorer picture – even a little blurred. (Was that why she chose it? Were there so many to choose from?) A slim girl in jeans and sweater and an old outdoor jacket that didn't look like her own. Sarah's? Bob's? It was in the garden at number fourteen. She seems to have been involved in some physical task – sweeping up leaves maybe. She's holding the handle of some broom or rake. But she looks as though the camera's surprised her, trapped her into an expression she can't quite manage – she would have looked better if she'd been caught unawares.

That first autumn (I guessed right), before anything had begun.

I found these same photos again among all that stuff I never burnt. The one of her is the bigger mystery. A poor photo, or something blurred in her? Who took it, and why? (It was Bob who took it, it was his jacket.) Italian, you'd think – who would say 'Croatian'?

She could be eighteen, she could be twenty-five. She didn't look like the woman I'd see three weeks later, if only briefly and never from closer than a few yards, stepping in and out of a black Saab.

But all that was after she'd – bloomed.

And anyway (trust a detective) people don't always look like they look.

I studied the photo and nodded. What was I supposed to say again? That she looked like trouble, a marriage-buster? That she looked like some lost soul anyone would have wanted to take into their care?

But I knew what we were both thinking (I think).

There they were on my desk, like a couple, as if they'd been picked. There we were like judges. Were they a pair, a match? Was that how it was meant to be?

I turn and drive along the edge of the Common. The light through the trees is like the light through the spokes of a wheel.

How do you choose? How do these things happen? I think Rita will go and run a dating agency. It's just my fantasy. The same job, but in reverse. One day, after extra-careful consideration, she'll say to one of her clients: I've got just the woman for you.

I heard Rita cough, that afternoon, outside. She can't hear what's being said in my office – any more than I can hear what she says on the phone – but she can hear when things get heated, desperate, hysterical. Nurse Rita. Or when nothing's being said at all.

I shuffled the photos matter-of-factly. Perhaps I coughed myself.

'Good,' I said. 'Now I've seen. And now we have a date and time.' Perhaps she noticed the 'we'. 'If the flight's at seven-thirty and check-in's an hour earlier . . . Fulham to the airport, that's a straight run – but at that time of day . . . Will you have a way of letting me know when Mr Nash will pick Miss Lazic up?'

She gave me a look as if I was being slow.

'He won't "pick her up". He'll be there.'

'I see.'

She took the photos and slid them back carefully, like precious objects, into the envelope. Then into the bag. There they go, back into their nest.

'Yes – now you've seen.'

A strange look, as if there'd been some flash of naked-ness.

All I'd seen were her knees.

She zipped up the bag.

I said, 'I'm about to shut shop anyway.' (Sometimes Rita locks up too. And she could think what she liked.) 'Would you like a drink?'

12

YET ANOTHER THING I never expected: that they'd thank you for it, like you for it, when they ought to hate you for it. You're the one, after all, who gives them the bad news, the messenger who ought to get shot.

Yes, it's pretty much as you imagined, yes, it looks like your marriage is wrecked . . .

And what's more, you're a man. One of *them*. Another of the bastards.

But if you start off their enemy, their hired enemy, you become, bit by bit, their ally, their friend, at least with some of them you do. You're in this thing together, it's between just you two. And who else do they have who's going to tell them this painful, intimate truth?

Some of them of course don't ever drop their guard. With some of them it's always mind how you tread.

You have to learn to make allowances – to develop a bedside manner (not something you pick up in the Force). Part counsellor, part comforter. They've all had to nerve themselves, they all think they're unique, and it wouldn't do to set them straight: My bread and butter, sweetheart, you're not alone . . .

'In your own time . . . In your own words . . .'

(Who else's words would they be?)

Their ally, sometimes, their accomplice. It almost turns into an adventure. And sometimes it's at the very moment they learn the worst that they most become your friend. They thank you for it – they even pay you for it. Who else could have spelt it out to them so plainly? You see them in their humiliation, their anger, their first rush of revenge. They're on the rebound. And before you know it, though you're ready with the Kleenex, the whisky bottle, the well-practised words, it's not you who's putting out an arm (though you could be forgiven for it, it's even the best thing you could do), it's they who've reached for you. They've come to hire you to be their detective, to do this and do that, but before you know it what they most want you to do is give them a hug.

'They're mostly women, Helen . . .'

When I fell into disgrace many years ago – when I left the Force and Rachel left me – it was Helen who came to my side. I don't mean she thought I was blameless, but she came to my side. The strangest thing, when we'd been such enemies. When you might have thought she'd have relished it, gloated over it. At least have taken her mother's side.

But she took my side.

The strangest thing. She's almost thirty now, and I'm turned fifty. The years between us haven't changed, but when we see each other now it feels like we're just two contemporaries, two grown-ups. So different from when, say, I was thirty-something and she was just fifteen. She used to make my life a misery – as if police work couldn't be tough enough – she used to give me hell.

I think she hated me. She might have hated both of us, but I know she hated me, and it was my being a cop that put the seal on it. 'My dad's a policeman': it simply wasn't a cool or easy thing for any teenager to say in those days. Even if I wore plain clothes, even if it didn't show that much. My dad's a policeman and therefore one of the ones on the other side. My dad's a policeman and therefore one of the pigs.

I'd sometimes wonder – small comfort – if it wouldn't have been worse if I'd had a son. On the other hand, sometimes I wished I'd had a son – as well – to take away some of Helen's heat.

The sulks, the tempers, the silences that burned. Where does it all get brewed? And Rachel, a primary-school teacher, used to the tantrums of little brats. But Rachel and Helen, I thought, had some kind of bond that was beyond me. How does it work – a policeman's daughter, a policeman's wife? I always thought they were friends.

Maybe it wasn't that I was a cop. Maybe that wasn't the main thing at all.

And it wasn't that she just took it out on me, she took it out on herself too, or so it seemed. She took it out on herself to take it out on me. She'd wear those awful clothes and dye her hair a different colour every month and make it go spiky like the bristles on an old brush. God knows how she got away with it at school – but we got the letters, the cautions, about the code for dress and personal appearance. And me a policeman. And Rachel up for Deputy Head. But the strange thing was her school-work was always pretty good.

Not like me, in my day. Poor marks all round.

(I've told Helen most things now, of course, most of the story.)

Then she had a stud stuck in the side of her nose. Then another on the other side. In those days that sort of thing hadn't yet become a kind of uniform.

Her business, her nose. But at weekends she'd go out with some gang, some gaggle – we never knew who they were – and sometimes disappear all night. Being a policeman doesn't stop you worrying, the opposite if anything. And sometimes I'd think that sooner or later I'd have to go and fetch her from some nick. Me a cop, and her in a nick. Drugs, whatever. And that would be it, that would make her day. The perfect piece of retaliation.

So when real scandal came my way, when I got drummed out of the Force and proved to be, after all, a dodgy cop, a bad cop (but a good one too – I'd made DI), shouldn't that have been her moment of triumph?

But which way did it work? If being a policeman was bad in the first place, then being a bad one . . . Do two bads make a good?

We both knew which way it worked for Rachel. Rachel decided – almost overnight – that I wasn't just a bad cop, I was a bad husband, a bad deal altogether. Rachel decided I was no longer for her and went her own way. That's how it worked, in a word, for her. And Helen, I would have thought, would have jumped the same way too.

But by this time she'd left school and left home. She'd already gone her own way (to be honest, it was a bit of a relief). She was at college now, art college – so, hardly a tearaway. Underneath all the outrageousness, a good little schoolgirl, particularly good, it seemed, at Art and Art History.

Though even that she'd use like a stick to beat me with. Me, the brainless clod of a policeman.

(But I'd been to college – police college, day-release. Sweated through police exams.)

It's true, I didn't know, or care much, about Art. I didn't see the point of looking at pictures. Or painting them. Though I'd have said to Helen – if it had ever come to it – that that's just why we have policemen: so that law-abiding people are safe and free to go to art galleries and look at pictures. Or whatever. Stick pins in their nose. What else is civilization for?

But I didn't say it, of course. Red rag to a bull. I even tried, for her sake, to get interested in Art.

'You're a detective, Dad. But you don't see things. You don't notice things.'

I even went to art galleries, and looked – and yawned. I even mugged up on her favourite painter, Caravaggio (they all looked like waxworks to me). And found out he was a bit of a tearaway himself, a bit of a thug on the side, always running up against the law. (Was there a message there for me?) A bit of a nancy too.

Then she left home. Then two years later I left the police. Then Rachel left me. And then Helen came home. I mean, she came home to visit me, to take my side against Rachel, who became, as far as Helen was concerned, the real culprit in the whole business, for turning her back on me.

'It's your mother you're talking about, Helen.'

'Is it?'

She never forgave Rachel but I think she forgave me, pretty quick, even when I was still putting my hand up to say it was all my fault, I shouldn't have done it, blame me.

*

I still see Rachel's face (though it's dim now, strange and floating, like the face of a woman I wonder if I really knew) when she said to me, 'I can't stay with you now, George. Do you understand what I'm saying?'

Her eyes more judging than the eyes of any judge I've seen in court.

'I can't be your wife any more . . .'

And I still remember the feeling – until then I hadn't had it, even if the ground had been opening up – of falling. Just falling, in the way you fall when you know there's nothing to land on, endlessly falling, the way people must fall in outer space.

I still have dreams of falling, like I used to have then. Everyone's supposed to have dreams of falling. What dreams does Sarah still have?

Falling. Off the edge, off the cliff of life. But in my dreams, though I fell, I could always see, above me, the point I'd fallen from, as if I wasn't just falling but always feeling that first sick rush. And there, at the top of the cliff, looking down, would be Dyson, laughing at me. Laughing himself sick. Laughing his fucking head off. He hadn't even had to push.

And sometimes Dyson would turn into Rachel, who was never laughing at all.

But Helen came home, to visit me, when Rachel was gone, when I was alone in the house – till we sorted out who got what. Before I migrated to Wimbledon. Alone with no job. Helen came just to see if I was all right, to make sure I was looking after myself. She'd look at me and then glance round at the place as if for signs of cracks in the walls.

The strangest thing. This renegade daughter of mine,

who used not to waste a chance to make me wince. Now she was turning into the sweet little (but drop the 'little') half-mother of a daughter she'd never been. She'd even toned down the clothes, the hair. She'd finished college by then and had some kind of design job. She was twenty now. Not little at all.

When she left I'd stand at the door (the neighbours, of course, knew: there'd been some changes at number three) and watch her get into the old Renault she'd bought and throw it into gear and give a last wave, and I'd think the obvious and simple thought: she's a woman now, her own life. But she cares about mine.

I'd watch her tail lights disappear, then turn to go in. Autumn nights, shivery and raw. Smoke in the air. 'You don't see things.' The neighbours knew I was a detective (and who really wants one of them up their street?) – though not any more. So now they were snooping on me.

The feeling of being alone again in the house. Like water flooding into a ship.

She'd even cook meals for me – pretty good meals – as if I never ate. (I drank – she noticed that.) That old wisdom in times of trouble: you've got to eat. This was my daughter, Helen. And that's how it began. My own cooking, my own mugging up on food. (Art too, but food mainly.) Something else they don't teach you in the Force.

I learnt to cook. First simple stuff, under Helen's eye (and where did she learn?), and then by myself, in the long empty hours, with the aid and the company of recipe books. Bright cheery photos of food. I decided I had a knack. I moved on to quite challenging stuff.

But, frankly, it kept my life from falling apart. The

way a whole day can hinge round a meal. And it was all to please Helen. To prove to her I was really looking after myself.

That's how the routine began. Helen would turn up one evening a week and I'd cook a meal for her. Three courses, the full works. And I'd set a table nicely: candles, napkins, wine glasses. She was my sole guest – and guinea-pig and judge. But the fact is I impressed her. I out-classed my teacher. She'd even dress up a bit. We'd eat and talk and drink wine.

The best day of the week – the days Helen came. Days that hinged round meals and weeks that hinged round Helen's visits. I didn't sleep so much then – that was the time. Though when I did, I dreamt. I fell. Days and nights of being awake at all hours, ready to do a job that wasn't there. The old job.

It doesn't stop, I'd tell Marsh, it doesn't go away. It's not a job, it's something inside, it's how you are. Better a washed-up detective, tracking down stray husbands, than no detective at all . . .

Helen wasn't keen, I knew. Going private. She thought it was just a bit obvious, a bit uninspired, like putting on a badge that said 'Failed Cop'. She even thought it was a bit mucky (but wasn't police work?). Her old dad.

So what should I be, Helen? An artist? A chef?

Marsh now, in the lap of retirement, still gets up early – when he can lie in all morning – as if he's on call. He's told me, when we play golf.

I thought about it for a long time: taking him on. I thought: maybe only if he asks. And besides, I had Rita.

*

Days when Helen would come, the best days of the week. When planning a meal was all the food my mind wanted or needed or could handle.

Of course I had the simple thought – and so did she: she's become the woman in my life now. My regular date.

I was going to go private, put myself up for hire. But that wasn't the only issue, and when it was settled – when I was out on the snoop again – the other question didn't go away. So, was I going to find somebody else? It happens. It's what men in my position do.

A new woman in my life, who wasn't my daughter. I was only forty-two. Only. And if I was getting all this – practice. If I could wine and dine. Get them round to try your cooking. Refill their glass.

'Nearly all women, Helen . . .'

But by the time I said it, by the time I made this not wholly honest or accurate remark, Helen had already come round to my being a private investigator – and she'd moved on herself, after all, from art to interior design (a switch I felt I shouldn't say too much about). And being a private investigator had a dimension she hadn't reckoned on – and nor had I. Full of potential for me and full of interest – entertainment? – for her. Her old dad.

I think she knew by the time I said it that I was already getting up to things.

'. . . More women than men.'

'So – are you complaining?'

13

I PASS PARKSIDE HOSPITAL. The trim front hedge, the neat forecourt, the glass doors. It could be some discreet, unshowy hotel. Then I reach the roundabout at Tibbet's Corner. I take the slip road for the A3, where it sweeps down between Wimbledon Common and Putney Heath. Richmond Park ahead. These chunks of tame wilderness – parks, commons, heaths. A pressing-round of trees. The road hard, humming and ruthless, six lanes wide.

I don't know if Rachel still thinks of me, if she's curious as well. She would have read the papers, I suppose, two years ago – the Nash Case – have read the reports which, in some cases, mentioned me. A private investigator acting for Mrs Nash . . .

My God – that's George. That must be George.

Curious? But I was 'out of her life' now, and she was out of mine. As if when someone's out of your life they might as well be dead.

And if she could see me now – if she could see what I'm doing now – what on earth would she think? That I've lost it altogether, passed way beyond the bounds?

*

The road drops away in front of me. There's hardly any distance to go. The sun is almost straight ahead, so everything in front has a glint, a metal sheen, like some great glistening slide.

A head teacher now, of course. Up there on the platform at assembly, addressing the little sparkling faces on this sparkling day.

Sometimes I think she *can* see me – she's watching over me – like I imagine she must imagine I can see her. It's a right, an ability we both have, by virtue of having been together, once, for so long.

Watching me slide.

It's nonsense, of course. She can't see me. Even Sarah can't see me. Though that's different: I try to lift Sarah from where she is, I try to be her eyes.

But Rachel can't watch me. Why should she? How do we choose? The truth is we meet, we part, we go our way. There aren't any laws, there aren't any rules. We're not here to follow each other, to guard each other's lives.

14

I TURN INTO the cemetery. It's past an Asda superstore. There's a slip road, a roundabout, a gateway. Then, inside, you double back along a narrow straight avenue. A sign says 10 mph, as if you might speed. As if the contrast with the frantic A3 wasn't obvious. Here everything is slow. Not to say still.

Putney Vale. In this dazzling light the gravestones look like bits of confectionery, wedding cake. But there's the black taste in my mouth. The grass glitters, cobwebbed with melting frost.

I remember the way. Along the avenue; park near the crematorium, which is already doing brisk business. A cluster of mourners emerging, another party gathering, waiting in the car park, nodding to each other, looking at me as I pull in as if I might be one of them. The inevitable comment, among the few comments available: a beautiful day. A beautiful day for it. Cold but beautiful.

The crematorium doing a roaring trade. But he didn't want to be burnt. He'd specified, apparently. You wouldn't think it: a man of science, a doctor. His little bit of super-stition.

I step out, take my coat and scarf and the roses from the back seat, lay the roses for a moment on the roof of the car. The emerging funeral party, spreading out, looks cautious and dazed, like a coach party on a mystery tour finally put down at its destination.

I pick up the flowers and start to walk. It's not far but it takes me, by paths lined with trees, to where I seem to be the only soul around. Living soul. The leaves on the trees are bright as paint. The frost-chewed flowers on the fresh graves look like leftover party decorations.

It's a plain grave: a polished granite slab. It still looks as if it was put there yesterday. The name, and the dates. You'd say to yourself: not a long life. There's nothing to indicate it's the grave of a murdered man.

I step nearer, slowly – as if there's some line, some edge. I want to feel at least calm, at least considerate, but I feel the hate rising up, the same sudden mad hate – maybe it's even fiercer – that I felt a year ago.

The grass where the frost has melted looks rinsed clean.

I pause, step forward, take the flowers from their paper, crumple the paper into my pocket, then lay them quickly, no fuss. No gestures, no words (what should they be?) muttered under my breath. But I can't just turn away. I have to stand and look for a while, my chest working up and down, though I'm only standing still.

The second time.

I came. I came again. I'm here, for her sake. I marked the day.

I'm paying respects, if that's the right phrase, when what I'm really doing is hating him, accusing him.

Look what you've done, look what you've done to her. Look what you did – letting her go and do *that* to you.

The sun's shining down on me and I'm black with hate.

Perhaps in eight years, nine years – or however long it takes – when she's served her time, I'll come here and I won't feel it. I'll come in peace – or I won't come at all. I'll have served my time.

The bunch of roses lying there looks like some accident, some freak. I think of the girl in the florist's. Her smile.

'Think of all the reasons . . .'

The son – Michael – arranged it all. Two years ago, or not quite. All the way from Seattle, on compassionate leave that lasted over three months. I don't know how many times he saw Sarah. I know he did see her, and I think it was bad, I don't think it was compassionate. And I know I was jealous, because Sarah, all that time, wasn't seeing me, wasn't sending me any word. Though who was I, after all? A detective, hired for the day. I wasn't a son.

I know he saw her lawyer. What does a lawyer say to a son in such circumstances? I know he took his dad's side. Why shouldn't he? Like Helen took mine.

And of course he never saw me – though I tried. But who was I? His mother's spy.

Jealous of a son who went his own way in the end, back to Seattle, and hasn't done what I've done, every fortnight, for over eighteen months. No more word from Michael. Just me.

A second punishment, like a second death: you're not

my mother any more. She took it hard, I know, I can guess. If Helen had never—

But could she blame him – *she* blame *him*? And how must it feel? Your father, your mother: to lose both. *She* should take it hard.

Hard enough for him just to have been there – here, on this spot, two autumns ago – with his father's relatives all around him, all in a state of shock. The body held in the morgue for nearly three weeks.

Sarah wasn't there, of course, wasn't free.

But I was here, right here. The mystery man who showed up from nowhere to watch things, then slipped away. To make his report.

A day in December. Not like today. Moist and murky and mild. Wet clods of earth, trampled grass.

I think of Rachel, as if her eyes are on my back.

How can you hate the dead? Absurd. As absurd as supposing the dead can feel fire. But I do, I can, even after two years. Look what you've done to her, look where you've put her. I stand here and hate him, and never tell Sarah. Yes, I'll take flowers. If he were alive I could kill him. Absurd, but I could. I'll never tell Sarah that. I could kill him – but, now, I can't.

Yes, I went. I laid the flowers. A beautiful day, brilliant and clear. The rows of trees like flames.

No, no message.

And if he could speak he might even say, 'No, you don't hate me, do you? It's not hate at all. It's not hate you feel. You're glad, aren't you? I've done you a favour. You're glad you're where you are now, and you're glad I'm here.'

15

How did it begin? And when? Even Sarah couldn't answer that. Only that she knew it had – knew in the way that you first know things, in the nostrils, and then the signs come later, the clues, the traces, to confirm what your nose has already told you.

For a little while she was like me, a detective, a private nose, on the scent, on the trail, but not wanting to be on it, not wanting to know what she knew.

Then one day she gave him a look – gave Bob a look – the kind of look, she said, she never thought she would or could ever give. And he cracked under it, crumbled, had no choice but to confess.

And the strange thing was that he made it seem like he was the helpless victim now, he was the one to be pitied.

An old dodge perhaps. But was there a period at least, an initial stage, when he'd felt himself slipping, sliding, and tried to resist? That sweet good period – autumn slipping into winter, three years ago – which, for all of them, seemed to be about something else. This new presence in the house, this new soft mood. The urge to protect. He should have been tougher perhaps, more callous – more clinical. Wasn't he used to that? Pity and charity sliding, melting into something else.

Or it was just a single moment? Maybe. One of those moments that turn everything upside down. No preliminary period of veering, and arguing with himself, no watching her every day like some substitute father but at the same time like a spy in the dark. A moment, an opportunity. They were alone together in the house. The dead of winter. Curtains drawn. They caught each other like startled animals. A door left open. A look that passed between them, a look that wasn't so much like two looks colliding and instantly bouncing away, but like a single bolt sliding shut, a look as unmistakable as that look Sarah would give him just weeks later.

'I just gave him a look, George . . .'

She didn't demonstrate, but I think I knew what it was like. Like that look she gave me on my first visits. A look like a knife. Don't play with me, George. I don't need your pity.

If life puts something in your way, what do you do? Deny it? Close your eyes, turn your back? Pretend you've walked through the wrong door. This wasn't for me, it was for somebody else . . .

Pity crashing into something else.

And afterwards the possibility that it was all a 'moment of madness' – that old get-out, that tired old formula – and they might carry on as if nothing had happened. As if it wouldn't be for him (and for her) like some infection that was inside him now.

And, anyway, by then, the scent was thickening in the air.

The charitable case: for him, for Bob. It hit him from nowhere, like wildfire. And he hadn't wanted to be burned.

And Kristina? So poor and helpless. She was twenty-two. Life had plucked her up and thrown her back into temporary childhood – perhaps – or made her grow up quicker than most. Older than her years. And so: an older man. And, in any case, she'd bloomed. Plucked up and set down in the land of comfort and plenty. Wimbledon.

Enough to make her burst, at first, into girl's tears. In that kitchen. But what did she care now, when she'd lost so much? What did she owe the world? A stateless person, only half within the law.

All those months, years – all the time – she must have thought it: I might have been there and not here. I might be dead too, worse than dead. I might have had to watch while they shot the others first, raped the others first, then shot them. She'd always know it. But here she was, in a warm bed in Wimbledon. Lawns and trees. What were the rules now? The feeling of protection sliding, for her too, into something else.

A rebound: you were robbed, now you take. And are the young so easily damaged anyway? So soft? Helen: she knew she was hurting me. You're only young once and there's a kind of savagery in it. That brother, the dead soldier, the handsome waiter. He'd been gunned down. But he'd fucked all those foreign girls, as many as he could, as if he knew he didn't have long.

'I asked her what she'd thought, George – of her brother just having his way like that, treating them like prey. You know what she said? She said it wasn't like that, it wasn't like that at all. She said if he hadn't been her brother she'd have joined the queue.'

I still think of these things, still on the case. The job that never stops. It's not enough sometimes just to watch and note. You have to put yourself into the picture, into their shoes.

His shoes – the man lying under this slab, under a bunch of roses. I think of him falling through his life.

How did it begin? How did it carry on – once Sarah knew and before there was, by tight-lipped agreement, that flat in Fulham? They – she – couldn't just kick her out. She was an asylum seeker: she had their asylum. The rules of charity. But hadn't they been smashed?

A simple question. Where did they *do* it – Kristina and Bob? You have to ask it (Sarah must have asked it). You have to ask, in my job, these simple squalid mechanical things. And put yourself in the scene.

Under their roof? Hardly – not any more. In his office? In his gynaecological consulting room? In Harley Street. In the Parkside Hospital. Signing on as some bogus private patient? The strictest privacy. It always teeters (I know, I've seen) into farce. A senior medical man with his trousers down.

In the black Saab? Or, for God's sake, wherever they could. On Wimbledon Common for God's sake. Just up the hill. Handy. Just over the road from the Parkside. It's big enough, you can get hidden enough. Enough thick trees. And even a relish in it, the danger of it – now their cover was blown anyway. An extra thrill. They might have fucked against a tree like people who own nothing. Part of her wants it, likes it like that, and he understands. (It also drives him crazy.)

On Wimbledon Common. Why not? Things happen there, in broad daylight. People get mugged, raped, killed. Or pump themselves full of chemicals. These chunks of wilderness.

Just a stone's throw from his grave – just over there, beyond the cemetery fence. Wimbledon Common next to Putney Vale. He's smiling at the thought now, at *my* thought, he's reading my thoughts. Yes, just over there, like mad things. In the woods, in spring. Don't give me flowers.

I'm standing in a cemetery thinking of two people fucking. You have to picture the scene. Even when they had that flat in Fulham. Because of the mad thrill of it. Even that last autumn, after the picture had changed – after the Croats had won. A last walk in the woods.

They shuffle through last year's leaves. September: this year's leaves still form a screen. He brushes bits of leaf, twig, bark from her back. A sort of ritual by now. She's wearing that old outdoor jacket. It's his. They're still wet and bruised with each other. And she's already aware how this may be a memory soon. An English wood. Bracken and brambles and silver birch. There was a reason once why she came to this country. But she's still a student of English words – and he's her teacher now.

She scuffs at something at her feet and stoops and looks. The hair parts from her neck. She knows the word 'mushroom' but she's forgotten, if she ever learnt it, the other word. 'Toadstool,' he says, and they both have to think about it while he explains a bit more.

'Toadstool.' The mystery of words. Toadstool. Fox-glove . . .

But which ones are these? The safe ones or the poison ones? He's not sure, he doesn't know. And she pretends to pick some up and cram them into her mouth. Then steps back, clutching her stomach, rolling her eyes – pretends to be sick. A joke: she laughs, but sees the look in his face and stops. He thinks (maybe she reads his thought, maybe she has the same thought at exactly the same time): suppose she got pregnant. What then, what then?

16

MARSH SAID, 'What was it to you?'

But maybe he had the scent already in his nostrils too. Maybe I was giving it off in clouds, along with (I could see the phrase in his report) my 'evident state of distress'.

'. . . witness in evident state of distress . . .'

An interview room. The smell of stale smoke. From down the corridor the muffled ring of a phone. How strange to be there, to be back.

'It looks pretty odd, you see. Our officers are barely on the scene and then a third party, a member of the public, turns up, in an agitated state, demanding to be let through. And, what's more, saying he has a right because he's really one of us. Meaning, as it turns out: *was*, once.'

A quick flinty stare.

Sandy-haired, greying around the ears. Grey, watery eyes – with the hidden flint. Late forties. The type who can look harmless and mild and then come on strong. The type that's well placed for being a detective because he doesn't look like one. He might be a schoolteacher. And he must have done his homework. A bell ringing somewhere – or he'd have chased it up, as soon as he knew I was ex-CID.

He leant back a little. A simple, tired expression. Had he finished with Sarah yet? He held his tie like a referee holds his whistle.

'This must be the first time that two DIs have sat down on either side of this table.' The soft approach that can suddenly bite. 'And the last – so far as I'm concerned. I'm being let out in four weeks. My time's up.'

So: this was his last case of any consequence. And only his because it looked wrapped up. Confession and arrest within minutes of the deed. Hardly four weeks' work. But then – there was me.

Your last case. How would it work? You'd want it to be no bother, you'd want an easy ride? Or you'd want to make a meal of it? Chew every detail.

And he knew what *my* last case was. I could read it in his eyes.

'But it seems' – a quick smile at his own joke – 'you want to be let back in.'

Had he finished with Sarah yet? What was it to *him*? She was just a case. And you don't get involved.

But his last case. He hadn't had to tell me that. Maybe he was proud. His last case, and it was a murder. Going out with a bang.

'You weren't exactly "let out" the first time, were you? You didn't exactly just leave.'

So there it was. Another flash of flint. He might even be more interested in me (since Sarah was in the bag), in playing games with me. The way you needle a suspect (I remember) you already know is marked down. Your last case. Make a meal.

Grey, weary eyes. Soft then sharp, then soft again. A touch of the headmaster, a touch of the dad. A family man. A wife and kids (I guessed right), the kids grown up now. He'd made it through – and so had they. They didn't see him in police mode: leaning on a suspect, stepping round a corpse. He'd come home and somehow make the switch. Soon he'd be home for good.

I might have been him (he might have been me). Two DIs. Except he had the seniority – by years of service – and I wasn't even a real DI.

Though he had to call me 'sir', technically speaking. But didn't that much.

And if I'd been him I'd have made DCI. He'd got where he was – which wasn't so far – by graft and slog mostly. I could tell. He could tell I could tell. And if he'd made DCI he might have been talking to me differently, he might really have pulled rank. Instead of being so keen to let me know that in four weeks he'd have no rank at all.

'Eighty-nine, wasn't it?'

This might have been me. Raking over old dirt and thinking of my retirement while some poor sad cow was in on a murder charge.

He let it drop, for now: ammunition he could bring out later.

'So – what was it to you?' he said.

'Mrs Nash was my client.'

'But you'd done the job – more than done the job. The job was done when you watched Miss Lazic go through to Departures and you phoned Mrs Nash to tell her.'

'La*zitch*,' I said. He kept saying it wrong.

'La*zitch*. That was all Mrs Nash had asked you to do.'

'What she actually said was "Watch them".'

Watch them, George.

'"Watch them"? So you carried on watching just him. You followed Mr Nash all the way back – to "make sure", so you've stated – till he drove into Beecham Close, then you turned round and drove home.'

'Yes.'

'But then, minutes later, before you reached home, you turned round again and drove back.'

'Right.'

'Why? Why should you have done that?'

Another flinty stare, as if he'd practised it over the years – and as if for a moment I'd become prime suspect.

And why not, why not? If it could have halved Sarah's guilt, or taken it away: all my idea, my mad, murderous plan. Seeing Bob into the trap then making myself scarce. But I'd got cold feet. Driven back. Too late.

And I must have been giving it off in waves.

'An – intuition,' I said.

'Intuition?'

'I thought – I've stated this already – I thought something bad was going to happen.'

'You mean you thought Mr Nash was going to be murdered?'

(Suppose I'd said, 'Yes'?)

'I thought I might prevent it.'

'It? You didn't.'

'How is she?' I said.

I heard the crack in my voice. I might have been saying to him: And here's my motive, loud and clear.

'She's not very happy. She's in a state of shock.' His

eyes flicked away for an instant. 'The constable's notes say' – he put a finger on his file – 'that you said he should let you through because, quote, you "knew what you were doing". Do you remember saying that?'

'I suppose so.'

(Let me through, I'm a detective.)

'And *did* you – did you know what you were doing?' He hardly left a pause. 'It seems to me you didn't know what you were doing, you didn't know what you were doing at all. Because if you knew what you were doing, that suggests you knew exactly what had happened.'

The eyes back on mine. Bad tactics. A full stretch of service and hadn't he learnt to go easy on the fixing stare? Look away, get up, turn your back, let silence pass. Then they blab.

But they weren't nerveless eyes. Flint not steel. Not in for the kill. Your last case: what do you do? Come on strong and extra tough, or show mercy?

'You didn't know what you were doing': like something held out, dangling.

And how he wrote his report, how he assessed, for example, the arrested party's reactions – immediate confession (she herself had made the call), immediate submission to custody – might, just might, affect the sentence.

It must have been well past midnight.

'You're ready to sign the statement you've made? That you followed Mr Nash to Beecham Close, then drove away, then drove back. Those were your movements tonight?'

'Yes.'

'You don't have a record of taking truthful statements. I wouldn't want to take an untruthful one from you.'

So. He couldn't help that. Ammunition. But fired over my head.

I might have said, 'Phoney statements can be true, even if they're not what the witness ever said.' And he might have said, 'That's what all the bent cops say.'

I didn't say anything. Be the humble, scared Joe Citizen. Evidently distressed.

And maybe he'd been there too: close, near the edge, near the limit. Some other time, in an interview room.

'Nothing you wish to add?'

'No.'

'About "intuition" . . . ?'

'No.'

'A true account of your movements – which you even happened to time precisely.'

'Professional habit.'

'Of course – like one of us. Technically you committed the offence of impersonating a police officer. I shan't press that.'

(But 'I'm a detective' wasn't a lie.)

'You "thought something bad was going to happen". That's to stand as already stated?'

'Yes.'

'It could still read as if you had prior knowledge . . .'

'Then why should I have *suddenly* turned back?'

'Quite. Of course. And then there's another point that hasn't been mentioned. It's my impression, it's my distinct impression, from all you've said, that the thing you thought was going to happen – the bad thing – was going to happen to Mrs Nash.'

'But it has, it did.'

I must have been giving it off in waves.

17

A CORNER TABLE in Gladstone's. It's a thrown-together place with a pseudo-Victorian feel. Music-hall posters on the wall. In Wimbledon you can go to Rio or imagine Jack the Ripper is prowling outside.

She asked for a white wine. I ordered a beer. Sipped it very slowly, watching the level in her glass like you might watch an hour-glass.

In life there's a sound principle: make a little do for a lot. Don't expect much. This may be all you'll get.

She said, 'He'll be there now, he'll be with her now.'

She didn't have to say it. I might have guessed: six o'clock on a Tuesday afternoon, and she had time to spare for me. So they were there and we were here. But she didn't have to say it. Maybe I had the thought that for them too – him and the girl – time was running out. They were watching the glass, even now. Only twenty more days – if it was all true.

'He has consultations at the Charing Cross on Tuesday afternoons. Up until five. Handy.'

A sour kind of smile. As if to say: See what I've come

to. Or as if we were like prim parents thinking of the children at play.

Except we were the children, maybe – whispering in our corner while the grown-ups did their thing.

And this look she had – as if the girl inside her was just beneath her skin.

How does it work? Your life comes off its hinges, so you go back to where you were. Not grown-up and forty-something after all. Like Kristina, forced to be a child again. But now Kristina had become the woman – Bob's woman. All the other way round. So Sarah had become the girl – the girl of long ago who didn't yet have Bob. A student, being driven through France. Flashing trees, the road south. Don't bank on it. A little for a lot, this may be all you'll get.

Is that how it is (I ought to know): a mid-life disaster takes away the years?

Or (another on-the-spot and fumbling theory): she was getting him back again – so she believed. Counting the days. Back to the start again with him, back to how she once was.

Flashing trees, the windows down.

So, I thought: she loves him still. And I was seeing what Bob had once seen.

Or it was just her anyway. How she was now. Young – and forty-three. A teaching thing, maybe. The gap getting wider between you and your class, but something rubs off. A connection – like the one she'd made with Kristina.

And yes, I could see it. 'Lecturer': it sounds old and strict and severe. But in the middle of a class something might happen – a spark, an excitement, something in her face. The student still inside the teacher. And some surly eighteen-year-old, in the middle row, would surprise himself, catch himself. He'd look at her hips, her knees. She stands by the window. The curve of an armpit, through the sleeve of a blouse, like the twist in a rope. The hidden layers in people. And girls his age could only be – girls his age.

What a fool this Bob Nash was, not to see what was under his nose. Going for the young girl. And him a gynaecologist too.

But now he was coming back – so she believed. It showed, it shone. She loved him still.

It hadn't turned into something else.

I watched the wine in her glass.

'He'll be home around nine. For supper – yes.' Another bruised little smile. 'That is, if he doesn't decide to stay the night.' A glance. 'I can't stop him, can I?'

As if she expected some sharp answer. Other women wouldn't do it like this, would they? Other women would have put up a fight long ago. I ought to know – in my line of work.

I kept quiet.

'It's a concession, you see. A concession. He only has so many days now – nights now. Only so much time.' She looked bleakly into her glass. 'Actually – it's all been a concession.' She looked up. 'When does a concession become a surrender?' She took a swallow of wine. 'You concede because you really want to keep, don't you? The risk is you're only letting it all slip away.'

The girl had vanished from her face. She held her glass just under her chin, as if it was there to catch her words.

'Are you married?'

'Was.'

A faint smile. 'It's what I thought.' A detective too. 'In any case – I know what you're thinking. What would be the usual thing, the usual option? You'd send her packing, wouldn't you? You'd tell her to get lost and never show up again. Then keep a close eye on him.'

I must have kept a straight face. Yes, that's what many would do – and the close eye might include mine. Not counting those who'd go the whole hog and send him packing as well.

'An asylum seeker,' she said. 'You see.'

I nodded. Yes, I'd got there already, followed that line. All the same, there's a point where all the rules might go hang.

'I know what you're thinking, George. If I'd never let her in. If I'd never let the poor – thing – into my house . . .'

I looked at my beer. She'd called me George. It's what I say, in the early stages: 'You can call me George.' They don't always take it up.

I looked at her knees.

'"What a fool", that's what you're thinking.'

I'd been thinking Bob was the fool.

'I wasn't thinking that,' I said. I sipped some beer.

'And I don't even hate her now. Even now.' She looked straight at me. 'And I still love him. I still love him and I don't want to lose him. There,' – a little shiver of her shoulders – 'that's my statement.'

As if she'd been called in for questioning.

'What does she do?' I said, as if I hadn't heard. 'I mean – if she's there in this flat all the time.'

'How does she *live*, you mean? He pays for that too.

The rent and everything she needs to live on – plus a bit more. And last March she enrolled in a professional interpreter's course. She's not stupid. That's what I did once – she's actually copying *me*. He paid the fees for that too.

'I know what you're thinking, That's a lot of money going in her direction that should be going in ours. But Bob makes a lot of money these days. "We" can afford it. Ha. There's a word for it, isn't there? Do you still think I'm not a fool? She's being "kept". So much for charity.'

A sip of wine as if it was some bitter medicine.

'I didn't want to go to war, George. I didn't want to make a war of it. I know . . . we're supposed to fight, aren't we? Tooth and nail.'

She looked into the air. George.

'What I'd say is – if you're going to be unhappy, better an unhappy peace than an unhappy war.' She looked straight at me again. 'Ha! I mean – compared to *her*. We're not exactly victims, are we? We're sitting here, having a drink. We've got homes to go to. We're not exactly refugees.'

I thought: She's forgotten who I am. Just her hired snoop.

'Anyway,' she said, ' – *anyway*. In three weeks it'll be all over. One way or the other. It's my little gesture. Not war but – intelligence. If they've got some other plan, then I want to know, straight away. I don't want to wait like a fool to find out. My concession – to myself.'

Another swallow of wine, the biggest so far. I thought: she's going to drain the glass then dash. But she looked at me hard.

One day, later (in a place where they don't let you do too much kissing), I'd tell her: I wanted to kiss your knees.

'Am I making sense, George? To love is to be ready to lose – isn't it? It's not to have, it's not to keep. It's to put someone else's happiness before yours. Isn't that how it should be? So if that other person goes a different way, what can you do?'

She blinked. She saw me looking – how couldn't she? – not into her eyes but at them. The eyes that went with the knees.

They say it can happen all at once, in an instant, in a flash, and you think that's just talk, a story, that's for kids not for grown-ups. But I think that was the moment.

Maybe it was me all along, something happening in me, that could make me see, detect, the girl in her. Maybe I was the one feeling young.

And it's still, amazingly, how I feel.

Something's come over you, George.

18

Rachel said, 'Goodbye. Goodbye.' As if once wasn't enough.

As if I might have mistaken this for some ordinary morning, one of those ordinary but not so common mornings when I was off duty and could have the luxury of a late lazy breakfast while she had to scramble to work. 'No, don't get up.' A blown kiss. She'd stand there for a moment, all set, in the kitchen doorway, and I'd think of how in half an hour or so she'd walk into her class – 'Good moorn-ning, Missis Webb' – and none of them would imagine how just a little earlier she'd stood in another doorway while a man in a dressing-gown, buttering toast, had sent *her* off to school.

'Goodbye, George.'

As if twenty years were just another day and it had all been anyway like some long, non-stop test which I'd finally failed. Teachers! Don't you just love them?

I didn't move. She didn't say, 'Don't get up.' And I was damned anyway if I was going to give her that last bit of satisfaction. Of seeing me get up and beg. So she could turn even harder on her heel.

Damned anyway. That was the word: damned. Judged – doubly judged now. Worse than being simply left. Or replaced. If there'd been someone else (was there? I'll never know) . . . But just to be judged – damned.

She buttoned her coat, gave that little lift and shake of her head that settled her hair. Yes, she was really leaving. It was all settled. But where had she *come* from – this woman in the doorway? How come I'd never seen her before, never known she was there? She'd missed her vocation, surely. She shouldn't be teaching sweet little infants. She was made of tougher stuff than that.

And when had she last blown me that breakfast kiss?

She stood there like some departing official visitor – like someone who'd only ever visited my life.

I even had to admire her. The firmness, the steadiness. The way you couldn't help admire them sometimes, whatever they'd done, when they kept their composure, didn't move a muscle, after you told them they were under arrest.

But hold on, I was the one on the charge.

So I didn't budge an inch, didn't even scrape my chair. I might even have taken a bite of toast. The small crumb of pride you grab when the cliff is giving way.

And everything, anyway, was suddenly up to her. I didn't have a case, a leg to stand on. She might have made *me* do the walking, with no leg to stand on. But she wanted to be the one to make the exit, to slam the door (I'd hear it in a little while), put me behind her. Didn't even want to stay where there'd be my taint.

No taint. That was all mine now, and I could keep it. No taint to her dealings with those rows of little faces, or to her clean smooth path from Deputy to Head.

Though for twenty years we'd lived with it, the taint

I'd come home with, the slow creeping taint. Married to the Force, as they say, and all that goes with it. But hold on, the taint was the taint – the taint wasn't me.

A clean slate. A clean blackboard on that bright Monday morning. A fresh white stick of chalk and a fresh brave smile, even as I kept on sitting there in that kitchen. Still as stone and off duty.

Off duty now for good . . .

And now it's such a strange, sad, far-off word – 'duty'. Now Sarah's made me think about words. When once it used to be just something floating in the air. 'Duty officer', 'duty roster', 'in the course of duty . . .'

I suppose Rachel was doing her duty that morning. 'Good moorn-ning, Missis Webb.' Well, she'd have to ditch that name.

Maybe I took a defiant bite of toast. Crunch. But I must have looked straight at her, as straight as I dared, consciously taking that last picture of her, framed in the doorway. Yes, I *had* seen this woman before. Yes, of course I recognized her, this bold, decisive woman. She'd done this before once, rejected someone else. Someone I could hardly ever have competed with.

'Goodbye, Rachel.'

What else could I have said? What else was she expecting?

She turned and disappeared. Her bright swirl of hair. Became the sound of her steps in the hall, the sound of a slamming door (maybe she just closed it, maybe the slamming was me). I heard the noise of the car. Then I felt myself falling. Doubly judged – and for the double drop. Falling, though I sat there at the kitchen table, toast stuck in my throat, sat there not moving, but falling all the while.

19

She didn't drain her glass. An inch or so left.

'You think he loves her?' I said.

The questions you come to ask. That even a best friend wouldn't ask. The part of the job I'd never imagined.

She sipped – barely a touch of the lips.

'I think so.'

She might as well have said, 'I know so.'

'And – she loves him?'

'Harder. Oh – I can see that she *could*. Ha!' Her face brightened, went dark again. 'She's the one who's leaving. She can't not go back. That's what she says – what Bob says she says. It's her country – homeland. Maybe she's torn: it and him. I'll tell you something, I've never followed the news so closely. I blessed the day when the Croats started fighting back, pushing back the Serbs, and the whole thing looked like it could soon be over. I thought this could be my – our solution. I wanted to cheer them on. Never mind they were killing each other, never mind they were doing as bad things to the Serbs as the Serbs had done to them. I was on their side! Our solution. Never mind the international solution. Crazy, isn't it? Wanting a war to be won just so it might save your day. And Bob . . . I think Bob was praying for the opposite, that the Croats would lose, that the whole bloody thing would go on, just so Kristina would never have that – way out. She'd always be – *his* refugee.

'Appalling, isn't it? And it all happened. I mean, it happened *my* way. The dust had to settle, she had to be sure. It all happened in August – it's almost November now. But you can put yourself in her shoes, can't you? A refugee here – a free citizen there. In her own country. Back where she belongs. Terrible, isn't it?'

Gladstone's. The corner table. I go there still, of course. It's a blow when the table's taken. It was a blow when they changed the upholstery from red plush to smoky blue.

'Of course, it gives her the chance to look virtuous, to look as if she's doing it for us. To look sorry. She'll give up Bob, she'll get out of our lives. She'll let everything go back to what it was.' A dry little laugh. 'Her sacrifice. *Her* concession. She can't go on causing all this – mess. It's a possibility. According to Bob, it's what she says. I haven't exactly talked it over with her. We haven't exactly all sat down round a table. The other possibility is that she sees where her life is now, where her future is, and she's ready to say, "Goodbye, Bob." Bob wouldn't tell me that, would he? Maybe Bob *wants* her to go. For her sake, for ours. It's *his* sacrifice. He's the peacemaker. He tells me that too. It's another possibility.'

She gave me a long steady look, the look of a woman who no longer trusts her husband, but hasn't stopped loving him. I'd seen the look before, come to recognize it, like a symptom, in clients.

'Have you heard of the Empress Eugénie?'

I looked at her. Maybe I looked lost.

'I do translating, as well as teaching. I've been given this book to translate – from French. It's a life of the Empress Eugénie. The wife of the Emperor Napoleon III.'

Maybe I looked completely foxed.

'One of the weird things about the Empress Eugénie is that she was Empress for twenty years but when the Emperor died she lived on for nearly fifty years. She died aged ninety-four. As if she had two lives really – an empress life, another life.'

'I know about the Empress Eugénie,' I said.

'*Do* you?'

Sometimes, maybe, fate steps in.

'She lived in Chislehurst. She and Napoleon III lived in Chislehurst. They were—'

'Rich refugees.'

Her eyes were suddenly alight. Sometimes fate steps in just for you. You're there in the class, in the front row, and the only scrap of anything you know is just what the teacher has asked.

'Napoleon died there,' I said. 'Eighteen . . . seventy-something. He was the Napoleon who died in Chislehurst.'

Not just a detective, not just a pretty nose.

'I lived in Chislehurst – grew up there. It's how I know. It's the only reason I know.'

'George, *I* lived in Chislehurst – well, Petts Wood – when I was a girl.'

Sometimes fate comes and gives you a pat on the back.

'They lived where the golf course is now,' I said. 'Chislehurst Golf Course. Their house became the club house. My dad used to play there. They were the Emperor and Empress who lived on a golf course.'

She actually laughed. Her face all alight. A woman holding a glass of wine, laughing. For a moment it seemed there wasn't any other agenda. We were sitting here in a wine bar in Wimbledon on a Tuesday evening to swap notes on an Emperor and Empress who'd lived over a century ago. This could be how it was with us.

For a moment, I had a picture of her and Bob, their regular life. The end of the day, the kitchen. He's opened a bottle of wine, rolled back his shirt cuffs. The smell of something cooking. And she's telling him about this book she's signed up to translate. The Empress Eugénie. Did he know (he was a gynaecologist) about the Empress Eugénie?

It's how their life should always have been.

I saw her eyes come back to the present.

'And the other possibility is . . . Is this just me? That it's *their* way out. *Their* escape route, their plan. All the other stuff is a cover. That they'll drive off together, or fly off somewhere, and he won't ever come home again. I don't know, I really don't know – or I wouldn't be sitting here with you.'

She smiled, as if she might have known me for a long time. She swallowed the last of her wine.

'So you were born in Chislehurst?'

'Brought up there. There was a plaque on the wall – at the golf club. I used to think it was *the* Napoleon. I never knew there was more than one.'

She put down her empty glass. I picked it up quickly, tilted it towards her. She nodded, no hesitation, but her eyes kept me in my seat. On her seat, beside her, on the red plush, the black leather shoulder-bag – the two of them inside.

'And the other possibility is that they don't know themselves. They really don't know what they're doing. What they'll do. They'll only find out at the airport. So even if he does say goodbye to her, even if that's where they say goodbye, I want to know how he does it, how they do it. I want to have been there – but invisible – for that. Do you understand?'

I must have nodded.

'Watch them, George. Watch over him for me.'

20

How does it happen? How do we choose? Someone enters our life, and we can't live without them. But we lived without them before . . .

The Empress Eugénie. Fifty years to go.

As if we were only half ourselves and never knew it. And maybe it's best not to know. Maybe that's what Rachel thought, standing in the kitchen doorway, in the exit from my life. That I was only half the man she'd thought I was.

I was half myself again. Or less.

But how does it happen? 'Meant for each other', 'made for each other', we say. And my granny Nora used to say when I was small, before we moved to Chislehurst, that 'there's a girl for every boy'. Maybe it's what grannies have to say. But didn't her own boy – my dad – prove it? Not just in marrying my mum, but in what he did for a living. His bread and butter: wedding photos.

My grandpa Ted was long dead. I never knew him. My granny Nora's other half. Nora and Ted. And my granny Nora never lived long enough to know what I knew about her boy, my dad.

Matrimonial work. I see it from the wrong end, the bad end.

I used to go with him to the golf course, Sunday mornings. It lasted maybe three months, my golfing phase. I wasn't so keen but I learnt the basics. I was only thirteen. But mostly I just used to caddy for him and his golfing mates. 'Caddy': a word that till then had meant a thing for holding tea. And mostly I went to please him. Because it was his high point, his triumph, becoming a member. I knew it even then. His golf was pretty shaky – he'd learnt as a visitor, as a guest of other members – but now he'd truly arrived, the Club had let him in. And he wanted me to slap him on the back.

Now that I look back, I can see that I wasn't a rebel, like other kids, even at thirteen, can be. Rachel, for example, in her way. Helen, of course. I wasn't gunning for my dad.

A rebel at school, maybe. Maybe not even there. A shirker – a shirker on principle. I just hated teachers, schoolwork, homework, deskwork. A man of action, me. It was Mum who tried to keep my nose to the grindstone: 'Brains, Georgie, you've got brains.' But my dad, I knew, was a self-made man, he'd worked up from nothing. What had school ever done for him? And my mum had fallen for him, hadn't she? She hadn't turned him down.

Golf – it's not exactly action, but it isn't sitting on your arse. And I was pleased for him, really, I was on his side.

A high-street photographer. Chislehurst High Street. Frank Webb. As much a pillar of the community by then, in his small way, as any solicitor or bank manager. And now they'd let him join the golf club.

But once, I knew, he'd been a beach photographer, before I was born. Broadstairs, 1946, after he came out of the army. Living all summer in a cheap back room with an old laundry-cupboard attached which he turned into a dark-room. Working the beach by day, the cupboard by night. Round-the-clock work, but that was how he learnt his trade. How to snap and make them smile. A camera and a bit of army know-how. And that was how he met my mum.

I used to think it was how he'd deliberately gone about it. That he'd gone down to Broadstairs just for that. She was the one he'd carefully selected. But first he'd built up his catalogue: beach girls, hundreds of snaps. They were all there with him, in the dark, in that laundry cupboard. It was how he chose.

My mum never said it was otherwise. It was her glory, after all. 'I was the one,' she'd say. There were all those others, in their summer frocks and swimsuits, the first real summer after the war, but he'd picked her.

Now and then they'd both mention, with a certain look in their eye, 'Mrs Barrett's place' – 'Mrs Barrett's place in Broadstairs', as if Mrs Barrett was some guard-dog they'd more than once tiptoed by.

'I was the one,' she'd say.

They got married late in 1946. I came along the next year. So my dad began his steady progress, with my mum beside him, from beach photographer to high-street photographer, and so we moved, in '52, from Lewisham to Chislehurst. A notch or two up and a better class of customer. Once again – like Broadstairs – he picked his patch well.

A pillar of the community. More than that: its record keeper, its curator. Weddings, christenings, sports teams, annual dinners, whole schools stacked up three-deep. Not to mention the countless studio portraits, commissioned for countless proud and loving reasons. We'll get Webb's to do it.'

But more than that. There was that other thing he could bring about – even when the mood might be dead against it, even when the kid had been dragged in screaming, or the couple who'd made the appointment had had a bust-up that very day. Different ways of doing it, but in the end it was something in him, in his face, his eye, as if he only had to say the word and the result would follow. As if he was still standing there on a holiday beach where everyone knew how to do it anyhow.

'Smile!'

Each photo with his name on it – stamped on the back or embossed on fine-grade card, depending on the presentation required. 'Webb's, Chislehurst.' His name on all those memory lanes.

Strange, how those photos would find their way into other places. In the Force, when you needed a photo – 'Is there a photo?' – what you'd often get would be the studio portrait, high on quality if not exactly up-to-date, handed over with a little proud echo of its former purpose: 'It's a good photo, isn't it?'

(I'd look on the back. If it was one of my dad's I never said.)

Missing persons . . . Copies would go out – the person would be missing but the photo would multiply. And whatever the result – a body, an arrest, a blank – the photo would still be smiling and unharmed.

Or the local papers. Reporters must do the same: Is there a photo? The same odd pride. The child killed in the accident: posed in a new school uniform with an angel's smile (though in fact, on the day, there'd been a hell of a tantrum). The rapist who'd once gone to college . . .

Bob's photo, next to the headline.

It's still the same now – in my high-street trade. Is there a photo . . . ?

Sometimes there seems to be only the one. The one that shows the two of them together, beaming and never to be parted.

We'd load the clubs into the car. Sunday mornings in Chislehurst. I knew what it meant to him: the golf club. I didn't want to mock and sneer. I even thought, in a small way, he was Mr Magic, coming from nowhere with a camera instead of a wand. Finding my mum.

Caddying, dogging him from hole to hole. There were his chums, of course, his golfing pals. And I'd listen to their chit-chat. Ears pricked, even then. There was a bench about halfway round, by a clump of pines, a place to pause, the brown needles at your feet peppered with cigarette ends like cartridges round a gun post.

I can't remember his name – Donald someone maybe – though I can still see him, crinkly-haired and confident-looking. Someone else who was someone in the High Street, or who ran some business, maybe, out on the factory estate by the Sidcup bypass.

I can't remember his name, but I remember the name he spoke – Carol Freeman – and I knew it could only be one Carol Freeman.

I'd been at school with Pauline Freeman. If the truth be known, I'd fancied her – an eleven-year-old's fancying: this was still primary school – and I'd thought it was mutual, just for a bit, but she'd gone off me all of a sudden. Girls for you. (Though maybe now I knew why.) And it had been long enough while it lasted for me to know that her mum's name was Carol and her dad's name was Roy. I'd even seen Pauline's mum outside the school gates. She'd looked like a woman – a mum but a woman. She'd given me a smile, a wave. I even knew where Pauline lived: Gifford Road.

I think they thought I was out of earshot. A breeze stirring the pines. I was looking for a ball this Donald Someone had whacked into the rough.

He said, 'Are you still seeing Carol Freeman? Are you still taking her pic?' I know that Dad looked up to see if I'd heard – he shouldn't have done that – and I know that I made a good pretence of carrying on what I was doing, combing the long grass. I know that he changed the subject pretty fast. And then everything was as it was, but not. A bright blue day in May, when golfers need to shield their eyes. But now there was a cloud.

And up to then I'd thought he had it all made, he knew how it was done. There was Mum and him and me – and only me because that had been enough. A perfect happy triangle.

Caddying. And being taught a little. Golfing lessons. Now I knew – I carried on scouring the grass – I'd have to go on pretending.

Golfing lessons. Eye on the ball, swing from the hips. But on the very first visit, weeks before, there'd been a little history lesson and even a French lesson as well. The plaque on the club-house wall. It was written in French. So Dad could pretend he was translating. A hidden talent. 'Napoleon III, Emperor of the French, died here.'

Napoleon? Hadn't he died on some island in the middle of the ocean?

'Not *that* Napoleon, George.' (So there was more than one?)

It all came back to me, in a rush, in Gladstone's.

Not just any old golf course, not just any old step up in the world. I could almost see it running crazily through his mind: now *that* would have been a photo! If only he'd been around then – to have had such clients.

A photo – and a hell of a challenge, a hell of a test. The Emperor and the Empress exiled in Chislehurst. Him with his empire gone and soon to die, her (though she didn't know it) with fifty years still to come.

'Ready. Look at the camera. Smile!'

How do we choose? Napoleon and Eugénie. She was a frisky Spanish beauty – Sarah's told me – and he could be a bit of a glum old stick.

Nora and Ted.

And Mum used to say, even after he was dead, 'Never mind all of *them*, never mind all those pictures he took – he knew how to make *me* smile. My God, he could make me smile.'

21

THE LEAVES ON the trees lining the cemetery paths are yellow as lemon peel. They don't move, as if they cling by a miracle. The next breeze, the next shift in the air will free them all.

I don't know what will free me here. I stand, I look. My feet are cold. How long do you give it? A minute? Five? I said to myself: Just do it, lay the flowers – go. But it's not that simple. How long is right, how long is fair, when you only come once a year?

Put down the flowers. Now beat it before the hate, or anything else, rises up. The seethe in your throat. But it's not up to me anyway. I'm here for her, for her sake. Her agent. How long would she give it, if she were here? For ever? Before she turned her back, closed her eyes, walked away. Suppose they let her out, just for this purpose, just for this one day. The taste of freedom. Lemon light. Cold air in the mouth. The freedom of a graveyard, where they never let you out at all.

But I have to do it for her, taste it for her. This life we cling to. As if she might be right here beside me, clutching my arm. Both of us looking down. The gall, the nerve of it.

I have to be here for her. To receive any messages. And that might need waiting – that might take ages – coming from the cold hard ground.

No word. Not today.

It's not up to me. And now that I'm standing here, not knowing how or when to go, I have the same feeling I had last time. It's up to *him*. He's got me now, in his grip. It's his one chance, I've walked into his trap.

You're glad, aren't you? Glad to be alive. He's smiling at me coldly down there. Nice flowers. Beautiful day.

He's not going to let me go in a hurry, not going to make it easy for me: this stranger he never knew, who turns up now like some phoney friend, some fake well-wisher. This stranger who followed him, shadowed him, though he never knew, when he was alive. Spied on him – in his pain, in his misery. And now comes to spy on him even in death.

22

RACHEL CHOSE ME, that's what I think now. Chose me – and unchose me. Though I thought I was doing all the choosing, making the move, sizing up the situation and stepping in, just like the well-trained cop I was.

Though I was something more than that by then: CID, if only just. A detective constable. Plain clothes. So she didn't know, the disguise must have worked. And it was the first and the best time I'd ever used it like that, to my own advantage, like some magic mask, like some suit of invisible armour.

I said, 'What's the trouble here . . . ?'

Police training. A little bit of presence and authority. You can break up fights (book them if they hit you back), you can stop traffic, you can act like a little god – if you're in uniform.

But she didn't guess, she thought it was just me.

It's how I met your mum, Helen, long ago. I was Detective Constable Webb. But I was Saint bloody George riding to the rescue.

*

I said, 'This lady would like a cup of coffee.' ('This lady'!) And I sat right down at her table. The nerve.

It was called Marco's. It was new and it was just a little way from the County Courts. I might have gone to the caff in New Street where all the cops on court duty hung out. I might have gone to a pub. But I mooched about and ducked into Marco's just as a shower was starting.

Eleven-thirty on a Friday morning and my weekend off was coming up, and the judge had called a sudden adjournment. My lucky day. And the sergeant said, when I called in, 'I'd hop it if I were you. See you Monday.'

Sometimes fate is on your side.

You can sniff an atmosphere straight away, you know when something funny's going on. Off duty? Maybe, maybe not. I sat at a table by the window. The shower had turned into a downpour. A waitress with a strange, hounded look seemed only too pleased to serve me. Three tables along, a big man (Marco? – I'll never know) was standing, towering over a girl who was sitting facing me but not looking at me, looking hard at her hands, one of which held a just-lit cigarette. The big man was speaking – under his breath but as if he might suddenly bellow – and she was ignoring what he was saying. He jabbed a finger towards the door. She wore a raincoat – unbuttoned, dry – but looked like she didn't mean to budge. He wore a grubby T-shirt, a tea towel tucked into his belt.

She took a drag on her cigarette, blew the smoke quickly and straight up, tilting up her chin.

And I got it all straight away. Ten out of ten for detection (and for that other thing that goes with it, sometimes: intuition). A waitress too. But she'd just been given her marching orders. For something she'd done, in the kitchen perhaps, just moments before – or hadn't done. Something *he'd* done (the details would get filled in later), and she hadn't complied. You have to put yourself in the scene.

There was a waitress's apron hanging untidily from one of the hooks by the entrance to the kitchen, as if it had been flung there in a hurry. So: she'd been all ready to storm out. Stuff your job. But then the rain had started outside and she'd had a better, angrier, braver idea. She'd sat down at the table.

If she didn't work here any more, she could be a customer, couldn't she? She could order a coffee, couldn't she? And he could damn well bring it.

Brave, angry girl. She looked straight ahead without even seeing me. Brave, angry, blonde girl.

He leant over her, his voice rising. His hands gripped the edge of the table as if he might tip it up. I don't remember *my* decision, I don't remember getting up, but one moment I was sitting at my table, the next I was standing by hers, saying, 'What's the trouble here?' And the next moment I was sitting down opposite her, but looking at him, and saying, 'I think this lady would like a coffee . . .'

The nerve. But who knows what I'd have done without my fall-back, my invisible shield? The ID in my breast pocket and the word waiting ready, which, as it happens, I didn't have to use: Police.

'. . . and I'd like to buy it for her.'

She looked at me. I could almost hear her think: Now what? What *now*? Who was this bloke from nowhere?

He glared. A moment's stand-off. Then he turned (I'd

done it!), whipping the tea towel from his belt, back to the kitchen. More words under his breath.

A sudden certainty inside me.

She looked at me. Studied me like something that had dropped from the sky. Outside the rain was pelting. April – Easter coming up. My move, but it was my audition too. A drag on her cigarette, the smoke straight up.

I said, 'The thing to do, when he brings it, is not to drink it. Not to drink it and walk out.'

She said, 'I was planning on that.'

He brought the coffee, but he wasn't going to be nice about it. Half of it was in the saucer already, more after he'd plonked it down.

We got up together, scraping our chairs. 'A shilling,' he said, folding his arms. She stubbed out her cigarette. I took a shilling from my pocket, slapped it down. A cheap round, a bargain. We edged past him while he stood like some tree. Then we were out of the door – and the rain was suddenly stopping, switching itself off like a tap. A gleam in the sky. As if that might have been part of a plan too.

I remember everything – everything, Helen. The way she grabbed my arm, straight away. The shine of the wet road. The films of oil, little coiling rainbows, in the gutter. The puddles she stepped round, the flecks on the backs of her ankles.

You don't see things, Dad.

Later, I'd say, 'Only women smoke like that – blowing the smoke straight up – women who are angry. Like a kettle on the boil.'

She looked at me. 'You notice things.'

'It's my job,' I said. It had to come out some time. 'I'm a cop,' I said.

But she didn't go off me, didn't change her mind.

And she was a trainee teacher (and I hated teachers) though I didn't know she was a trainee teacher yet.

'Plain clothes,' I said.

'Or no clothes at all,' she said.

Rain outside again. Its hiss. A kettle on the boil. I notice things.

In her room, on the first floor, stuck to the wardrobe door, was a poster, a photograph: a man in a singlet, a cigarette dangling from his wide mouth, a pistol in his hand, held up near his cheek. A bad guy, a good-looking bad guy. Every night she let him watch her undress.

I said, 'Who's he?'

She said, 'That's Jean-Paul Belmondo.'

I said, 'Who's he?'

I stayed all that weekend. Before I left she took the poster down.

It's how I met your mum, Helen. What do you think of my chocolate *roulade*? There was this other man in the room, a French geezer with a gun.

A trainee teacher. I wouldn't have guessed. Nakedness: it's a good disguise. Her last year of training – working in her Easter break as a waitress. Though not any more. One day she'd be a headmistress, a whole school under her thumb. Now she was holding my balls in her hand, cupping them like a pair of eggs.

I'd never have guessed. But nor could I have detected in her the girl of just three years before, who'd walked out

on her parents (that's what she did, Helen), and been
disowned by them.

It was months before she told me, the whole story.
Perhaps she thought it would put *me* off. The thing is
they'd been religious, the whole family – one of those
strict peculiar lots. In her bedroom, in those days, there'd
been a picture of Jesus.

But she'd rebelled (your mum, a rebel too). One day
when she was seventeen she'd told them. She didn't believe
in it any more.

The nerve, the bravery. Even now I try to picture it, years
after she walked out on me. Brave, tough-minded bitch.
I still see her when she was seventeen and I never even
knew her, taking that first brave step. As if she's up on
some high wire, about to put her foot forward. And God's
up there, even higher, glaring down.

A great walker-out.

But didn't I know it – hadn't I seen it, in Marco's,
that afternoon? She'd walked out on God. She was on the
rebound, a long slow rebound, via Jean-Paul Belmondo,
to me.

How do we choose? I should have been in court. If the
judge, and the sergeant, hadn't let me go free . . .

And in those early days I even liked court duty.
Strange, when words weren't my thing. Action, me. Having to get up there and be made to look dumb. Having
your evidence pulled apart. Seeing them get off. But I used
to think it was a kind of reinforcement nonetheless. It was
what we were for. Those things that might be just words
were part of the fabric round you there: justice, law.

Nineteen sixty-eight. We got married early in '69. I was up for detective sergeant by then, she was a qualified teacher. Model citizens. But her parents didn't show up (I think I was glad). My parents were there, of course.

Georgie, marrying a teacher! And he'd always hated school!

They stood side by side, arm in arm, remembering their own wedding, I suppose.

A registry office. A civil ceremony – it had to be. But there was confetti and flowers. And photos, of course. And who else could have taken them?

He had to step out of the picture for a while.

'Smile.'

How do we choose? My dad had gone about things thoroughly – so the story went. As thoroughly as a policeman, combing the beach with his camera.

But up in that first-floor bed-sit that wet afternoon it came back to me, that passing, nudging phrase: 'Mrs Barrett's place. Mrs Barrett's place in Broadstairs.'

Rain fell outside, all weekend it seemed. April showers, April rain. The swish of traffic sloshing through it. Buses passed, their top decks level with the window. Once – was it Saturday or Sunday morning? – she got up, quite naked, to peer through the crack in the curtains. A bus was coming and, just for the hell of it, she gave them a flash, whipping back the curtains, whipping them shut again. Her front view for them, her back view for me.

It's how I met her, Helen. More *roulade*?

And now I think about it, I think Rachel never really gave up her god. Or, she gave him up but something that went with him, or her family's version of him, stuck. I think the word is 'righteousness'. That's the right word. A sense of what's right and what's wrong. A cop. She'd never have guessed, never have imagined either. A cop. A knight to the rescue who turned out to be just a cop, but that was okay, that was all right.

She chose me, and I was always in court.

I should have seen it even there in Marco's. The sticking to her ground, the coolness. Not just a girl with balls who'd told some bloke to take his grubby mitts off. So when she walked out on me twenty years later I shouldn't have been surprised. *My* mitts were grubby now, so to speak. She was unchoosing me. Slipping her arm out of mine like a ship unties from its moorings. Sailing on.

Right and wrong. And I'd done wrong.

Never mind what Dyson did.

23

I TURN, I WALK away at last. It's only the thick taste of hate that lets me. As if I need to go and puke.

Look what you did to her, look what you made her do.

Even as I walk I feel the tug, the pluck at my back.

But don't be fooled. It's only a grave. Don't look round – a last glance, as at some abandoned victim. The roses like a blotch of blood.

Don't be fooled by the words you think you hear, whispered and icy.

'Go on, walk. You can do that, can't you? You're free, you're glad. But you haven't got her yet, have you? Not exactly. Eight more years, if you're lucky . . .'

Keep walking, close your ears.

But is that where he *is* in any case, in that grave behind you? Is that where the dead are, locked up in their graves – prisoners in their cells as well? Aren't they the freest ones of all, watching us maybe, wherever we go, like perfect unseen detectives, when we think we come to stare at them?

'So you can't ever walk away, not from me, can you?

And you haven't got her yet. Eight more years . . . You poor sad bastard.'

But I reach the line of trees and feel safe. Out of range, in the clear. Only a grave, only a slab of stone.

From the region of the crematorium, the sound of car doors shutting. One party leaving, another arriving – even in the time I'd been standing there.

And it's only the old old question, the common question. How long have we got? What's our sentence? Eight, nine years . . .

My God, there was a time when a year yawned for ever, it was time you could waste. Now it works both ways: *only* eight years.

'When I come out, George, you won't want me. I'll be years older, you won't want me.'

'It's not like that, it doesn't work like that.'

(It would work on *his* side, if it did.)

I breathe deep, the black taste subsiding – thank God for this crisp bright air. And now it's past mid-morning, there's even a faint hint of warmth when you lift your face to the sun, like warm water in a cold glass.

I walk on. Twenty to twelve. Time on my hands, even allowing for the drive to come. I find a litter bin and get rid of the balled-up wrapping paper. The cemetery is a grid of paths and plots that someone must have planned once, like you plan a town. But not far from the crematorium is a separate laid-out garden, a wall at one end, facing south – a terrace beneath, with benches. In summer the wall must be a mass of climbing plants. Even today it looks like it's being granted a brief midday bask.

Women in the Tanning Centre, doing both sides. The sun in my empty office, touching my desk.

I sit on one of the benches, hands in coat pockets. A graveyard tramp. Beyond the flower beds, through more lines of trees, the ranks of graves. But they're okay, seen at a distance, seen all together: harmless gravestones taking the sun. They're almost reassuring, these well-behaved guests, given their space here in the land of the living.

Who on earth are they all?

24

But Helen didn't clear out. Right or wrong. There she was, once a week: my daughter, my dinner date, my food sampler.

'What's it tonight?'

'Wait and see.'

Chicken Marsala (though I use sherry). The secret is in the scrapings from the pan.

'Have some wine.'

I lit the candles. A little vase of flowers. I'd put on a good shirt. It's not just the cooking, it's the presentation, the whole thing.

When had Rachel and I last done this? When had we had the time?

I'd bring in the serving dish with a flourish. '*Voilà!*' (I can speak French.)

'Dad – this is really *good*.'

You can tell when someone's pretending, only saying what you'd like to hear. She'd let the first bites linger in her mouth, give me marks out of ten. Below seven was rare.

But if Helen had become the woman in my life – if

that was the unspoken fact – who was the man in Helen's? A fair question. Another unspoken fact.

'You know . . . if one of these days you wanted to – bring someone. I'm sure I could manage for three.'

Clumsy maybe. Helen had her own life somewhere, what did it have to do with me? And why should I want to upset these precious weekly visits? A lifeline, simply: they kept me afloat. The mercy, the miracle that, after everything, she and I should be friends.

'If there *is* someone . . . at the moment.'

But it seemed she'd been waiting for the subject to come up.

She put down her knife and fork. A quick sharp breath, a slight wobble of her chin.

'Yes, there is someone. There is someone. She's called Clare. We've been living together for over a year.'

What do you say when you hear such a thing? The truth is, when I heard it – she said it perfectly clearly – I didn't feel anything much. No jolt, no shock, no lightning reaction, unsuspected inside me, leaping out. I was pretty numb in those days, maybe. But anyway, why should I be shocked? I was a policeman – I'd been a policeman. I'd seen some things.

I suppose what I felt was the great airy gap of my own ignorance. My blindness. 'You don't notice things.' This is your daughter Helen, who you hardly know.

And then what I thought, suddenly, rapidly rewinding years, was: it makes no difference (it hasn't knocked me off my seat), yet it does. Because this is something that Helen has taken all this time to tell me, something she hasn't been able to tell me, for fear of how I might react. So now if I *don't* react, it will be like a disappointment, a humiliation to her, it will be like saying all those years of being my enemy were just a waste.

She'd *like* me to be a blustering, ranting dad.

I suppose what I thought was: my own daughter has been afraid of me, most of her life.

And now I was washed up, now I was no threat . . . Now I wasn't a senior cop any more, or even a successful husband . . .

Unless it was Rachel she'd been afraid of.

I don't know how long I just looked at her.

'Sweetheart,' I said.

I don't remember choosing the word. It came out of my mouth like a bird: 'sweetheart'. A word I'd never used to Helen before.

There was a tear – no more than a glint in her eyes. Like that glint I see in clients' eyes.

I must have smiled at her, because a smile spread over her face too. The tremble of her chin. How brave.

'I never knew,' I said.

'You do now,' she said.

I wouldn't have taken her hand, wouldn't have known if that was the thing to do, if she hadn't pushed it first across the table.

And then (then and afterwards) I thought all the thoughts that you think. How long had *she* known? But was it like that? A point when you knew? Or just a long awful time of not knowing, of not knowing which side you were of a line?

'Well,' I said at last, 'it doesn't alter what I said. Bring *her.*'

She looked thoughtfully, seriously at me.

'I think maybe that's not a good idea. Not now.'

'But – tell me about her.'

And now she became flustered, awkward – as if she was a boy and the question was from her mum.

'She's . . . She's . . . brilliant at interior design.' She couldn't help one of her quick searching glances round the room. We're thinking of setting up – as interior designers, I mean. Of going into partnership—'

She laughed at the phrase she'd used. I laughed too.

I thought: so it was simple. Your big love was Art. Big pictures in frames. But you'd settle for interior design: that was your big love now.

Maybe she could tell what I was thinking. She looked down at her plate.

All those years, I thought, all those years of not saying. And now, in a few moments, it was said. So it wasn't about me being a policeman – though my being a policeman can't have helped.

And later I thought, half guiltily, half excitedly, of Helen in bed with another woman. Clare. In much the same way, I suppose, as Helen must have thought of me and Rachel, her parents, in bed together.

'This is delicious,' she said. She meant my Chicken Marsala.

I must tell her, I thought, I must tell her about Rachel and me.

But maybe she won't come any more – not now. Now it's over with, now she's said it. Maybe that's what it's all been about, these visits. Not about my cooking, my managing, my proving I could look after myself.

But she did keep coming. (She hasn't stopped coming.) In the fullness of time I even got to meet Clare.

Though it was after that evening when she made her

announcement that she began to get more direct, more pushy, even more plain damn nosy, about me finding someone else, someone, that is, who wasn't her.

I went on a weekend cookery course. She nudged me into it. I had a real talent, didn't I realize? Buried by twenty-four years in the Force. It needed bringing out.

Though I didn't need that much nudging, I was keen myself. This new me, this unsuspected me, this kitchen me.

'How was it?' she said.

'Fine. I picked up lots of tips.'

'Did you pick up anything else?'

I wasn't going to act dim.

'I was the only bloke there, if that's what you mean . . . they all admired my pastry.'

But it was only after I went into private detection – which she hadn't been pushing for at all – that facts began to race ahead of her little teasing schemes.

I think she was glad for me. And I think, the way it turned out, *she* was the one to be shocked. Her dad. Not just finding another woman in his life but, so it seemed, more than one. But it was my life, like it was hers. Fair exchange, and let's be frank (and she'd have known if her dad was having her on), I slept with clients. There. One or two. Difficult not to. Breaking all the professional rules. But hadn't I taken that turn already? Already been branded?

Corrupt, through and through.

I think she didn't know how to take it, I think she was a little ashamed. Do you remember, Helen, when *you* were a rebel, impossible to handle? But I think she was also entertained. She hadn't known this man before (nor had I), this – what's the word? – womanizer. I think she was taken aback but I think she found it mainly comic. And maybe, mainly, it was.

Life was a comedy after all, maybe. As opposed to all that tragic teenage stuff. As opposed to all that grim stuff you find in police files.

'This is really delicious.'

Lifting her fork daintily. Like a woman on a date again, like a man's woman making sweet and obliging comments, testing the ground. But she meant it too. And there'd been all those wretched months when I'd struggled round art galleries, an off-duty policeman, staring at pictures, trying to see in them some clue, some lead to my daughter.

Chicken Marsala, followed by lemon tart. A bottle of wine. A man and a woman at a candlelit table. Interior design. Don't knock it – what's civilization for?

Beyond the window, the back garden, hidden and dark. My last days in the old house. Rachel, Helen, me. I turned and pointed at the glass, at our two faces looming in a pool of light.

'Caravaggio,' I said.

25

I NEVER FOUND that lost golf ball, hidden in the rough. And now there was something else that would have to stay out of sight: the little wild black ball of what I'd heard, that had come slicing, whirring towards me. I'd caught it and put it in my pocket, and that's where it had to stay.

I wish I could have found that missing ball – the white, the right one. Held it up with a smile, like something that put everything back where it was.

But you know when you've crossed a line.

'Never mind. It's only a golf ball . . .'

They got up from the bench. We moved on to the next hole, me pulling the bags on their trolley, a little way behind. Before we reached the tee I'd already made my decision: that I'd have to pretend – so Mum would never know. Keep mum. That was my mission now.

I'd never been this way before – where words, that were just bits of air, could turn scary and black and hard. The word 'wrong', for example. It gets chucked all the time at kids, gets chucked at you all the time at school. I'd never caught it, never felt the weight of the word 'wrong'.

We got to the tee. He drove first and I handed him his club. I felt the weight of the word 'club' in my hand.

Pretend, keep silent. I couldn't even tell Pauline Freeman, who must know already — because she'd given me the brush-off. Tell her that I knew too. Though that might have been a way of getting back together with her. Partners in secrecy. Like her mum and my dad . . .

I thought of the little black ball of knowledge Pauline had been carrying around with her for months already. And it would have to go on. Because you'd never not know.

And the other thing I decided, even as I followed Dad to the next hole, was that I'd have to *follow* him — other sense. Watch him, trail him. Because if you knew something then you had to *know* what you knew, you had to have proof. Otherwise you might be tempted to think it was all a mistake, everything was like it had always been.

But I didn't follow *him* — how could I follow him? He'd turn and recognize me at once — I followed her: Mrs Freeman. Though she too might recognize me. That smile, that wave outside the school gates (had nothing been happening then?). And once, later, I'd passed by Maynard's estate agents in the High Street where she worked part-time (Pauline told me), and I'd looked in through the window, past the photos of houses, and seen her, Mrs Freeman, dressed like a secretary, and she'd seen me, I'm sure, but hadn't waved or smiled. And I'd thought that was because Pauline and me weren't friends any more.

But that's how it came to me, how a whole rush of things came to me. Part-time at the estate agent's — Wednesdays to Fridays, Pauline had said. And Maynard's was just fifty yards or so from Dad's studio, on the other side. So during that three-day stretch each of them would know that the other was there, across the road, near yet far. Was that how it began? He'd invited her across? 'Taking her pic.' What kind of pic? The old beach photographer. After hours maybe. But it couldn't carry on like that (if it was going to carry on) in his studio.

So . . . ? Three days a week in Maynard's, which left two days when she was just – to use the word then – a housewife. Free to come and go. And Mr Freeman worked all day in town. And Dad worked in his studio of course, but he still went out on jobs, even though he had assistants, packing his gear in the back of the car. And he could pretend. Though he'd hardly go to the Freeman house in Gifford Road.

But she worked in Maynard's, and working in an estate agent's she'd surely know about places that were briefly empty, waiting for buyers, tenants. She might even be able to get, or get a copy of, a key . . .

There are always these simple, mechanical questions. Where? When? How? Often they're half the battle. For them, as well as you.

' "Matrimonial work", Helen. That's what they call it.'

I looked in his appointments diary. Not difficult. He carried a pocket-size version of the one he kept on his office desk. In the evening he'd often leave it, for ready reference, by the phone in the hall. Nothing suspicious inside – unless you already had a theory and saw that on Monday afternoons for two weeks ahead there was a gap between one and four. And once on a Tuesday.

Detective work. It's mostly graft and slog but there are times when a light comes on in your head.

I couldn't follow him: he drove a car. I followed her. She didn't drive, but they'd make separate journeys, I was sure. He wouldn't risk picking her up. Gifford Road joined White Horse Hill, a bus route, so I waited near the bus stop on White Horse Hill, reckoning that if they rendezvoused soon after one, I should be on watch from about a quarter past twelve.

Summer. The school holidays: I was free too. Summer, but pouring with rain. But that was a blessing. I could wear the hood of my anorak up. I could loiter, as if sheltering, under the awning of the newsagent's some twenty yards from the bus stop. And when she appeared, round the corner of Gifford Road, she was carrying an umbrella, which is like a kind of hood too, a barrier to knowing you're being watched. Rain: the detective's friend.

She might have crossed, to take the bus in the other direction – I'd have crossed over myself – but she stayed on my side. A bus came. I dashed, at the last moment, to get on. Then it was a case of sitting with my head turned mostly to the window. And if she saw me – well, it was a coincidence and I'd have to settle for studying her face.

She didn't see me. She got off at the Spencer Arms. I timed my exit neatly, hung back while she walked on. Then I followed her round two, three corners, remembering the names of the streets.

At any moment, of course, Dad might have driven by and spotted me, hood or no hood. But I was lucky in that too. She was well ahead of him.

Collingwood Road. She turned into a house – number

twenty. Yes, it had an agent's sign outside. Yes, she had a key. I scurried to the other side of the road and walked on a little – carefully eyeing each parked car. This was the tricky part. A residential street: where do you hide? But some way along was the entrance to a little park, a recreation ground – deserted in the rain – and I tucked myself in the gateway, under the branches of a chestnut tree.

And it was from here that I saw Dad's Wolseley drive by and park, not so near number twenty, though there was a gap, and saw Dad, a blurry figure in the rain – half hidden, too, by an umbrella, but unmistakably my dad – hurry to the same house. He didn't have to wait to be let in.

I stood, not moving, under my tree. You know when you're committed, when there's no going back.

I suppose I had the thought: now I could pounce. I could go to number twenty, bang on the door. Open up! I had him – them – trapped. It was even, maybe, the right thing to do.

But I didn't move, as if I was on guard. The mysterious urge to protect. My shoes were leaking, my neck was damp. I thought of the sound of the rain from inside. Gurgling gutters and down-pipes. The smell of a room that isn't yours. The feeling of shelter, of taking shelter wherever you can.

And was this their only shelter, here in Collingwood Road? Did they have – according to their strategy and the state of the housing market – a whole string of shelters, in Chislehurst, in Petts Wood, Bromley, all round the not-to-be-trusted suburbs?

I suppose that's what I felt, under my chestnut tree: that I didn't have any shelter, real shelter, any more. I was shelterless. Rain dripped from the leaves.

I could slink off home now but I didn't have a real home any more, just a pretend one, and I'd have to work hard – just me and for as long as it took – to stop the pretend-walls and pretend-roof from tumbling down.

Until the thing that was going on there in number twenty died a death. Whenever that might be. But even then – because I'd always *know* – I'd have to go on pretending, even after it had died a death.

26

AND KRISTINA? What did she want? Did she really love him – that man over there under the slab, with the roses? And so was it really her 'sacrifice'? To go back. Not to destroy him – him and Sarah. To get out of their lives.

Destroyed anyway.

So much of it I've had to piece together gradually, on my visits. As much as she's wanted to tell, as much as she's wanted to talk. A special room for talking, like an interview room, like several interview rooms together. It's not ideal, it's not private, but it's all we have. You haven't got her yet.

And we write. I write, my 'English lessons'. That's where Kristina came in. If she'd never walked into Sarah's English class . . .

In the beginning, when she didn't want to see me or speak to me (no Visiting Order, no visit), it was all there was suddenly: writing. I'd never done it before, put down things like that on paper.

Please call me . . . Please see me . . . Please answer this letter . . .

As if I was the one on remand.

*

How much could I ever have learnt then – in Café Rio, in Gladstone's? Our few moments, our time together, in the free world. You haven't got her yet. But a little for a lot in this world – the only rule.

It might have been Bob's rule too. It's all on remand. This can't last, this will end in disaster – but I'll always have known this madness.

And even then, in Gladstone's, trying to make a glass of beer last for ever, I wasn't thinking so much of what she was telling me. A lapse of professional concentration. I was thinking: I may not see her again, not like this. This job – this simple job – and then?

And I wanted it to be a success – I mean, I wanted it to turn out as she wanted. I wanted to see her get her husband back, to be a witness to that. So that then, at least, I'd see her happy.

She'd have settled the bill, thanked me. Thanked me like some good uncle.

And then? I might never have seen her again. Unless I loitered continually by the Fine Foods section. Unless – crazy ridiculous thoughts – she asked me to dinner, to sample her cooking, to meet her husband. To say, 'Bob, this is George, the one I paid to watch you, to spy on you. You and Kristina – just in case. George, this is Bob. Bob's been dying to meet you . . .'

Crazy thoughts.

But I was a detective, wasn't I? I could always see people, be with them, follow them. I could follow her, just as I'd followed Bob and Kristina. Just as I'd thought, years before, when the divorce was on its way, of follow-ing Rachel, of viewing this impossible thing: Rachel in another life, her own life, without me. Rachel as she once must have been, before I'd ever met her. Rachel with somebody else.

How do we choose?

She must have someone else – she must have *had* someone else. So all that getting on her high horse, all that being the judge of me . . .

I might even have stopped following and watching and butted in.

A detective, wasn't I? A detective still.

'It's my choice, Helen, it's up to me . . .'

Choice? It's in the blood. It's what I do, I *am*.

It's what we all do, I think, in our different ways. Something in the blood, in the nose. Under the chestnut tree, the sticky breath of summer rain. We're hunters, that's what we are, always stalking, tracking the missing thing, the missing part of our lives.

I might never have seen Sarah again, not properly. Just followed her, dogged her, snooped, spied. But that wouldn't have made me a detective, would it? It would have made me something else.

27

AND KRISTINA? She disappeared of course. Became a missing person, an absent witness. Marsh wasn't going to have her traced. The trouble, the expense. Not worth it for such a sewn-up case. (Just a few loose threads.) Not worth his remaining time, ticking away till they let him out. And, anyway, for all immediate purposes she was out of the picture, uninvolved. She was up in the sky when the crime was committed – or coming down to land, in Switzerland. Neutral territory.

I think of her on that night, in that plane. Tears all the way? (Did someone sitting next to her have to take pity?) Or dry-eyed, hard-eyed, sipping her free drink?

Thinking of what was behind her, or what was ahead?

I see her arriving in Geneva, producing her wad of papers and credentials, the proof of who she was. The passport from a country that no longer existed.

And she didn't know – how could she? – that Bob didn't exist any more either, whether for her or not. The lights and announcements of an airport, the flow of people. Didn't know (it was meant to stop things being destroyed) the destruction she'd left behind.

But then – she'd always been leaving destruction behind. The story of her life. Five years in England while everything she'd known was torn apart. Going back now to see what was left.

Hard-eyed and hardened? But blossomed and softened and beautiful, with the embrace of another woman's husband still with her like the clasp of a ghost.

Switzerland. Airport shops full of watches and chocolates.

Over and over I've thought it: she might *never* have known, she still might not *know*. Would she have looked at the English papers? Or even noticed, if she had, the not so big story (only a murder, only a simple murder) on the inside pages? Would that have been her first concern? Out of their lives – that was the deal? So, no follow-ups or backward looks, no further communication. Dead to each other.

In Switzerland, or in Croatia, you don't think of a street, a house in Wimbledon. Any more than people in Wimbledon think of a street, a house (a ruined street, a burnt-out house) in the former Yugoslavia.

Some things it's best not to know. And if she *does* know, if she did find out, she's never come forward, never declared herself. Lived – wherever she is – like an exile with the knowledge.

And she's never appeared here, in this cemetery, considering it worth the journey, the expense, considering it necessary to come all the way back, to stand – shed tears perhaps – lay flowers.

Though how would I know? Who keeps a constant watch on a grave?

*

The sun here, by this wall, has a papery warmth. The sky is as blue as a summer sea. Holiday brochures. Dubrovnik . . .

I see her sitting too, at some pavement café. Geneva? Zagreb? Dubrovnik? Winter sunshine. Steaming coffee cups, glinting table tops. Her eyes are hidden by sunglasses. You can't follow her gaze. You'd look and think: no child. A woman of the world.

What did she want? It's easy to say she got what she wanted – as if it was all done by calculation: loss and gain. The bright-eyed girl who'd come to London to study, to get a life. Well, she'd got her compensation. A refugee? A flat of her own, for God's sake. Seeing how they lived in comfortable Wimbledon, in comfortable Fulham. Oh she knew how to turn everything to havoc. Compensation? More. All the time, after all, she might have been living through a war. Atrocities on both sides. Fair's fair.

And then when it seemed at last she had a country of her own to go to, she went back with her loot, her credentials, a veteran of the English suburbs.

How could it have been like that? His last hug still warm on her.

She'd become a hunter too, in Wimbledon. The missing part of our lives. She'd watched him, he'd watched her. Which way round did it work? Some moment must have come. And she, at least, must have known, when it came, that there weren't any rules. Life happens outside the law.

Did she love him – however it began? Did he love her? There's no recipe, it's not like cooking. It can last for life, it can burn out in months. He hadn't wanted to be burnt.

They walk in the woods. On Wimbledon Common. They fuck against a tree. But she's still the student of English words.

They were the best times, Sarah said, when they'd begun to teach each other: English for Serbo-Croat. The teacher being the student, starting from scratch. In the kitchen, the different words for food – 'nutmeg', 'pumpkin' – or in Sarah's study, overlooking the garden. The best times: learning each other's language. Even the feeling that Kristina envied her. Was that so surprising? This study, this safe calm place. Translation work. The garden outside, wintry, littered with dead leaves. As if Sarah was what Kristina wanted to be.

Well: that had come true. As near as could be. Her English was perfect. She had her degree. A qualified interpreter too. That passport of a skill.

She'd even shared Sarah's husband.

'Toadstool,' he says. A mad word.

She stoops (so I picture it: I'm watching, a detective, hidden by trees), pretends to eat, pretends to throw up. How will it end? Suppose she got pregnant – they both have the thought. But they both have the other thought too. How will it end? This is how it could end anyway – something like this. With poison, with death.

They look at each other as if they've both eaten for real.

To love is to be ready to lose, it's not to have, to keep.

So: she made her sacrifice? She was the one who always

had to lose everything? Arriving – dispossessed again – in neutral Switzerland.

What became of her? Where did she go? I could follow her too, track her down. An international assignment. Find out the truth: did she ever *know*?

But that's not my job, that's not my case. That's for that man over there, it's his case. That's for Bob to do.

28

Dyson did it. And if there were any justice . . .

And I'm still shocked – the reverse of other people's shock, the reverse of Rachel's shock – at how the story, the crime almost, became how I'd shown myself to be a crooked cop and had to be made an example of, and not the story of how Lee Dyson had stabbed Ranjit Patel in his Handi-Store on Davis Road. Stabbed him three times, almost committed murder in fact (and not for the first time), but was going to walk free.

But I'm still shocked at myself, it's true.

A Sunday evening. They called me out. September '89. Helen had left home – so I couldn't blame her. Needling me, pushing me near the edge. Remarks that stung. 'You don't *see* things.'

So what am I saying? It would have been all Helen's fault?

Three witnesses – or none, depending on how a court would see it, and if it reached a court in the first place. But Dyson did it – his handiwork, as the saying goes – and now I had him. It ought to have been a sewn-up case.

Ranjit Patel. But he'd passed out in seconds, and

hadn't been in a state to talk (it was touch and go) for two days. By which time ... And any defence lawyer would have torn holes in the reliability of his memory. Even if he hadn't said anyway (since it was Dyson): I don't remember a thing.

Mrs Patel – Meera Patel. But she'd come on the scene, from behind the shop, just too late to see Dyson (if it was him). What she saw was her husband lying in a terrifying pool of blood (and Dyson, maybe – a blur that was hardly in her vision – disappearing through the door). Her first thought hadn't been to look out on to the street – which seemed to have been surprisingly empty of passers-by – or to look down the passage leading to the Callaghan Estate. But she was ready enough, now, to testify that Dyson – she even knew his name – had abused and threatened both her and her husband several times before, had even once, though she wasn't present, waved a knife at her husband. She was as ready to say it was Dyson as I was – and she was relying on me.

Which, given the minimal forensic, left Kenny Mills. Given that the weapon was as yet unlocated, though it was reckoned to be a knife with at least a four-inch blade. Given that Dyson (if it was him) had managed to lose it very efficiently and, in the time it took for police and ambulance to get to the scene, had (to reconstruct) gone back to the Dyson place on the estate, put all his clothes in the washer ('So? It was wash day'), disposed somehow of a pair of probably blood-stained trainers, put on fresh clothes, then set off for Mick Warren's flat, across the estate, where, according to Warren, the two of them had been since seven, watching a match on TV.

All this, a defence lawyer would say — all *this* in the time it took for police and ambulance to be on the scene . . . ?

Yes, if it was Dyson, yes.

It left Kenny Mills, in Room Number One. Who wasn't having a happy time. Who said he'd only gone up to the Patel shop for some cans and fags. Yes, up the passage from the estate, and he hadn't seen a soul, and then he'd come upon Mrs Patel with Mr Patel bleeding and unconscious.

I said he was lying and he said he wasn't. Either way, he looked scared.

Not one of the true hard-nuts. Not one of Dyson's little core. On the edge — wanting to be let in, perhaps. Though not any more.

Some cans and some fags, which he never got to buy. And for this innocent little errand, and though Meera Patel swore he'd walked in *after* she'd called 999 — maybe a minute after she herself had come in from the back of the shop — he was hauled in by Uniformed and strip-searched, as if a four-inch knife might be hidden up his arse. Then grilled long into the night, including by DI Webb who arrived — from the Patel shop — at nine-fifteen.

And took one look at Mills and had them haul in Dyson as well.

It's a well-known game. You have the two of them in and you play the one against the other, hoping for a quick result. Especially in those precious moments before either of them has a lawyer beside them, telling them when to shut up.

Not so much detection as spinning plates. Till one

breaks. But sometimes you just get impatient, you get excited – you get near the edge. The scent of a quick kill under your nose.

Dyson did it, Mills didn't – I knew that. But I didn't have to tell him. I even believed the beer and fags. The only bit I didn't believe was that he'd come up the passage from the estate – at just that time – without seeing Dyson coming the other way.

More than one reason he was looking scared.

'You didn't see anyone – coming the other way, from the shop?'

'No.'

'Lee Dyson, for example.'

'No.'

'Pity.'

'Yeh?'

'Yes, because if you say you didn't see Dyson you're smack in the frame.'

'I never got there till after. That woman—'

'Mrs Patel? Yes, that's what she *said*. But maybe she was confused. She thought her husband was dying. He still might die, you know. And, maybe, she was scared of *you*.'

'Scared?'

'Yes. Wasn't that the idea – the old idea? Scare them. See how far it could go. You, Dyson and the others. Scare them a little, scare them a lot. You look scared yourself, Kenny.'

'Fuck off.'

'You wouldn't have stuck a knife in Ranjit Patel, would you? Not by yourself. But you were there when Dyson did. Let's suppose. And that put you in shit. But then you

came back. Smart – and not so smart. You thought you'd
clear yourself, you'd make it look as though you'd just
arrived—'

'That wasn't how—'

'How? How what, Kenny? What are you saying? You
really did it yourself?'

'Piss off.'

'So who did? If you didn't, why are you looking so
scared?'

'Fuck off.'

Interview rooms. Grey boxes. There's a point where
they can become like clearings in the forest. The thrashing
and gnashing could start. There's a tape running and a
DC sitting in, but you can forget both are there.

'Shall I tell you something? We've got Dyson in here
right now. Just along the way.'

You watch their eyes closely.

'But – we'll keep you apart.'

'Fuck off.'

'You're scared of Dyson, aren't you? That's okay, that's
sensible. Dyson's scary. I'd be scared of Dyson – but I'm a
cop. It's your chance, Kenny. While the two of you are
here. You nail him first. One of you walks, one of you
gets to stay.'

It's what I said. On the tape.

'He did it, didn't he? You were there.'

'No.'

'You were with him.'

'Fuck off.'

'Okay. You weren't there, you weren't with him.
Here's another story – tell me if it's any better. Yes, you
went to get some beer and fags. No, you didn't do a thing

wrong. You were just going to get some beer and fags. But you saw Dyson coming the other way, down that passage. Bad timing. Or good timing – maybe. He looked pretty fired up, didn't he, and you couldn't step out of his way, could you? And he couldn't step out of yours. Just the two of you. So he grabs you and he *tells* you what he's done. He's full of it. I'm prepared to bet he even waved the knife in your face. He's a nutcase, isn't he, Kenny? Off his fucking head. And he tells you that you never saw him. He tells you that you never saw him and that you should piss off out of it. And he disappears fast himself.

'Then you've got a choice, haven't you? Big choice. Disappear yourself, that's the easier option. But you reckon – smart thinking – that if you do that and it comes back round to you again, you're an accessory. So you walked on. You walked on to clear yourself, but you walked on for another reason – let's hope. You'll say you never saw Dyson anyway, but you walked on for another reason. There was a man dying – maybe – just yards away. He still might die, Kenny. You did the right thing. You didn't piss off. A different kind of bottle. You behaved like a good citizen. You get points for that. You don't need a brief, Kenny. Sometimes briefs take ages to arrive . . .'

I watched his eyes. You can tell. Ninety-five per cent true. Sometimes it's not detection. It's being in the picture. As if I'd been standing there all along, watching, in that passage.

'A good story? You haven't said anything. If you like, we could make it your statement. You could sign. And I'll make another bet. If you don't have a better story and Dyson gets to know you went on to that shop, he'll stick you right in it, that's for sure.'

Interview rooms. They can be like another world. I got up, turned my back, looked, hands in pockets, at the wall. Like the teacher when the class is doing the test. But I think my heart was thumping, measuring the silence. Those first few hours. Dyson, at last.

If you look away, it's sometimes when they talk. But the silence dragged on, thick with Kenny's thinking.

Finally I said, 'Okay, I'm going to speak to Dyson.'

Kenny said, 'Stop.'

29

I sit on the bench. Not yet noon. Time to kill. But if I leave soon and take it slowly . . . And I always allow time, I'm never late. As if I'll earn privileges, too, for good behaviour.

The usual routine: park in the side road, walk first in a different direction. Not that I'm ashamed. Ashamed to be seen to be a visitor, a prison visitor. For God's sake, I'd be over that by now.

And anyway: the most precious moments of my life.

Twice a month they see me. An old hand by now, a regular. His home from home. A women's prison. Something must keep him coming back, coming back for more. When you think about it, it can only be one thing . . .

And he can't be her husband, can he?

'George' they call me. Or 'Georgie-Porgie'. Or sometimes, because of the 'homework' they know I hand in and collect, they call me 'The Schoolboy' or 'The Teacher's Pet'. And they all know as they frisk me (they can't touch you in certain places, they have to get a male warder) that I was a cop once, a DI. Now I'm a private dick.

A regular. Never misses a fortnight.

But I was so nervous, those first times, of being late. So she might think – what? That she'd been stood up? Though she wasn't thinking much at all, then, wanting to be like ice.

So nervous, I've long since got into the habit of being early. A bite to eat first. I walk, the other way, to the main road. It's 'Snacketeria' usually, which, despite the name, does good stuff.

'What was it today, George? The mozzarella and grilled vegetables? Or the spicy ham?'

She wants to know these things. Every detail, every crumb. Life outside. As if I can live it for her, ordinary blessed life. The smell of good coffee. Lunchtime bustle. A sandwich, well made.

It was a good sign when she started to ask (a little like Helen): what was I cooking, what was I eating? A good sign when she said: the food's crap in here.

It might be a good spot to munch a sandwich, right here. A bench against a sunny wall. It's what benches are for: a bench, a sandwich. But can you eat, should you, do they let you, in a cemetery? Crumbs for the dead.

What do the dead most wish for – if they're watching? The feathery warmth of a November sun on their eyelids? The taste of fresh bread?

Bob could tell me. But how do you ask?

Patel was lucky. Stabbed, scarred – out of action for months – but alive. He'll have known what it's like to come back from the dead.

Lucky? Well, yes and no. Enough to make him put aside the smaller factor: that he never got any justice. The law let him down. And he and his wife would finally quit that shop – that shop that had become part fort anyway, trading post and fort, in enemy territory.

Even though he would say to me it was Dyson, no mistake. He'd got a good look.

Well, we had him, Mr Patel – I had him for you. But we had to let him go. A police fuck-up. Twisting the rules. Perverting the course of—

I went in to see him. A big bunch of flowers. I wouldn't have been surprised if he'd spat.

A cop gets the boot, Dyson goes free. Patel gets the nightmares and the scars.

As it happens, Mr Patel, my life is pretty much in pieces too, pretty much up the spout – if it's any consolation.

But I couldn't say that. Nor could I say to him: There was a moment, Mr Patel, a mad blood-thirsty moment when I actually hoped – so much the worse for Dyson – you might die.

30

I WENT ALONG TO DYSON. Room Number Two. He should have been stewing, but Dyson wasn't the kind who stewed. The face like some soft stone.

His brief was there beside him. Who'd be Dyson's brief?

I said, 'We've got Kenny Mills in here as well.'

Not a flicker.

'That cunt.'

'We had to bring him in. He was there, you see. He'd walked into the shop. He must almost have been there when it happened.'

I watched Dyson's face.

'So – have you arrested the cunt?'

'I've been chatting to him. The thing is, he says he saw you. Before he got there. He says he saw you coming away from Patel's shop.'

Not a flicker again. Just something clicking into place at the back of his eyes, as if it was Kenny he was looking at, not me.

'How could he have done if I was round at Mick Warren's watching the game?'

They were searching Warren's place still. As if they'd find a blood-stained knife stuffed down the sofa.

His brief was quick. 'Do I understand correctly? Your other witness has made a statement to this effect? A statement on the record?'

'Yes.'

A small word, but the tape picked it up.

'My client and I would like to consult.'

I went back to Number One. Sometimes, if you're lucky, the chase can all be over inside four walls. Sometimes it's you who gets caught.

The duty solicitor was there. I didn't like the look on his face.

I switched on the tape.

'Okay, Kenny, you've done a good night's work . . .'

His brief said, 'Mr Mills wishes to withdraw the statement he's made.'

I looked at Kenny. Kenny looked at the table. So: more scared of Dyson than of me. With justice maybe.

'Mr Mills informs me that none of the words in the statement he's made are his.'

I looked at the lawyer. You cunt.

'They were not volunteered by him. Mr Mills alleges that he was coerced into making his statement by intimidation and deceit.'

It's true. That's how the tape might show it.

'Kenny—' I said.

He gave me a quick look. A brave look, in a way, a brave coward's look.

I'll swear it still, to this day. Everything was true.

Ninety-five per cent. Even the bloody knife waved in his face.

But looks don't get picked up by the tape.

I couldn't say it in front of the brief, with the tape listening. I made my eyes say it: He'll get you anyway, Kenny.

But he wouldn't get him. Since Kenny would get Dyson off. The two of them would crow about how they'd got *me*. Kenny would move in with the big boys now.

The brief saw it, I think. And Ross, the DC, must have done. That I was on the edge, I was teetering. But the tape doesn't pick up teeterings either.

And still the hope – the hopeless hope – that Dyson might cave in anyhow.

The smell of interview rooms, like contaminated zones.

I went back to Number Two, with Ross. The gist of Dyson's chat with his brief? I knew it. Try it out first: call the fucking copper's bluff.

And now he could even say – and did – he was the victim of police malpractice.

But Dyson wasn't a victim of anything – take it from an old DI. A victim-maker, a victimizer, full-stop. None of that sob-stuff victim-makers are supposed to be victims of: deprived upbringing, et cetera et cetera. He stabbed Patel because he wanted to, wanted to and did.

He didn't speak. His brief spoke. 'My client has nothing further to add . . .'

Dyson just looked at me. Now, when I remember it, it seems he was already up there, looking down, watching me fall.

And Gibbs, the new Super, would say he couldn't help

me. No cover-up. In the circumstances, and with the Force getting public flak. The word was 'corrupt'. He was going to drop me too. He wanted Dyson banged up as much as I did, but he was going to drop me down a big hole instead.

The smell of police stations – even in a Super's office. Who'd want to work in one?

And I'd been hoping – it's true, it's true – Patel might not pull through.

His brief spoke. Dyson just looked at me. He looked at me as if he might have been waving that knife in my face too. Come on, grab it if you can.

I went back to Number One.

Kenny's brief said, 'Mr Mills wishes to reinstate his previous statement.'

Beer and fags.

I said, 'Think again, Kenny.'

He looked at the table.

'Mr Mills—'

They say you see red. I can't remember seeing red. Something came over me. I can't remember seeing anything but my hands round Kenny's throat.

I grabbed Kenny, with his brief and Ross as a witness – so his brief had to intervene. I grabbed Kenny, the innocent one. I didn't even grab Dyson.

31

AND IT DID DIE a death. Or so I thought. The Freemans moved, in any case, to Bristol, in '65, the year I joined the Force, so I assumed that was that, even if it hadn't stopped beforehand. Though there was still the fact of it, the secret of it, lurking.

I watched his face for signs of – I don't know – sadness, heaviness. Something Mum might notice. What's up, Frank? And of course, I know now, obstacles, distances (London to Bristol?), they aren't necessarily the end of anything at all.

But he was always Mr Smile, Mr Breezy. 'Smile everyone, please.' So how could you tell?

Monday afternoons, once upon a time, with Carol Freeman, never anything serious. Did that make it better or worse?

And then – twenty-one years later – he died. Twenty-one years of the secret lurking and never surfacing and of me becoming a cop, a boy in blue and then a detective, and getting married myself and having a family – Helen – and popping round every so often for Sunday lunch (Rachel's parents not being part of the picture). And even now and then finding time to play a token round of golf with him, even sitting with him on that bench with that scatter of fag ends. A secret smokers' place. Husbands who were supposed to have quit, wives who'd never know.

He died. 1986. He was only just sixty. But I supposed they'd already reached the point where the thought was real between them: one of us one day must go first. And I suppose Mum had reckoned, as I suppose women must reckon, going on the evidence, on widowhood. But not yet.

April '86. Alongside all the other thoughts, I couldn't help thinking: well at least she'd be safe now, and I'd be safe – my secret would be safe. Her memories wouldn't have any scars. Except the scar of seeing him there on that bed, when he should have been good for another twenty years, who knows? Working his way towards death.

We kept watch while his chest heaved up and down, and he slipped away from us then back again – if he knew we were there, we couldn't tell – sometimes muttering things, sometimes just groaning and wheezing.

And then he said (with only hours to go in fact): 'Carol . . .' His eyes were shut and God knows where he thought he was, but he said it clearly and he said it again and again: 'Carol . . . Carol . . .'

It's almost a treat, here on this bench. You can close your eyes, the sun like a gift on your eyelids, lift your face and think it's spring.

You couldn't mistake it, couldn't ignore it. 'Carol . . .' Couldn't avoid the meaning.

I thought: Now I'll have to pretend again, a different

kind of pretence. I'll have to pretend, for her sake, to be shocked, bewildered, like her.

But not heart-broken: that was for just her.

You couldn't mistake it. Both of us there. I was a witness. And if we hadn't been there – or if he'd died quicker, if he hadn't laboured on like that, so that the delirium, or whatever it was, hadn't set in . . .

'Carol . . .'

Of course, I had to say it: he's delirious, just delirious. But I could read her face. Like hell, George, like hell.

Just delirium. The chestnut tree. The way he scurried through the rain and was let in like a bird swooping into a nest.

Just those few hours. Cheated, right at the end, by a few hours.

I think that became her position: she might never have known. She might never have had to know. If she could trade it all back, not the fact, just the knowing, the having to know, she'd have settled for that. I never said a thing.

And now she'd have to pretend, too. To be the brave grieving widow. To cherish his memory. All those photographs.

But was it such a pretence?

'He could make *me* smile, George – my God, he could make me smile.'

It was a few weeks later. Something had shifted in her since the funeral, an adjustment, a decision. We'd stopped talking about, even skirting round, the subject of Carol.

'I've got an idea, George. Will you help me?'

She wanted to buy a bench – have a bench made. One of those wooden benches – you see them everywhere – that have little plates or inscriptions: 'In Memory of . . .' She wanted to have a bench made in his memory, and she wanted it put on Chislehurst Common, just up from the High Street. Because, after all, he'd been a public figure in his way, the local photographer.

It would be a gesture. A public bench, for everyone. But of course she could go there and sit on it too whenever she wanted – if it was free. 'Hello, Frank.'

She didn't know how you went about it, nor did I. There must be some procedure. Of course I said I'd see to it.

'Thank you, George. And will you do something else for me?' she said.

She looked at me for a while. 'When – I go, will you make sure that my name goes on the bench too? So it says "Frank and Jane"?'

Of course, I said, of course I would.

I saw to it. You have to apply through the Parks Department. A solid wooden bench, the best teak, a silky deep-brown then – grey and weathered now. There was a simple unceremonious moment when it was put in its designated place and she went along to be the first to sit.

I go there still, myself, when the mood takes me, just to sit. Wimbledon to Chislehurst. The points on your map, the poles of your world.

It's good to sit there. It was a good thing to do, the right thing to do.

On the far side of the Common is St Mary's Church where the Emperor Napoleon – Napoleon III – was first laid to rest, when he died in 1873. Then his wife Eugénie lived on for almost fifty years.

But Mum didn't have a long stint of being ex-Mrs Webb. No second life. It surprised me: I thought she would simply go on, the resigned, enduring, steady type. And, by the law of averages, since my dad went early . . . But she died only three years later, only months, as it happens, before I was kicked out the Force.

And whether if she'd never known – about Carol – she'd have lived on longer, whether it was like a sentence for her and so better made short, I don't know. I don't know about these things.

But she never knew I knew. I'm proud of that. And I carried out her wish to the letter, of course.

'Frank and Jane.'

If there's someone else sitting there, I'm miffed, I'm even a little affronted, for a while. Then I relax, I'm strangely pleased. They don't know who I am – how could they? I watch them not knowing who I am. I walk around, I take my turn.

It's good to sit there. It's a good thing to do. Never mind all the other things that happen with public benches. Dogs come and cock their legs – and as for some of the human users . . .

Public benches, golf courses. What's civilization for?

And whenever I sit there (I can't help it) I know I'm glad they're dead. I'm glad they died when they did. So *they* never knew, neither of them, about *my* scandal and disgrace. Their boy, getting on in the police – a good job, for all the mud that got slung at coppers nowadays. For all the talk of corruption.

They never knew, they'd never know. Nor about Rachel and me. About Rachel and me not being Rachel and me any more. About my life falling apart.

And as for me now: this – visitor. This man on his way to prison, resting on a bench: what would they have made of that?

32

I went to the Fulham flat. A dry run, just to check it out. To see what the parking and the sight-lines were like.

A first-floor flat, bay-windowed. Below: an arched porch, steps leading up over a basement.

As if she could have known it, a girl in Dubrovnik. The points on our map.

A small front garden. Dead roses. A laurel bush, a privet hedge. A front path and gate, a little bunker, draped with ivy, for dustbins, just inside. The house number on the gate: forty-one.

I was there again the next Monday, at four o'clock. November 20th. The earliest they would leave would be around five. But you have to be in position, ready. Detective work is fifty per cent waiting.

And the black Saab was already parked outside.

A dank raw afternoon. Almost dark even at four. A light already on, behind the curtains, on the first floor.

A concession, Sarah had said, and now, perhaps, in the gloom of a November afternoon, the concession was running out.

Well, let them have their last eked-out moments, let them use up their concession. Then leave each other for good. If that is how it was.

Or let them disappear, the pair of them together, into the night.

How can you tell – from a lit-up window? All the windows, saying nothing, lights on, lights off. All the houses that stare at each other across streets. Read my face, guess what I've got inside.

The street lamps changed colour, pink-eyed then amber.

At five-fifteen (I note these things exactly) the front door opened and Bob Nash appeared. He was manhandling two suitcases, one large, one small, moving with concentration. He looked like a man carrying out some dangerous task, as if the cases might be full of explosives. I remembered what Sarah had said: how he'd carried up the boxes while Kristina had sat in the kitchen, about to burst into tears.

He was wearing a suit, no tie. The flop of dark hair that, with his hands gripping the suitcases, he couldn't smooth back. The cases looked new. He shut the door behind him and carried the cases to the car. I couldn't tell, from where I watched, if there was already luggage (his own) inside the car. He re-locked the car, walked back to the front door. He seemed to pause and breathe hard for a moment, standing in the porch – but then he'd been lugging suitcases. He let himself in with a key.

Five minutes passed, maybe more.

You look around, take it in: take a last mental photograph. Home, and not home, something different from home.

The light went out upstairs. Then they both emerged

below. He had a tie on now. She was dressed – as if to make an impression, as if she had some appointment, some role to perform – in a simple elegant dark suit, a pale round-necked top beneath.

It was the first sight of her I'd had, not counting that photograph. Different people you might have said. A transformation had taken place.

My first sight. There was only that brief moment when the light from the open door caught them, I could hardly see her face. I looked for some dizzying, devastating factor that might, in an instant, explain everything.

But didn't I know, by then, there's no telling how it strikes?

A scarf, deep red, hung loosely from her shoulders. Glossy black hair. Something foreign, yes, and intense. Italian, yes, your first guess.

They both had coats over their arms, for the few steps to the car. She had a bag, of the compact boxy sort you might carry on to a plane, another small bag hooked over her shoulder.

The door shut behind them. No meaningful pause.

A professional couple, you might have said – in whatever sense – with matters to attend to, some schedule ahead. Married, or not married, or just professionally linked. Two people about to set off on some business trip – a trip that might have been entirely for legitimate purposes or entirely not, or something embracing both.

You can't tell.

They descended the steps. She seemed the surer and quicker of the two. One of those man–woman partnerships where it's the man who is the anchor maybe, but the woman who takes the physical lead.

He would have bought her the suit, I suppose. A 'going-away' suit? She flicked the scarf round her chin like a mask. The scissory, clipping steps of a woman-about-town. A refugee.

He opened the car door for her, took her coat and bag to lay on the back seat. I lost sight of her after the quick inward swing of her legs. Good sleek legs. In four hours' time he'd be dead and she wouldn't know. He walked round to his driver's door and before getting in, and with an odd quick wrench of his head, looked up, looked round, looked back.

33

GONE TWELVE. ENOUGH. I get up from the bench. I've
given it time enough. Time enough for respect, time
enough to say I didn't hurry it. Time for all those messages, if they were going to come, from the dead.

No, sweetheart, nothing. (I wouldn't lie.) The dead
don't say anything. They don't forgive.

There's just one name on this bench: 'John Winters
1911–1989.' But it's made of good, weathered teak.

And my life got put back together again.

I walk back to the car. I shiver a little, now I'm on
my feet. Sitting around – in November. John Winters.
The day's still brilliant, the sky an almost burning blue,
but, even at just past noon, it has that urgent feeling that
even still and brilliant days in November have. It's waning
already, it can't last.

34

MARSH SAID, 'To *her*? Something terrible's happened to *her*?'

She was along the corridor. Nothing would ever be the same for her again.

He looked at me, reading my face.

'Something good had happened to her, hadn't it? Her husband had come back. This girl had gone. Everything she wanted.'

'Yes.'

'So – why?'

'That's not my business.'

'No?' He looked at me. 'I could say it's not mine either. When Mrs Nash came to you – to hire you – did she seem like a woman intent on revenge?'

'No, not at all. She wanted her husband back.'

'You're sure?'

'I see lots of women – clients – intent on revenge. You can tell.'

Sometimes as soon as they step through the door.

'Still, it's an explanation. It could persuade a jury. Why – at *that* point? Because she was going to do it all along. She waits till he gets back, till he thinks he's in the clear—'

'She'd cooked him a meal. His favourite meal. She'd laid the table. You saw—'

'Exactly. Revenge. A ritual element. People do weirder things. Did it ever cross your mind she might be off her trolley?'

He didn't believe what he was saying – I could tell. Cock-and-bull. He was testing me in some way.

'A jury won't come into it,' I said.

'Maybe not. It depends. You knew it was his favourite meal – she told you that?'

He looked at me.

'You *saw* her,' I said. 'She didn't *look* like she'd planned it. She didn't look like she'd meant to do it.'

(She'd looked – as much as anyone can look who's saying, over and over, 'I did it, I did it' – like she didn't know what she'd done.)

He looked at me and let a silence pass.

Not like *she'd* planned it, he might have said.

Your last case. What do you do? Go to town, follow the wildest goose chase, break all the rules?

And if it could have been made to fit the facts I might have said at that point: Okay, all right, I planned it. I conspired with Mrs Nash to kill Mr Nash. I put her up to it. I followed him, reported in – so she'd know. Then followed him all the way back, just to be sure . . .

A false statement (my real one was on the table waiting for me to sign): I really did it, it was me.

Cock-and-bull. But people do the weirdest things. They walk into police stations (every nick has stories) and confess to crimes they never did.

He fingered his tie. He might have been thinking: And if she's mad, he could be too.

But they can't arrest you for what's only in your head.

'Yes, I saw her,' he said.

Interview rooms. Two DIs. How strange to be on the other side of the law.

And wasn't it why we'd both of us joined – back then, back in those simple, certain days – to be on the right side of the law?

(Yes, he'd say, later – when we met up to play golf.)

A good thing to do, the right thing to do. A kind of insurance: get on the right side from the start. A sound choice anyway for us good-on-our-feet types who were never much cop at school. (Problems at home as well.)

Schoolboy misfits (Marsh too, I'd guess). Not much good on paper, but good enough underneath. Good enough to serve the law.

And now look at Marsh – coming up to retirement: he looks like a teacher, a weary teacher (a touch of strict flint). And look at me, back in a police station. All because of a teacher. Because even teachers now and then go and land in trouble with the law.

Those simple days, before the police became the pigs, the fuzz, the filth.

I think he read my thoughts.

'Can I see her? Please can I see her?'

That question – that word 'please' – like a confession.

He looked hard at me. The face of a tired teacher – the sort who, if you're lucky, will let you off. But even tired teachers can catch you out. Even friendly looking policemen can whip out the book.

It was the only way I'd see her – from then on: by permission.

'I can't do that,' he said.

More than his job was worth, his job that would soon be done. A wife waiting for *him* to come home, for good.

'That's not possible, you know the ropes.'

And Bob Nash was lying on a bed of stainless steel. I knew the ropes.

His last case. I might have tipped him over the edge.

It was me – I'll come clean. Have me, take me instead. What else is love for?

35

I START THE CAR. Another funeral party, a large one, is dispersing, whole gaggles of mourners returning to their cars, and I get caught up in the queue of their departure, feeling vaguely in the wrong. No, I'm not with you. Just here to look at a grave. I'm here with someone else.

A little arrowed sign says 'Exit'. There must be some system of traffic flow, even here – designed to stop a party leaving from obstructing a party arriving, from upsetting its slow but steady progress behind the hearse. So that on a busy day like today each party arriving can at least have its moment, can at least have the brief illusion that it's the only one that counts, the only one with serious business here today.

Like my clients coming through my door.

You're the only one who counts, the only one who counts for me.

How do we decide?

'Exit.' It's a strange word, when you think about it, in a cemetery. It ought to be the word you see, the final word, as you come in. Everything here turned inside-out.

And where Sarah is it's not a word that has much use:

exit. No helpful arrows pointing. Everything there is just inside.

Before Sarah became my teacher I never used to think much about words – hold them up to the light.

'You can do it, George. Write it all down.'

More than just letters. A correspondence course, home-work. Something more than just begging letters dropped into the dark. Please let me see you . . .

Special lessons, private coaching.

'Something for me each time.'

Not much good on paper, till now. Her eyes, her agent in the world. You have to have a motive. It's the same with crime. You never know what you've got inside.

The day she said, about my latest effort (I'd wait for the verdict, like when Helen tasted my cooking): 'I think you can do this, George, I think you've got something. You don't need me any more.'

'That's where you're wrong,' I said.

But I walked out that day – out of prison – my feet floating on air.

Look, remember, write it down. I carry a notebook, like every good cop. It's like being on a special full-time case, the one and only case, the only case that counts.

The line of cars I've joined creeps along between cypresses and evergreens, then between the rows of gold-leafed trees, then comes to an unexplained halt. Grave-stones glinting on either side. Here and there bright clumps of flowers.

I think of the girl in the florist's. The way she moved in and out of light. Somebody's daughter. They bloom (Helen seemed to grow thorns). And what are Sarah and me? Late-flowerers, like chrysanthemums. Flowers in

November – arriving from God knows where. Hothouse flowers. Jailhouse flowers.

The sun through the windscreen, as if I'm a plant under a frame.

'Putney Vale.' It sounds like some lost paradise. And it's true, there can't be much trouble-making here. No need for police-work. Minor traffic snags. No breaches of the peace. One safe little patch of the world. So why are we all lining up to leave?

We move off slowly again towards the gates, where everything will change speed. The gravestones seem to watch us, as if they're standing, still and silent, out of respect for us. Everything inside-out. Honouring the living as they leave, watching us depart like some doomed patrol.

Except Bob – if he's watching. He's not honouring me.

There he goes, the bastard, sneaking out with the others. Trying to look like one of them, the fraud, trying to look as if he's full of grief.

That last strange quick lift of his head before he got in the car.

There he goes, the creep, with his flowers delivered and his conscience clean.

36

THE WORD THAT got used was 'corrupt'.

A strangely physical word. A black taste welling in your throat, a thickness on your tongue, as if you have a disease. As if they've rooted out some foul stuff inside you and it's you, it's yours now, you're stuck with it for good.

I was found to be corrupt, to be party to police corruption. At another time, maybe, there would have been internal disciplining, reprimands, suspension. Shaming enough. But because the air was busy in those days with the word 'corrupt', because there was pressure from above and lack of public confidence and examples had to be seen to be made, I got the axe while Dyson walked.

Justice: another word.

And I'd have got nothing but commendation if (as I nearly did) I'd locked him away for a good long stretch.

Look what I *haven't* done, I said. I haven't used police powers to further my own ends, to line my own pocket. I haven't turned a blind eye. I haven't, for the sake of the tally, stitched up an innocent man.

No dice. Look at it this way, they said – or I could read it in their eyes – you're being sacrificed for the good of the Force, a bigger thing than you, for the sake of its reputation, for the sake of keeping its grubby face clean.

And, by the way, you're getting off lightly, you assaulted a witness . . .

Corrupt. A word with no half measures: you've got the disease. Pooled in with the worst. Like a criminal gets called a criminal, along with all the others, even if he only dipped his hand, once, in the till.

Not just a cop who'd overstepped the mark. I'd sinned.

The gravestones twinkle in the sun. And this place, when you think about it, must be riddled with corruption . . . Not such a sweet little community after all.

Always, of course, the taint – that everyday, workaday taint. A dirty job sometimes. Things you have to clean up. A filthy job sometimes – and the police were sometimes just the Filth. And sometimes you'd bring it home with you (when they finally let you go home), like a smell in your clothes, in your hair. Home to your wife and daughter.

After a while it doesn't wash away. You don't even have the decent dutiful smell of a uniform. It gets in your plain clothes, the clothes that let you mingle and blend with the enemy. Then you go home.

So it had really been brewing all along, with Rachel? She'd had enough, and this was just the final crunch? Or put it another way: she'd grown sick of my smell. And I thought I'd managed it, mostly, that work–home thing, that difficult trick, that crossing a border every time you opened the front door.

At least in *that* direction. Going back to the nick, as often as not, with a bruising from Helen.

But at least with Rachel. Okay, so sometimes I was a pain, a big pain. Bruisings all round.

But now she had the chance to make it all my fault. The taint *was* me. Not Mr Right but Mr Wrong. And not my wife, my judge.

My queue of cars reaches the gates, files out, rounds the roundabout, still like some stately procession, then turns, gathering speed, on to the A3 slip road. Then, one by one, we launch ourselves back into the world.

I think Rachel never really gave up her god, that's what I think. I mean, the big stern daddy part of him.

I never had a god like she did, I wasn't brought up (thank God) like her. Though my dad would go to church often enough – to snap the happy couples.

I used to think of how it must have been for Rachel when she was small. God looking down on her, and her looking up, being obedient and scared. Then one day, when she was bigger, her deciding: no, there's no one up there at all. Just me.

I wasn't brought up like Rachel. But you pick things up about God. You pick up his scent, like the smell of church. I remember some passage being read out some-where, that there's no sinner so bad, so worthless, that God will ever let them slip through the net of his love.

Rachel never quite gave him up, that's what I think.

And whether he's up there or not, and whether he's got a net, I don't know. But I think it's how it ought to be, just among us. There ought to be at least one other person who won't let us slip through their net. No matter what we do, no matter what we've done. It's not a question of right or wrong. It's not a question of justice.

There ought even to be someone for Dyson, even Dyson. I don't know who it is. I know it's not me.

I turn on to the slip road and put my foot down. I'm on my way now, I'm on my way. I whizz out on to the A3.

No matter what we do, no matter how bad. If we're found to be corrupt. Even if we do the worst thing ever, even if we do what we never thought it was in us to do, and kill another person. Even if that other person was once the person for whom we were holding out a net.

37

Marsh looked at me for a long time. His face was tight and hard as if he had me at his mercy.

Even tired teachers can make you squirm. Even kind-looking cops can give you a rough time. The power policeman have (why some of them join). The power that leaves them when they leave the Force.

Your last case. You can run with it any way. You'll be out in the clear soon.

Then his face went soft. It had that look of someone who needs to make a leap.

It must have been about one in the morning. My statement was still resting on the table, under his hands. He pushed it towards me.

'Okay,' he said, 'I think that'll do. Sign.'

38

I PARK THE CAR in the usual spot. Not quite one-fifteen. Over two hours to spare. But it's a lengthy process, they don't make it easy for you. You learn to build in time. The Parcels Office first, always a performance, then the visit itself. Report to the Gate and wait. Allow a good hour. And if you want to eat . . .

You learn to make a day of it. It only comes once a fortnight. Plenty of times when (without a grave to visit first) I've been earlier still, and gladly. Just to be near.

And never a time when I don't think, locking the car: One day I'll do this for the last time. One day I'll walk away from the car and when I walk back I won't be alone.

These routines that become part of us, like a sleeve, a skin. Climbing the stairs at the office. Rita with the kettle already boiled.

When you have a subject for surveillance, you have to learn their habits, their regular routes, so as to know when they step out of line.

Though this hasn't always been my route. For nine months it was Essex – day trips to Southend. Then, by a fluke, back here. And she could be shipped out again, we know, at any moment. No rhyme or reason.

But if it happens, I'm ready. I'll go. I've learnt where they all are, the ones that take female lifers, second stage, third stage. The points on your map.

I slip off my seat-belt and reach under the dash. A large brown envelope, unsealed. It's been there all day. My latest offering, my fortnight's work – to be opened and examined, of course, before it's passed on. I don't mind. I'm used to it. They can read every page, every word if they want. They're not love letters, not exactly. Twice-monthly reports from the world.

They can chuckle and think what they like. The female screws – screwesses, screwardesses.

Georgie-Porgie, coming back for more.

And an envelope, usually, to pick up. Drop and collect. My previous delivery, with my teacher's response. But Sarah doesn't have so much to report. The routines of prison – they go without saying.

Besides, she's writing something else: the Empress Eugénie.

(Was there a problem? Apart from the unfortunate – delay. She had a contract with a publisher, she'd already begun – and she waived any further payment. Not gainful employment. And did anyone need to know? The person who translated this book was a murderer. Murderess.)

Translators, they're shadow-people, halfway people anyway.

And anyway it's kept her afloat. A raft: the three of us. Her, me and the Empress Eugénie. Not forgetting

Eugénie's old Emperor husband. The four of us. We talk about them like people we know.

'How's the Empress today?'

I put on my coat. Inside the envelope, as well as my pages, there's a fresh pad of blank A4 paper. She needs as much as she can get.

I slip the envelope under my arm, lock the car. I walk in the wrong direction – away from the prison. Time to spare, time to eat. The main road is five minutes away. If not a sandwich on a bench, leaving crumbs for the dead – then Snacketeria let it be.

A street of houses, houses with a prison handy. Left at the end, then right. Then I emerge into shops and traffic and crowds. Safeway, Argos, Marks and Spencer. The sun flashes off cars. There's a tinge, a touch of coppery fire to its light. People's faces pass like flares.

Snacketeria is packed. It's like entering an engine room. The hiss and snort of the coffee machine, a gabble of orders being repeated. Lunches to go. A queue shuffling forward – six or seven in front of me – but I don't mind.

Something I see in myself these days: I don't mind waiting. I can wait. I've lost the knack of impatience, I don't mind queues, procedures, jams, delays. To leave a graveyard, to buy a sandwich . . .

When you stand in line you can watch, you can notice things. When you stand in line you can think of all the other lines you could be in, all the terrible shuffling lines.

Is there a life anyway which isn't half made of waiting? Studded with detentions? 'Worth the wait.' 'Give it time.' Nothing good can be hurried – like cooking. Though they're working flat-out behind the counter in this place.

Besides: a detective's virtue. If you don't know how to wait, to lie in wait . . .

They know me here, by now. A regular. Every other week. And sometimes I make separate trips, just to the Parcels Office. Clothes, bits and bobs, things they're allowed. Door-to-door service.

I reach the counter. I get a nod, a word of recognition. Whether they could guess my story is another matter.

That one? Him – with that packet under his arm? He's just been to stand by a murdered man's grave. Now he's going to see the woman who killed him. In between he buys a sandwich and a cappuccino.

Chicken, rocket and roasted red pepper. They're Spaniards here, the management. Sarah could speak their language. 'Snacketeria', a good old Spanish word.

There's a seat free – a stool by the window. The Café Rio. This international world.

How does she get through this day? Half-past one. In my mind's eye I see a gravestone – coppery light, the flecks in the granite like sparks – where no one will go for another year.

In twenty minutes or so I'll head back the way I came, take a slightly different route and join another queue.

39

THE SAAB PULLED OUT. I followed. Maybe a thirty-yard gap. When it turned into the busy Fulham Road I was almost nudging its bumper, anxious not to lose contact at the very start.

At night it's not so easy to follow a car. If you slip back, all you have are the tail lights – looking like anyone else's tail lights.

By the same token, of course, it's harder to tell if you're being followed. If that ever entered their minds . . .

Lillie Road . . . Fulham Palace Road to Hammersmith. Then the A4 for the M4: the route to Heathrow. Five-thirty: heavy and slow traffic to Hammersmith, which meant I could be close enough, often, to see the crowns of their heads.

And read their thoughts? If they were heading off into the night together – if they were about to make their escape – there would surely be a tingle, a pulse between them detectable even in the attitude of their heads. Whereas if they were about to say goodbye . . .

Fulham Palace Road. Past Charing Cross Hospital, where he worked – where he saw his women.

And would still work? Did his head turn, just for a moment, in spite of himself, or did he make himself look rigidly ahead?

When you follow two people – when you follow anyone – and they don't know you're there, it's hard not to feel a flutter of power. As if you can decide their fate. Your foot over the scurrying beetle.

The mysterious urge to protect.

The roundabout at Hammersmith. They swung left on to the A4. Now the traffic quickened: harder to stay close. But he didn't drive fast, he kept to the slow lane – two steady red lights. He didn't drive like someone eager to be far away.

I think I knew it even then. She was going. She was going to leave. Some things you piece together, some things you know in your bones. He hadn't told Sarah any lies. He was eking out the moments.

The A4, then the M4.

Even so, even so. The thing was still in *his* power, there behind the wheel. He might do something mad, as the exit for Heathrow approached. He might step on it suddenly. He might put his foot down, exceed all limits, for the sake of not letting her go.

A last wild hope. His hope? Mine? He was brooding on it, I was brooding on it – an ex-cop who'd done six months, once, on cars. Okay, sonny, if you want a race . . . Not a surveillance, a chase (wasn't *that* why you really joined?). In the end it's just hunting, it's the lawlessness of the hunt.

Dyson's face when I had to tell him: I'd exceeded limits.

And Kristina was going back – if she was going back – to where they'd ditched all the rules.

Three exits, on the motorway, before Heathrow – not counting the one for Terminal 4. The options close off rapidly, the moments whittle down. Then you get sucked into the mesh of a huge airport.

He kept to the slow lane. Indicated for the exit to 'Terminals 1, 2 and 3'.

Even so, even so. Things can still happen, they can turn right round at the last minute. And there was always Plan B: that they'd pass through the departure gates together – as always intended. They'd flash their boarding cards and be gone. Why should he have driven anything but steadily and calmly if that was the plan?

The link-road from the motorway to the airport entrance. The roar of a low jet.

In my bones I knew it, they were going to part. The way the black Saab seemed to drive as gravely as a hearse, down into the tunnel under the runways, as if there was no way out.

Part of me – my bones only? – must have rejoiced. The rest of me begging to be wrong.

40

WHEN YOU GO TO visit someone in prison it's like a small rehearsal of the real thing, a small taste of punishment. Doors close behind you. A system – a smell – swallows you, you're searched and counted and marked. You wonder vaguely if they'll let you out. Then, when your time's up, a small miracle occurs. You go back – it's okay – the way you came. You take that simple step which for those who stay inside isn't simple or even thinkable at all.

Everyone ought to be made to do it perhaps. A kind of education, a privilege. To know what it's like to leave the world then be put back in it again.

I join the line at the Gate. There's a brand-new Visitors' Centre, just across the way, but it's not yet up and running so we huddle like people without a home.

Familiar faces. Always the sprinkling of kids, kids without their mums, minded by someone else. Some nods, quick smiles. By and large, we're a silent bunch – except for the kids. We haven't come to meet each other, and it's only by accident that we look like some special, picked group, a chosen few.

The high brick wall rears above us. There's a hunching of shoulders, a shifting of feet – an impatience, to be let into a prison. But while we shiver in the shadows, the brickwork up above glows like the crust of a just-baked loaf. For the sun it's no problem either – that simple step that isn't so simple – it can just float over a prison wall.

A privilege, a chosen few. All the shuffling queues.

Except for me the privilege is in the wrong direction. The most precious moments of my life. As if I might say, when they send us out: Can't I stay? Do I have to go? I'd gladly stay if you could find a reason, an excuse. Isn't there something you can pin on me?

Except, small snag, this is a women's prison. No matter what you did to get a permanent pass, you couldn't find a way round that.

Five past three. It's time. They open up. We edge forward, and though it's the new, the unfamiliar faces they're watching out for, my stomach goes, as always, into a knot. As if they might stop me, as if there'd be the stern look, the finger pointing, then flicking away. No, not you. Not you today.

My stomach tightens. But, as always, I don't forget to fill my lungs. It's become a ritual, a superstition, an essential preliminary. Like a diver. A lungful of free air.

As if I could hold it for all the time it takes to get through the doors and checks and searches and into the Visits Room, and only release it when our lips meet.

As if we're allowed to kiss on the lips . . .

*

The screws say, 'Hello, George.' You have to leave your stuff in the lockers. Pockets turned out. It's like old times in the cop shop. No wallets, keys, money in notes, cigarettes. They look in your shoes, they look in your mouth. Sometimes they bring in the dogs.

They frisk me quickly, more by habit than purpose, not touching certain parts. We've got past the jokes about all-over massage, but part of the smell of prison, there's no doubt about it, is the smell of sex. Sex without sex.

Though it can't be as strong, I suppose, as in a male prison. The reek of perfume at visiting time, the dolling up. The best that can be done.

Like my clients – some of them. Wafts of signals being given off. Rita sniffs them, eyes them, then lets them in. And there are all the questions you can't ask, though you do (and they know it) in your head, and sometimes – sometimes surprisingly quickly – they answer them anyway.

You still sleep with your husband? When was the last time . . . ? So you still have sex with him, but you know, by the way he . . . ?

It's the same when the screws feel you up: a little flurry of unspoken questions.

The last time? There hasn't been a first.

They look at you. Well it takes all sorts.

And you're still holding your breath.

My screw's name is Bridget (I know some of the names). She's firmly built and forty, and looks like a female judo expert. There must be men who fancy female prison officers. Like men (I knew some) who fancy policewomen. Women in uniform, screwardesses. A touch of discipline.

Me? I'm more teachers, these days.

Bridget says, 'Hello, George. How are we?' As she pats me and I lift my arms. These days, it's true, we're past the silent-question stage. She looks at me these days with a sort of respect.

'Nice day out there,' she says.

And I wonder if she knows, if they all know, if they keep a special log. This was the day.

'But cold,' I say.

Just a step. But it's another country, another world. And if you've come to live in it, you have to survive. There are all kinds of ways, but one way is to accept it, to want it utterly – is there anywhere else you should be? You've done wrong (the worst kind of wrong) and shouldn't you be punished? Once upon a time – not so long ago – they wouldn't even have let you live.

Wanting to be locked away. Wanting to forget that you ever walked about in that other world, far away, just beyond a wall. It never existed, you were never really there.

She used to hate me, at first. I could see it – it was terrible – in her eyes. She hated me: this outsider, this intruder – this reminder – this breaker into her space. For the first three months, in fact, she refused to see me, refused to call, though they can call. The prisoner decides, their one bit of power, the prisoner invites. Come to my place.

And of course, I feared. A crime like hers, they'd put you on close watch.

Feared, and doubted? My own feet turning cold? 'Off her trolley,' Marsh had said. Feared, and couldn't believe.

Could she believe it? That it was happening. An old cop, and I'd thought, as if I didn't know the law: she can't get life, not life.

Letters only, my dumb letters. Letters only one way. Then one day a reply. I stared at it. Then one day that magic thing, that concession: a Visiting Order. But even when she did see me, let me see her: the look in her eyes! As if I was dead to her, she was dead to me.

He'll stop, he'll give this up, I'll make him. Then I'll be alone, then I can turn completely to stone.

I said to myself: Keep going, hold on. What did you expect? To be welcomed, rewarded, made to feel good?

I don't want your pity, George, I don't want your fucking charity.

It's not what you're fucking getting.

Me with my lungfuls of air, me about to burst. Me with the one bit of news she didn't want to hear: whatever happened, whatever happens, you're still *you*.

Keep going.

And I wasn't blind. I knew about prison, what it does to people. It turns them into people they never thought they were. On conviction, they go to the hospital wing. That numbness in her eyes: some of it sheer shock. Sweetheart, I wasn't naive. It used to be my job once, my duty, to send people to prison. Now look at me, banging on the door myself.

I thought of how I'd gone to see Patel. Off the danger list. I'd wanted forgiveness. As if I'd stuck that knife in his chest myself.

*

Don't give up. This will pass, it will pass. It's only natural. Only natural: to kill the man you love – love? loved? – then to want to be dead yourself.

Not prison but burial. As if she were in that grave with him. I couldn't drag her out. I couldn't smuggle out earth, I could only carry in air. How many lungfuls, how many deliveries – a whole cellful? – before the hatred started to die? Before she came back to me. And back to herself.

Back to being *you*.

There are times, there always will be, when you still wish you weren't, you'd never been you. Or when you could almost believe it really was some other person, not you – how could it have been *you*? – who did what you're supposed to have done.

But on this day, of all days, the anniversary of the day you did it, you know you can't believe that.

41

THE SAAB CAME UP out of the entrance tunnel and took the lane to Terminal 2. I was three cars behind. When I moved into the same lane I reduced the gap to two. Five past six. The sudden urgency of an airport.

They followed the sign for 'Short Stay Car Park – Terminal 2'. Short stay? A brief slow-down, then we both swung into the multi-storey and began the spiralling ascent. On the fourth level there were spaces and when the Saab pulled into one I drove by, turned back on the far side and parked where I could watch.

Almost a minute passed before either of them got out. The last moment at which there might have been a change of plan? Of heart? He still had the key in the ignition. She was still sitting beside him.

Though what *was* the plan? 'Short Stay': that might mean nothing. The car might just stay there, till somebody asked questions, till Sarah had to deal with it – with that too. An expensive decoy, a top-of-the-range Saab, if that was the plan – but only a small part of everything he'd be leaving behind.

You take a step, you cross a line.

But people do weirder things. And some people, he might have thought, like this woman still there beside him, don't get to choose. They turn their backs and life explodes behind them.

His excuse: she was his example? Why play safe? The world doesn't.

And she was sitting there now, perhaps, waiting. Watching him waver, watching him sweat. It was up to him.

I couldn't make them out, behind the glints and shadows. The Saab was parked facing away from me. It might already have been empty, except (wavering, sweating?) he hadn't yet switched off his lights.

'Missing Persons . . .' They'd often start with an abandoned car. In a multi-storey car park, say. The point of departure. The point where somebody hoped, for one reason or another, that they might become somebody else, they might walk right out of their own life.

Missing Persons: my bread and butter these days too. Missing Persons and Matrimonial Work: they sometimes amount to the same.

He switched off his lights at last. She got out first. His door opened, more slowly. Yes, she was taking the lead. She was coaxing him through this as if he might have been some stumbling invalid. She was the one who took command in a crisis.

And, yes, as she moved ahead of him, towards the back of the car, I saw something you might have wanted, if you were the right man in the right place, to obey and follow like some dumb dog. Dark pools of eyes. Her skin, in the harsh light, drained of blood.

He opened the boot as if acting under silent instruction. He took out the two suitcases – just the two, the same two. He might have been simply her driver, dealing with the luggage, anticipating a tip, except that when he put the suitcases down his hands went up, as if to something much more in need of handling, to the sides of her face. As if to some vase perched on a shelf.

I opened my car door. A rush of chill air. The roar of planes and the smell, keen but vaguely stomach-turning, of aviation fuel, mingling with the cold-petrol smell of parked cars. The scent – there is one – of emergency.

She took his hands from her face. Gently, firmly. Some yards away, near the lift, was a stack of luggage trolleys, and she walked across – deliberate strides – to get one.

A destitute student. In that sleek black suit that stood out against all this dingy concrete? You wouldn't have believed it.

She wheeled back the trolley. He was waiting with her coat. He put the suitcases and her carry-on bag on the trolley. He shut the boot and locked the car, then took the handle of the trolley and began to push.

I grabbed my own coat. Now their backs were turned, I got out and walked, like them, towards the lift.

It was a temptation, of course, a big temptation. To have stood with them while the lift came – to have stepped in with them. And how would they have known? A temptation: a breach of the rules. Never risk having your presence noted. Keep on your side of the line.

But now I wish I had. Entered – just for that brief journey down – their space. I'd have read all the signals close-up, in the bright light of the lift. Scented the scents. I might even have given that quick meaningless smile a stranger gives in a lift. As if I didn't have a clue.

I'd have looked at her, at him. He'd have looked at me. I'd always know that we'd looked each other in the eye.

I veered past them, took the stairs. A more-than-professional tact? The lift to themselves: those few seconds down to departure level. But every second, perhaps . . .

There's a word I've learnt about from Sarah, that goes with the closeness of people. 'Aura'. It's Latin or maybe Greek – like 'gynaecologist'. It means 'breath', 'breeze', 'shimmer'.

I'd have been in their aura. Kristina's aura.

Sarah's aura.

I took the stairs slowly. When I reached the walkway to the terminal they'd already emerged and were several yards ahead.

In airports there are channels and slots and filters like being in a production line. A great grinding system that takes away aura or – by the same token – makes it stand out. So many departures, so many arrivals: you can't tell the simple goodbyes from the agonies, the lovers from the friends. People get excited, they hug, they cling, they kiss. What do those wet eyes mean? See you next Saturday? I'll never see you again?

All this intimacy in public. But here it's not unusual, it's almost the done thing.

And, by the same token, it's a detective's dream. You're part of the crowd, you won't be noticed – even if you should brush right by.

And, anyway, it doesn't take a detective. Something in the blood. Who hasn't done it – stood, sat at the edge of some big milling space and watched? And who hasn't, just for the sake of it, picked out, like a spy, some single figure, some couple, followed their every move and gesture, tried to read their lips? Wondered: what's their story?

That couple there, for example – that striking girl (Italian?) with the handsome but anxious-looking older man.

Arrivals and Departures. Check-in was a level below – they'd missed a sign. I followed them down, watched them find their way to a line. Flight 837 for Geneva. So? A longish queue.

So little time left now (if that was how it was): to have to spend it in a queue. She was the steadier. He kept looking at his watch. The nervousness of a man about to be condemned? Or about to abscond? His hand kept going to her waist, her arm, her shoulder, sliding through her hair to the nape of her neck.

They shuffled forward. Perhaps this was more terrible than either of them had imagined. She was the steadier – almost a grimness, as if *one* of them had to hold on. They'd said they'd go through with it, *he'd* said they'd go through with it. But now, at the barrier, he was starting to crumble, back down, he was slipping away from her.

If that was how it was.

Shouldn't a gynaecologist have learnt to stay calm?

Two tickets or one? I still couldn't be sure. Those suitcases could mean anything – all part of the decoy perhaps. People walk out of their lives with next to nothing, with just the clothes they're wearing. His hand on her neck.

To lose, to have the one you love. To love isn't to have, to keep.

I still didn't know.

42

HER EYES SEEM to stare through me today as if at someone else in the distance.

She says, 'You went?'

'Of course. I took flowers. Roses. It's a beautiful day out there.'

And that seems wrong, of course – both to say it and the fact. Today, of all days, a beautiful day.

How does she get through this day?

There's a little hard knot in her brow, tight as a question mark. She stares into my face. At the same time there's a sort of shame in her eyes, a shy twist at the corner of her mouth, as if she's saying, I know this is absurd, George, I know I'm being silly, but—

And maybe she's thinking, like I'm thinking: this is how it was two years ago. Me with my mission, her waiting to be told.

What can I say? There isn't any message, I'm not his messenger. I'm just your visitor, like any other day.

'It all looked – good. It all looked – just the same.'

What can I say? That he hasn't budged? Not going anywhere. That he said he'd always be waiting, too?

And I know she doesn't believe in ghosts. At least on any other day.

'"Haunted", George?' she said once. 'That's too simple a word. That's not how it is . . .'

But I know she's been with him, she's told me, in dreams. With Bob in dreams, even though he's dead, even though she killed him. That seems just an incidental point, until she wakes up.

And I've been with Sarah in dreams – my dreams and hers (she's told me) – even though she's here in prison, which seems incidental too, where we can hardly touch.

In dreams there aren't any locked doors.

I say, 'I stood there, sweetheart. I can't speak for him. And he can't speak.'

It seems almost cruel, like explaining something dreadful to a child. And she's my teacher, usually – I'm the kid, turning up at this special school.

'I stood there quite a while.'

(I gave him time, I gave him his chance.)

And I know well enough the word she wants to hear – or something near it, just the promise, the glimmer of it. And she knows, well enough, she can't have it.

And, God knows, though some people might say she blew away that possibility completely (and what crime did *he* commit?), she's forgiven *him*.

But I can't say it for him. I can only say, and I have, that I forgive her. Thousands wouldn't, but I have. A thousand times.

And, God knows, it was always my feeling about murder victims (I've seen a few): why, if they could come back, should they ever forgive? I've seen the victims of lesser crimes, still able to speak. Why should they ever forgive?

Why should Patel have forgiven – Dyson or me?

'It's just a grave, sweetheart. I stood there.'

The twist at the corner of her mouth tightens. What did she expect?

There's no grille or barrier. A plain table, chairs fixed to the floor. They let you touch, they let you hug. Once a fortnight: a hug. Of course it's not private, there are all the others, and you're being watched. The screws can see your every move – hear, if they want, your every word. You're on CCTV. But, after a while, you don't let it bother you. It's not so different, really, from visiting in hospital. You can get a cup of tea. At some beds there are intense conversations, at others no one knows what to say.

A play area for the kids. The squeal of babies. Some of them live here. Hospital, nursery . . . You might be fooled.

She doesn't give up. She says, 'But what did you *think*?'

As if I should say I thought the gravestone was looking less hard, less stony, less unforgiving.

Or as if I should say, 'I hated him. Just a bit. More than a bit. I had this – foul taste in my mouth.' But she knows that. I know. She knows that's how I think. And how can she blame me – when she *killed* him – for just hating him in my head?

'I thought: I wish you'd been there. With me, at my side.'

The twist leaves the corner of her mouth. She smiles thinly. The ghost of a smile.

'I was. You know that.'

It's how we speak of things now. The arrangement we have.

'It was all – so clear and still. The trees, the leaves . . .'

Absurd, to believe in ghosts, on such a bright clear day. But I could wish they did exist, so he could come back and say, like any self-respecting dead husband who's been let out of his grave, 'It's okay, you two, you go ahead. Don't mind me.'

She can smile, even today. I must have my dad's old knack after all.

She didn't always smile, of course. No place for smiles here. Wipe that smile off your face. It had to come back, like a pulse. One day, one amazing day, it was there.

She says, 'Did *you* say anything, George? To *him*?'

'I said, "These flowers are from Sarah. With love."'

It's true, I said it. (Along with all the other things I said in my head.)

Her eyes look through me again.

But then – if he could come back he'd have the last laugh. Go ahead! She's yours, feel free! He'd laugh his head off.

Or he'd just shut up and know his place. A ghost, a shadow, the perfect detective, watching. He wouldn't let us know he was here.

The screws stand around as if they're on playground duty, ready with their whistles. But it's not a game. These visits – these smiles – like cracks of light in a wall. A whole world behind. Prison takes away aura too. My gulps of air, the smell on my clothes, in my hair, of a cold dazzling November day. A little for a lot.

'I didn't go straight away. I had plenty of time. I went and sat on this bench, in the sun. I sat and I thought . . .'

I've never told Sarah about my mum and dad, about Dad and Mrs Freeman. It never ended, after all, with anyone being stabbed – except my mum, by a name.

I don't tell her I thought about couples. How when one goes first and gets a resting place, it begs the question . . .

'I sat there, and – I did what you've been doing, sweetheart. I've been doing what you've been doing all day.'

She doesn't have to ask, she knows. I've been going through it bit by bit, that day, two years ago. Going over it again, like evidence. Every step, every move. Replaying it like a film.

Half-past three. The sun will be dipping outside – the band of glowing brickwork getting narrower. On this day, two years ago, I hadn't even arrived yet outside the Fulham flat.

On my birthday Mum used to say, to tease me: 'It's not your birthday yet' – since I was born at eleven p.m. As if I might not get a birthday before I had to go to bed, I might not get a birthday at all. Then she'd relent and smile.

But Sarah will take it literally, precisely, I know. Every hour, every minute, every detail.

And I'll be doing it with her, though I wasn't with her then, not till it was over. And I can't be with her tonight – at eight-forty. Holding her hand.

Still all to come, all to happen. Though I don't tell her how I drove up, this morning, in the sunshine, to Beecham Close – with still hours to go. But couldn't do it.

As if I were Bob, in the clear light of day, coming back.

Every moment, every clue. Reliving it. She was in her kitchen. I was in Departures. His hand on her neck. Every twist. Trying to find the point where the sequence might have been different, where it might have turned another way. So that this time around, at last, the third time of trying, she won't do it.

But I can't be with her when it happens. Holding her hand.

43

ONLY ONE TICKET, only one boarding card.

So, it was settled. She was leaving.

Only one passport too – her unfamiliar passport along with a wad of supporting documents. A small age while they were looked at. What was he hoping: they wouldn't let her on the plane?

I should have crumbled, maybe, crumpled like him: a pair of us now. But what I felt, in spite of myself, was the glow, the whoosh of success. As if I'd brought about this outcome, this incredible trick, all by myself. So: it was over.

And had I really thought I'd be making that other call? They've flown off, the two of them. It's just you and me now.

Mission accomplished. Be content with being the hero of the hour, with being bathed in thanks. To love is to serve, what else is it for?

The glow of virtue. Saint George.

In a little while I'd speak into my phone. She's leaving, it's all over. Then melt into the night. Another job tomorrow.

But for now, this rush of elation – as if, for this moment at least, I was feeling only what Sarah would feel.

She turned from the check-in counter, holding her boarding card, as if she'd received a prize. And now you saw it: the glow in her, that she'd never expected to feel, maybe, quite so strongly or quite just then. And the cruelty of it for him: she'd never looked so beautiful.

A concession, Sarah had said. But this was misery for him, torture. Worse than anything he'd imagined. It was obvious, it shone: she was going off to find herself. Of course. And he was losing himself. He was already like one of those lost souls, people in transit you see in airports. No place of their own.

Already I was thinking: in a moment I'd make the call, and I'd have to lie.

As they walked from the check-in counter they passed as close to me (a pretend-passenger, travelling light) as they'd ever pass. Close enough for me to have reached out and touched her shoulder, her hair.

The shimmer of people.

It was twenty to seven. Fifty minutes before the flight. Maybe thirty minutes before she'd have to board. What do you do with thirty minutes to go? What difference can thirty minutes make? They went to a coffee place – the usual clattery messy coffee place with empty cups and wrappers littering the tables, luggage parked on the floor.

They didn't have coffee. Neither of them turned to go to the counter. There was a moment that was almost like the beginning of a row. He gripped her arm and pulled her towards him, even as she was about to sit. They hugged clumsily, but she pulled away, as if they'd agreed not to do this, a pact – not until the very end. They sat.

They looked at each other. More like pausing opponents, you might have thought, than lovers.

I sat at a table ten yards away, twiddling someone else's plastic coffee spoon. He might have given, at that moment, all he had, for just one sign from her that her pain was as much as his, that she was having to tear herself from him. That at least, that – gift – at least.

And who knows what she felt? She was the one, you saw it, who had to be tough, to hold her nerve, to get herself on a plane.

Perhaps that clutching of his made up her mind. To shorten the agony, or hasten it – whatever. She could collapse later. To be cruel, to be merciful, or just to get it done. She would go through *now*. It had to be. She picked up her carry-on bag. Got up from her seat. He seemed to have lost all power.

They walked, a little like dazed people stepping through wreckage. The battle-zone of airports. But she knew the way. She'd been here, somehow, before. He followed as if to the place where he'd be shot.

They stopped where they could go no further without being drawn into the drift of passengers passing through into Departures. Now they were here, there was a sort of deliberateness, a ceremony to their actions. He clasped her and she clasped him, as if each wanted to fix the other to the spot for ever. It was equal, ferocious, fair.

Somehow it ended, somehow she turned and walked. For a moment you even thought, this is something splendid, magnificent, after all. She walked as if her name had been personally called. Showed her boarding card to the man by the barrier, who smiled, waved her through (what did he know?), eyed her casually – a mockery of Bob's stare.

Then she passed through the gap between the partitions beyond as if on to some hidden stage. She didn't look back. Perhaps that was agreed: no looking back. She was gone.

And my job was truly done. Even the second unofficial part of it. To be her eyes. *How* would they say goodbye?

Six forty-eight.

But he just stood there, his back turned to me. Just stood looking at the space where she'd been. Yes, fixed to the spot. So that even when I stepped to one side and got out my phone, even as I thumbed in the number, he was still there. Even as I heard Sarah's answering voice.

'It's okay, it's all right,' I said, my voice sounding oddly like someone at the scene of an accident. It should have sounded like some magician's.

'She's gone by herself. The flight to Geneva. Everything's all right.'

He just stood there, even as I heard Sarah's voice – the relief, the joy, yes, the gratitude in her voice.

'Thank you, George – oh – thank you—'

The unmistakable sound of someone speaking through tears.

All this I told Marsh.

He just stood there. This is the man – I had to say it to myself – she loves.

He stood there and stared, as if by staring he could make her walk back. Not Departures but Arrivals. All a big mistake. And he was waiting for her. The world turned inside-out.

'And Bob?' Sarah was saying in my ear. 'And Bob . . . ?'

At last he turned, looking like a man who'd forgotten who he was.

'He's on his way home to you,' I lied.

44

THE 'NASH CASE'. It became a story as well as a case, it made the papers. Nothing major, soon gone and forgotten, but a small splash. If splash isn't an unfortunate word.

Most murders aren't news. They happen all the time and mostly (ask an old cop) they're bleak, grim, depressing affairs (wasn't this?) that happen in some place where murders happen, where we don't have to go. A war somewhere far away. A body, weeks old, dumped in a patch of waste ground. And pity the poor cop who has to deal with such stuff, then go back to a nice clean home. A wife, a kid.

But when it happens, in the first place, in a nice clean home – not just a nice clean home but a pricey pad in the leafiest, choicest part of Wimbledon . . .

There's something just a bit pleasing about the disasters of the well-off. Look, even they go and screw it up, even they don't lead charmed lives. So we needn't feel so jealous, after all – let alone feel sorry for them. So – he was knocking off this foreign girl (where was she from again?) and she, the wife, didn't like it. Well, poor her.

Poor her with her luxury kitchen. We should be so lucky – being miserable in comfort.

And she didn't have to do it, did she, in the first place? Take that girl in, give her shelter? The stupid bitch.

And him a gynaecologist. Raking it in. You can't help having the thought: wasn't he the one who had women under *his* knife?

A story. A stabbing. A stabbing is always good – a nice juicy stabbing. A kitchen knife. A college lecturer and translator: words were her thing. She went and picked up a knife.

On top of all that, the extraordinary fact, the mystery (was there any mystery otherwise?), that she did it on the very night that he'd said goodbye to the girl (where was she from?). He'd seen her on to a plane. He was coming back to her, his wife. Everything was going to be as it was. And, for God's sake, she'd got all dressed up to welcome him. She was dressed – don't say it – to kill.

At that very point.

Mystery? It was all set up. A plan. The heat of the moment? Pull the other one. And he'd had it coming, you might say – but not *that*. She waits till he thinks he's safe, till he thinks he's made his peace. Then bam! The murdering bitch.

The Nash Case. It had all the ingredients: 'Top Gynaecologist Slain By Wife'. If 'ingredients' isn't an unfortunate word.

Since she was cooking a meal at the time – it's how the kitchen knife came in. And wasn't that the weirdest thing? It was his favourite meal, she said so, swore it. A meal that never got eaten, never got served. All the time she was waiting for him, all the time his last minutes (though he didn't know it) were ticking away, she was cooking him his favourite meal. *Coq au vin.*

(So how did that fit in with the plan?)

The heat of the moment, the heat of the kitchen. A good cook. She loved to cook. And with a kitchen like that. You might see her sometimes lingering by the Fine Foods section in the supermarket.

And that last meal, there's no doubt about it, was lovingly, meticulously prepared.

Coq au vin. It needs time, plenty of time. Strictly speaking, for best results, more time than even Sarah gave it (but then there was the element of surprise). A day in advance is best, so the whole thing can cook, then steep, then cook again.

(I know a little about these things now.)

But she began her task – did Marsh ever ask her? – early that afternoon, around the time that Robert Nash made his way to the flat in Fulham where Kristina Lazic was waiting for him.

While the two of them were in bed together (let's assume) for the last time – either that or preparing to flee – Sarah Nash would have jointed a good quality small chicken (forget a real cock, in Wimbledon). She would have set aside shallots, garlic, dark-gilled mushrooms, streaky bacon. Diced the bacon into little chunks.

Amounts for two. She would have known there was a chance, a real chance – it's how it turned out, but in a different way – that this meal would never be eaten, would go to waste. But it was as though (I can understand this) its very preparation and intention would bring about the outcome she wished. In the careful and loving cooking of a meal there is (I believe this too) a sort of healing power.

His favourite meal. And by association hers. They'd first eaten *coq au vin* together, I know this now, in France on that first long car journey together – the purple Mini Cooper – that might, who knows, have turned out differently, have all gone wrong (do I wish it had? All gone wrong – then?). Especially when on the very first day and in the middle of a summer downpour their windscreen had shattered on the outskirts of some unknown small town. So there they were, suddenly wet through and shivering, driving at a snail's pace through a storm. And it was Sunday too – no chance of a quick repair.

A blessing in disguise. The way things happen, get sealed. The owner of the ramshackle garage they finally found turned out to be a saint. As though here were his lost children. No, he couldn't get a replacement till Monday afternoon. And no, he didn't speak English (but Sarah spoke good French). But he took them to his sister-in-law (her name was Anne-Marie), who ran a little inn-and-restaurant where she herself did the cooking, and there she served them *coq au vin*. It might be best on a cold winter's night but it goes down well enough on a stormy summer's evening when you've been soaked to the skin. A miraculous *coq au vin*.

They fell in love, really in love (it's what she's told me), over *coq au vin*. And the next morning the sun shone – and live cocks crowed – over a green lush hidden part of France they might never have discovered. So they stayed for nearly a week, even when the windscreen was ready.

Forget St Tropez. And that's where Sarah first thought of learning to cook.

She's dreamt about that green corner of France, the restaurant, the inn – as if it only exists in a dream.

And she would have thought about it then, on that November afternoon – already growing dark – as she set aside, of course, that other principal ingredient, the wine. A bottle of Beaune. Since although the wine is for cooking, not any old plonk will do. A mistake to skimp on the wine. The better the wine, in fact, the better the *coq au vin*. It's half the secret.

And later on she would have placed a bottle of the same wine – only fitting – on the table in the corner of the kitchen where a half-partition with a counter-top (cupboards and a shelf or two of books underneath) formed a separate cosy alcove. Along with the glasses, the napkins, the vase of flowers (freesias), the candle.

She would have opened the bottle for breathing – it's my guess – a little after my call. Waited still longer to light the candle.

But earlier that afternoon she was only beginning the ritual process of cooking a classic time-honoured meal. Browning the chicken joints. Trying at that early stage not even to think, to hope, to guess. Another thing that cooking undoubtedly does – if you don't rush it. It soothes the nerves. It occupies the mind and stops it pointlessly roaming.

And it would have served that calming function as best it could until, come the evening, when everything would soon be made clear (when I'd already followed that black

Saab into the entrance tunnel at Heathrow), she couldn't have prevented herself looking at the clock, at the telephone, or prevented her stomach from tying itself in knots. You cook and you're not hungry yourself. It's sometimes how it is.

But then the call had come – at ten to seven by my watch and the clocks in Terminal 2 – and it must have seemed, after all, that all that preparation had worked. At that point – after wiping away tears – after opening the bottle, and breathing deeply herself, she would have returned to the simple civilized task of cooking as if it were a splendour, an act of celebration.

Not that there would have been so much to do. Time and slow heat. She might already have removed the chicken pieces, to reduce and thicken the liquid (a little flour-and-butter whisked in), then returned them to the pot and to the barest simmer.

She'd set aside vegetables. With *coq au vin* you want nothing much. A few small potatoes, a dish of French beans. Some crusty bread. She'd made a pudding – poached pears. They'd been left to cool. A wedge of Roquefort, some red grapes. All never to be touched. She would have laid the table – now it was safe – the same table where once she'd hugged a sobbing Kristina and thought: now it will be all right.

Kristina by then, perhaps, would have been boarding her plane.

At some point, after a tidy-up and a quick glance round, she would have gone upstairs to change. The sudden coolness of even a well-heated house when you leave the warmth of the kitchen. November dark outside. She put on, so the police would observe, a simple but

stunning scoop-necked dress of black velvet – a dress for
an evening out though it was an evening in – and chose
from the box on the dressing-table a pearl necklace (no
doubt, but I know it now, a present from him).

A simple question: do you get dressed like that if you
mean to—?

Now I run it all back through my head, as if I was there
(there in their bedroom), it seems almost the most unbear-
able moment. The last time, though she didn't know it,
she would do this. Make herself ready. Those practised,
almost unthinking and, recently, just token actions, now
once more performed with meaning, even a touch of
triumph. All that Kristina might have had to offer. Not
any more.

She touched up her hair, her face. Lipstick. Scent.
The last time she would do these things, this way. The
last time she would know even the commonplace pleasure
of a bedroom, a dressing-table, laying out a special dress.

And Mrs Nash, the papers would note (Marsh would
note it), was a striking woman. If that's not an unfortunate
word.

I should have been in that bedroom, fastening that
necklace, fastening that dress.

It was nearly eight perhaps by then. She came back
downstairs. Now all her agony had condensed into a single
minor uncertainty: when would she hear the car, his step?
The key in the door. She knew it might be a while. Traffic.
A weekday night. Heathrow to Wimbledon, it can take
longer than you think. She knew she might need this last
scrap of patience.

In the hallway, by the window, she'd have checked that the porch light, the light over the garage and the little low lights at the entrance to the drive were all on. Of course they were. She would have eyed herself in the mirror. The way we can look at ourselves as if we haven't met for a while.

And Bob – did she wonder? Would it be like meeting him all over again?

She would have gone back to the kitchen. She would have been doubly careful to put on the apron – the proper, wrap-around cook's apron, navy-blue with a white stripe – that was found, when the police arrived, bundled loosely on the work surface where she must have flung it quickly when she heard him arrive.

One of the cops (a tasteless joke): she should have kept it on.

But there had still been things to do. Final touches. A last taste, a last stir, a last adjustment of the heat. And there was the parsley to chop, for the garnish. And perhaps it was at this point – not waiting, after all, till she heard the car – that she lit the candle.

So that when the police arrived they walked into a scene that was not at first – till you saw the obvious – like a murder scene at all. The opposite. A scene of perfect welcome. A warm, inviting house on a cold November night. And a house that smelt, that breathed – this was the really striking thing – of something wonderful cooking. You couldn't help smelling it as soon as you entered (whatever your reason for being there). The smell of good cooking that goes straight from nose to stomach, from stomach to heart.

Look, it was still there, still on the gentlest simmer, it hadn't been touched.

Someone took it upon themselves to turn off the heat. And someone (Marsh himself?) – after Mrs Nash had been taken away but the body, her husband, was still there – might have raised the lid, looked, sniffed.

A wooden spoon was close by. Did they dare?

And over there, in the corner, the candle, the flowers, the napkins, the unpoured wine.

Even the murder weapon, a kitchen knife, a good one and recently sharpened, still had on it, along with Bob Nash's blood, some green smears and flecks of parsley.

A private detective, who blundered madly in, noted all this too.

The Nash Case. How could it have been cold-blooded revenge? But if not revenge, then what? On that very night, at that very point?

She hadn't planned an escape, a get-away. The opposite. She herself made the call, said the words. And there she was, still there, saying it over and over again, I did it, I did it, I did it, as if she was learning a new language, as if someone should have been there to translate.

She'd put down the knife. She'd put it back on the chopping board.

Revenge? He had it coming? But who was the real monster now? The real monster of the two? He was just a gynaecologist who'd crossed a line – and taken advantage (if it was that way round) of a poor helpless refugee girl.

No, he didn't look so pretty. But who was the real monster now?

But go back, go back to that kitchen before it was the scene of a crime. Before it was a case, a story in the press. Rewind the clock. Relive it (how do the dead relive?). It might be different this time.

It's eight o'clock. It's eight-fifteen. She begins to worry – ordinary clock-watching worry. Traffic. But of course – she's not naive – he might be having to do some thinking, he might be having to pull himself together. Taking his time.

All the more reason for this meal, for all this elaborate preparation. So that when he arrives he'll be instantly reassured. Instantly greeted by a smell, a smell speaking louder than words.

And it can stand waiting, one of its virtues, the longer it simmers, the better.

And, anyway, a little after eight-thirty she hears the sound that for her is like a confirmation, an embrace. A familiar and not often thought-about sound, which recently has meant little to her ears. But now it comes like music. The sizzly civilized sound of tyres on gravel.

45

'You know what he said once, George? He said, "I can't live without her."'

We sit at our prison table. She's never told me this before.

'Just before she moved out – into the flat. How are you supposed to take that? Your husband says he can't live without another woman. It's the sort of thing that should never get said – and he didn't have to bloody well say it – but once it's said, what are you supposed to think? He doesn't *mean* it?'

I think of a table laid for two.

'And what are you supposed to *feel*: it's wrong – that can't be? *I'm* the one you shouldn't be able to live without. But is that what counts, is that how it should be – to expect that someone else can't live without you?'

I look at her and try not to think too hard.

'And he *had* lived without her, hadn't he? All the time he'd never bloody known her. All the time he'd been living with *me*. So what *did* he mean?'

It's as though Bob's still here and she's giving him a grilling. All his bloody fault.

Or giving me a grilling in his place.

I should shrug and say it's just an expression, it's just a bunch of words. But I take words seriously these days.

Her face has gone grim and cold. Like it was in those first days I came visiting.

'Of course we can live without,' she says, 'we can live without anyone. If we have to, we must.'

I look at her, not blinking. It's like a test.

'Look at Kristina, George. Wasn't she living without? Without just about everything. And this place – my God – doesn't it teach you to live without, doesn't it teach that?'

I try to smile. 'I wouldn't know, sweetheart.'

The barest of smiles back. 'It's a luxury, isn't it? Having someone you can't live without?'

'But this isn't luxury, sweetheart.'

The screws stand around, keeping an eye. It's not a playground (despite the kids) but it's a kind of school. Here you have to learn. And here – she's explained it more than once, though any fool might guess – it's not so much what you have to live without but what you live *with*. More words that you have to take seriously, big wordy words that used to be just words in the dictionary or like words in someone else's language. But now (I feel their weight too) they're as real as rocks.

'Remorse', for example.

Today, of all days, they're real.

'It wasn't a luxury for him, either. I wish I could have said it was. You know – like men have another woman because it's a luxury. She's just his luxury. So – he'll get tired.'

The smile's disappeared.

'You know what I thought – ha! – he's the refugee now. He's the bloody refugee. The one who doesn't know where his home is. Now I'd be giving *him* shelter. I'd be sheltering my own husband.'

It's as though it's still happening now. It must be the day. The reliving.

Sometimes I want to say – and then it seems absurd: Stop punishing yourself. Today, of all days, it seems absurd.

On the wall in the Visits Room there's a clock with a red second hand that jerks round, telling you the time you have left. It always seems like a bad joke. Thirty minutes . . . Eight years . . .

If only they'd let her out, just for this day. So she could go to the grave and see. If only they'd allow her that – luxury. I'd take her, I'd stand surety, I'd deliver her back. I wouldn't sneak off with her, oh no. I'd even stand off to one side, like a guard – it's my job, to tag people – while she stood there looking.

A cruelty for her to look at it. A cruelty that she can't. So she could see. Just a grave.

"You know what I thought, George? Well, now you can't be greedy any more. You can't be greedy. If you can't live without *him* – then share. But don't stop loving him, don't stop loving him – that's not how it works.'

I say to myself: Do I want to hear this, do I want to hear any of this?

What do I want to hear? That Bob was a mistake, a long mistake? A smashed windscreen, *coq au vin*. Like I became a mistake for Rachel. Goodbye, George.

I don't know what she'd say now – after two years – if

she was let out, if she could stand by the grave. I don't know how it works.

I'd stand to one side straining my ears.

Goodbye, Bob.

The second hand jerks on. Nearly a quarter to four. Two years ago it was their last afternoon in Fulham.

I can tell you now, Bob – as the one who killed you, after all – I don't love you any more.

Her eyes look worn, as if she hasn't slept. The knot in her brow. She's not wearing make-up.

Don't punish yourself.

'She wasn't his luxury, was she – only his luxury? Otherwise he could never have said it, he could never have dared say it to me: "I can't live without her."'

She looks down at her hands. 'And, anyway, it was true, wasn't it? He didn't, did he?'

46

MY JOB WAS OVER when I said those words.

'He's on his way home.'

I could have gone home myself – cooked my own supper for one. Cannelloni with spinach and ricotta. It was already done (I think ahead), it only needed twenty minutes in the oven. A tomato and basil salad. A glass of Chianti. Don't stint yourself because you're on your own. Allow yourself a little luxury.

But I'd seen his face – or that loss of a face – as he turned, came stumbling, without knowing it, towards me. There was a moment when I lay right in his path and – had he been looking, had he been seeing anything with that emptied-out face – he'd have seen me, for an instant, no more than three yards away, phone to my ear. He'd have taken in a man he wouldn't have known at all, a nobody, but who was right then talking to his wife. While, in reverse, I was looking at a man I knew (I'd seen his photo – a holiday shirt) but who seemed to have become a nobody. So for a second or two it was like looking in a mirror. Is that *me*? That lost soul?

Then he swerved, lurched away from me. I pocketed my mobile. My job wasn't done. Of course not.

It's where Marsh's questions began. You didn't have to do it – keep trailing him still.

No, I could have been eating cannelloni.

As if it wasn't up to me to make it true. To stand surety. He's coming home. That leap in her voice – 'oh, thank you' – and that leap inside me, when I should have been sinking, like him.

The other's happiness, not your own.

He headed back towards the car park. In his shoes what would I have done? Found some spot that looked out on the runways? Pressed my nose against cold glass? All those taxi-ing lights. All those trundling planes, the people inside them like mere possibilities. At night it's hard to follow . . .

I followed him along the walkway. 'Followed' isn't really the word. I couldn't explain this to Marsh. 'Urged' maybe. Forced. None of the usual caution: see and don't be seen. As if I might have caught up with him – his own steps heavy and slow as lead – gripped his arm, dragged him along. Come on, do it!

How he found the right level, found the car, I don't know. At the best of times you get lost in such places, forget where you were. But less than an hour ago he must have known it, not wanting to think of how it would feel: he'd have to come back this way, retrace his steps, all by himself.

The mercilessness of a multi-storey car park. Cold concrete, blotches of oil. The scream of jets. She'd gone. He found the Saab, got in. A car can be like a bunker, a bolt-hole, a tomb. After a few seconds the interior light went out and he still hadn't switched on anything else. I couldn't see if his head was in his hands.

Five minutes must have passed. So the car became like a black hard shell again. Was there a person inside?

For God's sake, man. Start the fucking car!

47

I THINK: HE ONLY lived without her for a couple of hours.

I don't say anything.

And this has been two years.

Sometimes, on the other side of the table, she's as close as a breath, sometimes it could be a mile.

It's not the first time I've thought it: If I'm a good visitor, an unfailing visitor, if I serve *my* time (two years!), won't they let me take her home?

Shouldn't it work that way round? I'll look after her, I promise. No more killings. She's safe with me. Surety, indefinitely.

I'm nice to the screws, I'm always nice to the screws.

And it would be one less problem, one less chore for them. One less mouth to feed, one less inmate to house. A small easing of the public burden. Private charity work. I'll keep her, myself, under lock and key.

It's only what *she* did once – three years ago: she took Kristina in. Was that overstepping the mark? For pity's sake.

The screws stand around as if at any time they could

make their selection. Okay, you two, we've been watching you. Today's your lucky day. No – don't thank us.

But they simply watch. It's their job. You stay detached. As if there's a line for them too. All the lines.

It's nearly four. They're still in the Fulham flat, the curtains drawn. And in a moment I'll be down below, in the car, watching, waiting. The light fading. Okay, you two, time's up.

She looks at me as if she's looking for something beyond me, something more than me. It hurts me. As if today I shouldn't have come alone, I should have picked someone up on the way (I tried). Look who's here. Look who's with me . . .

And if that's what it would take, and I could do it, I'd do that too.

Look, it's Bob after all. Look, everyone: Bob Nash. It was all a mistake.

I'd say: Okay, you two – good luck to you both. Now I'll be slipping away, now my job's finally done.

But it hurts me.

I should feel hurt today. The absurdest things: I'm jealous of the man she killed. I want him out of her life. And he is. But today he has visiting rights. It's his day, I can't deny it.

Four o'clock . . .

But he's still with the woman he said he couldn't live without.

'Did you go to the office?' she says.

Small talk, casual talk, skirting the subject. You sit by a hospital bed and talk about the weather. Around us, maybe twenty other conversations. The one question that makes no sense in here: How was your day?

'Just for an hour or so – before I left for the cemetery.'

'Rita's there now?'

'At the office? Of course.'

'She knows where you were going?'

'Before here? Of course. She knows what day it is, she hasn't forgotten.'

Her eyes go a little edgy. Sometimes I think Sarah would like a word, a message, from Rita – another woman's word. And I'd bring that too, if I could, Rita's word.

Rita says, 'Hello.' Oh and, by the way, she says to forgive you.

I haven't told Sarah everything about Rita – not about the pink fluffy dressing-gown. But she knows, I know she knows, she can guess. It's a game we play. The absurdest things. A game of jealousy. As if Sarah should be jealous, as if she has a right. Or a cause.

But she looks at me closely, only a slight crease of a smile. As if I'm under interrogation. Another game. I'm the one under suspicion, even the guilty party. Sarah's had me in for questioning, a grilling. At her bare table. I'm the one who still lives in the world, where people go wrong. How can you go wrong in prison?

'And what does she think?'

'What does Rita think? About—?'

'About.'

'I think Rita thinks I'm mad.'

She looks down again at her hands. She often looks at her hands as if surprised they're still hers.

'And are you?'

222

'I'm not mad, sweetheart. You know that. I said she should have the day off. Since it's – a special day. Since I wouldn't be around much myself. But – Rita, take a day off? She's there now, working twice as hard.'

'As if you're skiving.'

'As if I'm skiving. Not mad, just skiving.'

The crease of a smile broadens. Her bare table. There are times on these visits when we forget which way round it is. Am I visiting her? Is she visiting me?

Another game we play: the big continuous game. It's not you who's locked in, sweetheart, it's me who's locked out.

'She's a loyal woman, George. You're lucky to have her.'

'I am.'

Though I could tell her, I could tell her even now: I think Rita's going to quit. That would end our game, our little jealousy game – it would mean Sarah would win. Rita's going to leave me, I've read the signs.

(Rita's read them too.)

But I know this isn't the time to tell her. They wouldn't be the words she'd want to hear. Rita's had enough, she's giving up, she's going to quit.

'Yes,' I say. I look her straight in the eye. 'I'm a lucky man.'

It's strange how in this place where there can't be any privacy you can learn to say so much. As if there's a code, a second language under the one you speak.

Strange, how here you can confess.

But I haven't told Sarah everything. Does anyone tell anyone everything? There are things I can't and won't tell Sarah yet. Perhaps I never will.

48

HE STARTED THE CAR, drove out of the car park. I followed him home.

Home? Where was that for Bob Nash, that night?

We threaded the tangle of roads inside the airport – where you might circle around for ever – then took the tunnel out under the runway.

Can you tell from the way a car is driven what the driver is thinking? Can you read a car like a face? Maybe not. He didn't speed – the opposite. The slow lane again. I should have thought: This is good, he knows he has to take care – given the state he's in. He's making sure he makes it safely.

When we came off the motorway on to the slower elevated section, I dared to drive right on his tail.

Did I want him to know I was there – urging him, escorting him?

If he hadn't been thinking of other things, his head might have jerked to his mirror. Who's this joker behind me who can't keep his distance?

A Monday evening. The traffic, in this direction, quiet

by now. He might have been back in Beecham Close in half an hour. But at the exit for the North Circular – the first option for Wimbledon, via Kew Bridge – he carried straight on, and when he took the Hammersmith exit he didn't take the second option – via Hammersmith Bridge – but continued round the Hammersmith roundabout and took the Fulham turn.

Still an option – via Putney – for Wimbledon. But he wasn't thinking beyond Fulham (I'd guessed it by now). He was retracing his route of two hours before, as if to turn time around.

I've never told Sarah this: that he went to Fulham first, on the way back. It wasn't that he was caught in traffic, that he took it slowly, had to stop, even, to collect himself. He went back to the flat.

And I've never told Sarah what happened before that – right there, on Fulham Palace Road, just a little way down from the Hammersmith turn.

There was a set of lights that had just switched to red: nothing between him and them except fifty yards or more of road. But he didn't slow down. For the first time that night he suddenly accelerated. For the first time that night he drove like a madman.

It's not a busy intersection, a minor road to left and right, but a long, high-sided truck had already started to lumber its way across. He speeded up – I'd swear it – when he saw the possibility. When he saw the side of the truck about to straddle the road like a wall.

A mistake? He hadn't seen the lights, his mind just wasn't on the road? No. I'm a trained observer – observation's my job. He speeded up, he went for it.

And only slammed on his brakes at the point where if

his tyres hadn't been good, if the road had been wet, it still might have turned out bad.

Fulham Palace Road. Junction with St Dunstan's and Winslow.

A cop again, composing an accident report, even before it had happened. The standard notebook phrases. Distance, direction, speed. It's your job – you stay detached. It was only when he stopped short and the truck lurched on, clearing the main road, that I noticed where we were. Charing Cross Hospital. Just south of Hammersmith. On the left, just ahead, on the far side of the lights: Charing Cross Hospital.

I never told Sarah. Or Marsh.

A necessary moment? A moment of truth? A self-administered shock? The life that used to be his, right there, about to pass in front of him.

They might have had to carry him in. It might have been handy. Accident and Emergency. Someone might have realized who he was. My God – that's Bob Nash.

But he came to a halt.

She might have had to go and visit *him*. *She* might have been the visitor. Never knowing how lucky she was – that this was really incredible luck in disguise. It might have saved them both. The danger list, then off it. It might have glued them together again as surely as his mending bones.

'Lucky to be alive.' Oh, but more than that. Doubly that.

And I'd have been nowhere to be seen.

Or he might have died. That way too. She'd never

know. Never have to know – what she was capable of. Thinking it the cruellest possible thing (and where could she have turned for comfort?). A 'tragic accident' – at *that* point. Thinking even – it had been her 'concession' – it was all her fault.

But she wouldn't have to be in this place now. Visiting time, like a hospital ward. Neither of us would.

A screeching, bucking halt. Pedestrians froze, turned, looked, walked on. But I don't think the truck driver, up in front in his cabin, even noticed what had happened.

Charing Cross Hospital: staring him in the face.

The lights were still on red. He'd stalled. He restarted. The lights went green. And now – if he was himself again, if the shock had worked – he might have driven straight on (I wished it, truly, willed it): Fulham Palace Road to Putney Bridge, then Putney, Putney Hill, Wimbledon Common . . . home.

But he turned left at Lillie Road and I followed him back to the flat.

Yes, I'm the lucky man.

The street just as before. Streets don't change, they don't breathe a word, they don't tell a soul. He parked, got out, walked to the front door and, as he'd done so many times before (did he keep a count?), let himself in.

Ten minutes to eight. I'd slipped into a space on the far side, twenty yards or so back. Now, more than ever, it could hardly have entered his head that he was being watched.

So – should I have stopped watching? Got out, crossed the street, tapped him on the shoulder? Made it my business?

Mr Nash? Robert Nash? Police. Would you step this way?

The front door closed behind him. The light went on upstairs. It might still have meant nothing: he had charge of the flat, after all. There might have been something he'd left there. Some simple unimportant matter. (After nearly driving into a truck?)

But anyway, could you begrudge it, if he couldn't resist it? A last look, on his way home. A last look while the room, the bed, still had a trace of warmth. While the scent of her was still there.

Nearly eight o'clock. She was in the air.

And here perhaps anyway he could truly say his farewell. Settle the balance of his life. Turn himself back into the husband of his wife.

I don't think Sarah would have begrudged it, if that was all it was.

But how long do you give it? How much time? A farewell. Just to that flat, to all it had meant? And I'd seen his face at Departures – his face like a departure itself. I'd seen him speed up at a red light.

Even so, I didn't move, I didn't leap from my car until at least ten minutes had passed. It's true, I just sat there. I let whole minutes pass. Settling, maybe, the balance of my own life. I didn't take prompt and decisive action based on reasonable suspicion and surmise, I didn't take due initiative – prepared, if necessary, to arouse neighbours to gain entry. Police. Police, open up.

*

It's true, Marsh. I sat there. Not being a policeman any more. Nothing to do with me. I may even have clutched the steering wheel as if I was clinging to a rock.

Five, ten – fifteen minutes. Dinner was cooking. The wine was breathing. Sarah was looking at the minutes ticking too.

You cross a line.

I opened my door, sprinted across the street. And it was then he would have seen me – seen me and not seen me – for the second time that night. I'll never know. He appeared at the front door just as I reached the front gate. I had to stop short, just like he'd done at the lights. Turn myself into some chance passer-by – acting a little oddly it's true, catching my breath. But he came up the front path as if he hadn't seen me, brushed past me, heading for his car as if he might have stepped right through me.

And that's what he looked like, already, a ghost.

49

'How's the Empress?' I say.

'She's fine. She's in the South of France. She's bought a yacht.'

'Good for her.'

'She's over sixty, but still going strong.'

'Life in the old girl yet.'

Small talk, dodging the issue. Time's precious – but you just play cards.

Nearly a quarter past four. In a couple of minutes they'll blow the whistle. No extra time. I'll have to leave before anything's begun. She'll have to live through it all alone.

Will there ever be a year when this day gets forgotten, like a neglected birthday, then gets remembered, afterwards, with a jolt? A stab.

No, I don't think so.

Nearly a quarter past four. I was outside the flat, the first time. She was sharpening a kitchen knife. Not even dreaming.

I say what I've said coundess times, when it's nearly time to go. 'I'm with you, sweetheart, I'll be with you.'

Though today, of all days, it can't be true. Because she'll be with Bob. His day. And ghosts aren't like other visitors. They can come any time, they can pass through walls.

Who'd begrudge him? Today. But the black taste wells up.

No, he can't make it, he's sorry – he told me. Unavoidably detained. You've got me instead.

As if I should stand in for him entirely: the whole re-run. His double. And she'd raise the knife and see it was me. And this time, really, she'd stop.

Jealous – of a corpse. She can read my thoughts. Her eyes can see inside my head.

'I'll be with you.'

'I know.'

But jealous of Bob *alive*. She knows that too. Jealous of all those years, good long years – twenty-four of them – ending like they did. And it might have been me and her in the first place. Me and Sarah. The absurdity. And Bob would have found someone else. And we'd all be happy, all still be alive. The absurdity.

And I might have been a gynaecologist and Bob might have been a cop.

You play cards, you shuffle the pack.

Twenty-four years. Except time doesn't work like that. Time doesn't make its meanings like that. Visits, moments, days. This day, this clear cold day, the air diamond-sharp.

Two minutes. What can you say with two minutes left?

A bedside closeness, a hospital hush. As if tonight's the night, when I'm gone, she'll go in for her operation. Touch and go. Ha – under the knife.

Though there's a knife, I know it, already stuck, grating and rusting, in her heart.

One day I'll pull it out.

I'm with you, I'll be with you. It's what I've always said, even right at the beginning – when she didn't want to hear. What tosh. This won't go on.

But one day she said (a smile like sunlight on stone), 'It's the wrong way round, George. Can't I be with you?'

I say it now. 'I wanted you to be with me, there, today. It's been such a – beautiful day. I wanted us to be standing there together by that grave. You know, sweetheart – there's a moment when you have to walk away, turn your back and walk away. I didn't know when to do it. How much time? I wish you'd been there beside me so you could have said when. Do you understand me? You'd have known best. I wished you'd been there so I could have heard you say, "Let's go now, George. Let's go."

'And the thing is, sweetheart, whenever you'd have said it, whenever you'd have decided, he wouldn't have stopped us.'

50

Marsh said, 'Wouldn't Mr Nash have got home safely without you following him?'

'I wanted to be sure.'

He looked at me sharply but patiently. A tactful senior officer dealing with an over-zealous junior. As if he were really my Super. An inside matter. Cop to cop. This needn't go any further.

'What did you think he would do?'

But I wasn't going to tell him. That he'd gone to the flat first, that I'd waited outside, a second time – maybe all of fifteen minutes. Waited even when I might not have waited, shouldn't have waited. Waited while something tilted and teetered inside me.

And up above (you have to put yourself in the scene), he would have thought: Where else was there to be? Where else was there to go?

It used to be how it was done once, in other times, in other countries, when some high-ranking officer had disgraced himself, done what he shouldn't. He'd be left in a room with a pistol, the door locked. His fellow officers waiting outside for the shot.

In a different world, a different age. Splendid uniforms, grim rules. The age of Napoleon and Eugénie, for example.

I waited.

And he wasn't the sort, was he? A sane and responsible medical man, a senior consultant. To be reduced to this. A room in Fulham, its four walls closing in on him.

I watched. Lights behind curtains. And we're all policemen, aren't we? Nothing's just a matter for the police.

Don't think, Marsh, you'll leave it all behind. Don't think you're a free man.

He stroked his jaw. Past midnight. Bob was four hours dead.

'You seem to have been very concerned for his welfare.'

I wasn't going to tell him. Or tell Sarah either. But she'd have known anyway: written in his face. All her patience, all her conceding – all her scheming with me – all her waiting and hoping: to welcome home a ghost.

And now she too was in a place of no escape. A locked cell – just yards away. Four cold clammy walls. How could she have come to this?

The fug of interview rooms. The matter-of-factness of police stations. In the background a smell of disinfectant.

'I wanted to be sure. For Sar—, for Mrs Nash's sake. For my client's sake.'

I saw the look on Marsh's face.

'She hadn't asked you to deliver him to her door.'

'I didn't.'

'No. A pity – maybe. Do you normally go to such lengths for a client?'

'I'm a free agent.'

'Sarah Nash's agent. You mean you didn't have to act like a detective just doing a job?'

Or not act, not move.

He means: like a good steady cop.

But I did act. I got out of my car. I crossed the street. I ran, for dear life.

And he found a way out, an escape route, somehow, down the stairs, out the front door. There wasn't any shot. We might have collided on the front path. I can't remember if I felt glad. He got to the gate before I did, stepped past me. I stepped aside. I let him go.

Let her go, Marsh, let her go. The words knocking inside my head, as if to burst out too from a little cruel room. Have me, put the cuffs on me. But let her go.

I should have stopped him. Shouldn't I? I should have arrested him – God knows for what. For being alive? A citizen's arrest.

A street in Fulham. Victorian red brick. A street full of comfortable law-abiding folk. A good part of town.

I'd have spared him, I'd have spared Sarah. I'd have kept the peace.

I should have said, 'Don't go home, not just yet. You don't know me, but—' I should have kept him in for questioning, for interview, to assist with inquiries.

'Not just yet. Let's find somewhere, let's go somewhere where we can talk.'

51

TIME'S UP. A sudden activity. It's like the moment when a ship leaves. All non-passengers disembark. Where do prisoners sail?

'Take care, sweetheart, I'll see you soon.'

It always feels like desertion. Today it feels like treachery. How will she get through these hours? As I make my way back with the others, through the doors and checkpoints, there isn't even that usual feeling of reprieve. You're lucky, they're letting you go this time. That was just a warning.

The screws count you out as if there still might be a catch. A catch? A concession? The tap on the shoulder: No, not you – you stay.

Do they know it was today, this very day? There he goes and it's two years now, to the day. It must mean something.

Bridget waves me through. Is that a special look in her eye?

'Bye, Bridget.'

'Bye, George. Be good now.'

'I'll try.'

And the world's still there. It's always a faint surprise: it didn't go away. And there's always the faint sweet rush of gratitude, of guilty gratitude.

Then it hits you, like another wall: another fortnight.

The cold strikes. I emerge with the others. For a moment we could be some strange class being let out of lessons (but I'm the only one who hands in homework, I think). Then we disperse quickly and silently, as if to blend as soon as we can into the surroundings and become just innocent passers-by.

A rule, a superstition: I never look back. Just in case the magic, the miracle, might work that way. An ache in my back. Just in case she's behind me and the tap on the shoulder is her.

George, it's me. Don't go without me.

It's twenty past four. The sun has dipped behind the rooftops. There's a red bloom low in the sky. Up above, it fades to pink, then gas-flame blue. A slice of moon. A vapour trail, thin and twinkly as a needle. Another bitter night coming, the air hard as glass.

Write it down for me, George, what it's like out there. Bring the world in here. Not like a police report, you understand?

A tall order. Asking the world. But I've done my best.

'You deserve the world, sweetheart.'

'No, I deserve what I've got.'

A piece of the world on a piece of paper. I'd never thought of it like that. The world brought in bit by bit, like prisoners – the other way round – chipping away, stone by stone, at a wall.

But no homework to collect today. Not today.

I cross the main road and walk on in the direction of

my car. The street lamps have come on. In half an hour it will be dark. I think of his grave, the smooth granite glinting like ice. He has to get through these hours too. If she does, he does. If things can be relived.

What do they do in cemeteries when night falls? Close the gates, lock up? All visitors out. No funerals after dark.

The trees along the side of the road are turning to silhouettes. Against the sky every twig and last leaf is distinct. Cars becoming just their floating lights.

Dusk. Twilight. She taught me to look at words. The way I think she once taught Kristina. Strange English words. Their shape, their trace, their scent. Dusk. Why is it so strangely thrilling – winter dusk? A curtain falling, a divide. As if we should be home now, safe behind doors. But we're not, it's not yet half-past four and everything becomes a mystery, an adventure. Now everything we do will be in the dark.

I turn the corner into the street where I've parked. One day I'll do this a last time.

I unlock the car. It's like a fridge. It's like a bed in a disused room.

It's my punishment too – but I don't say this. I never say it. To have and not to have. But, this way, you could say I *do* have her. She's not going anywhere. You could say I have her where she can't get away.

My punishment and my reward.

And my remorse. An ache in my back.

If I'd carried the job through to the end, delivered him back – special delivery, to the door, like a gift. Matrimonial and Missing Persons. Here he is – there were problems on the way, but here he is. As if he was the prisoner set free.

Was it possible? And she might have been happy. Was it ever possible?

I turn on the ignition with the heater full on. It throws out a freezing blast.

So happy she'd have come in to see me, a last time, to settle the bill, to thank me in person, a few moments in my office instead of years – of this. To sign a cheque and thank me ('It was nothing – nothing, really') and suddenly hug me, maybe, kiss me even, on the cheek.

She'd have walked out free and happy. Was it possible? I'd have watched her heels, the backs of her knees. Departures. I'd have watched her from my window, crossing the Broadway, walking back to her life. And that might have been and should have been gift enough for me.

52

SINCE THEY DO THANK YOU. Thank you and more. The strangest thing – I never expected it – they thank you even when the news is bad.

'It's not just that they're women, Helen . . .'

'No?'

Suddenly all ears. 'Well, you can't leave it at that – you've got to go on.'

Chicken Marsala, Sole *Véronique* . . . But it wasn't just the cooking. This dad of hers that she'd never known.

Rita said, 'Are you married yourself, Mr Webb?'

'Was.'

A cock of her blonde head.

'A long story.'

(Though it wasn't really: a quick goodbye then off she went to school.)

'You don't have to tell me.'

She glanced round my office – the way Helen had glanced round at the house. The tiniest hint of a tut-tut.

There are all kinds of motive: information, confirmation, desperation . . . Sometimes it's an act of war. It's savage, it's rough. And there's always the rebound factor. I'd got wise to that.

The tiniest hint of a sigh.

I'd already given her the news: the who and the where. She'd already half-known. The no-nonsense, dry-eyed type. She worked in a factory – cardboard products – manager's PA. I imagined she could do the job for him, do it all with her eyes shut, but she had to know her place.

She sat now in my office, legs crossed, eyes clear, the black point of one shoe now and then prodding the air.

And I'm a detective. I'm not a fool. I can read signs. I ought to have had a sign on my door: 'George Webb: Private Investigator and Rebound Consultant'.

And wasn't I on the rebound too? A long story. A long, slow rebound.

She wasn't finished, so it proved. She wanted me to go one step further. A little extra job. She wanted me to take her to the house, the address – while the husband was there – and just wait outside while she went and knocked. That was all, a simple job. She'd only be a moment.

Would I do this? She'd pay.

The point of her shoe poked forward, like something being aimed. She took her eyes off me and looked along the stretched-out line: knee, ankle, toe.

So we went. A modern house on a new estate. Nine in the evening. They thank you, you become allies.

I parked outside. A cold January night. She was all grim, steady silence, but before she got out, while my hand rested on the wheel, she reached across and pressed her fingers against my wrist. 'Wish me luck,' she said – as if no particular reply was needed. Then she took away her fingers, leant across further, took my face in both hands and planted a kiss on my cheek. 'Wish me luck.' I did.

She got out, straightened her skirt. She might have said, 'Keep me covered.' What was she going to do? Pull a gun? (From where?) A knife, a jar of acid? While I sat here drumming on the steering wheel?

She walked up the front path. It's an inspiring sight, a magnificent sight, the striding hips of a woman who hasn't got much to lose and, right now, means serious business.

I waited. The door was opened, a shaft of light. She was actually let in. I waited to hear yells, screams, breaking glass. Remembering my police training. Put in your call first. It was more than a moment, it was almost ten minutes. Then she reappeared.

I'll never know what she did or said in there, but she walked out in a way that was magnificent too, but different from the way she'd walked in. She held her head up high, breathed the air. She might have swiped one brisk palm against the other. Her moment of glory, of make-do glory, of hollow revenge. I thought of Rachel: where was she now?

Though the revenge wasn't over yet.

She got back in. She said nothing. For an instant she sat still and rigid as a statue, then she went into cascades of tears, she went liquid. I put a hand on her shoulder. She shook it off. I felt I shouldn't have been there. Then she pulled herself up, groping in her handbag for a tissue, and said, 'Drive! Drive! Get us out of here!' So I drove. She said, 'Put your foot down!' as if we'd just robbed a bank.

I drove – in no particular direction. I drove like an ambulance driver, like a cop who'd done time on cars.

Then after a while she said, 'Stop! Stop!' There was a dark empty side street, a grass verge, dimly lit. 'Stop here, George, stop here!' I thought she was going to be sick – she'd fling open the door and throw up. So I stopped.

Then she lurched across towards me and – how to put this? – dived into my trousers.

In the morning, in her bedroom: more tears. She oozed tears. 'I'm sorry. Oh God, I'm sorry.' As if she'd dragged me there by force. A hand clapped over her face. 'Oh God, what a mess. You'd better go.'

But it was a Sunday morning in January, grey, bleak and cold, and after a while she got up and was gone for maybe half an hour. She'd paused and turned in the doorway first. 'How do you like your eggs?'

She came back with a tray. Tea, toast, marmalade. She'd taken a shower, she'd done things to her face, her hair, slapped on some scent. And she was wearing a pale-pink fluffy dressing-gown, inside which her tits huddled and snuggled up to each other.

An empty bed, George.

Mr Rebound.

The truth is she wasn't the first. Who else do they have to lean on, to console them? And, God knows, you have to have a heart. And sometimes it's just at the point that you think they'll collapse completely, they'll go to pieces, that, strangely, they brighten up, they bristle, they find a new fire. Their friend in need. Mr Quick Revenge.

I'd never have guessed it. It's supposed to be a loner's job, a loser's job. A shabby, shady, dead-end job. Matrimonial work.

And I'd never have guessed there was this other person inside me: a womanizer, a woman specialist. Sleeping with my clients. Each one with the same worrying complaint: they aren't getting loved any more. All part of the service. Your agent, your confidant, your bosom pal.

Though it's true: not every one. One or two – well, three. Some of them wouldn't have touched me with a barge-pole.

I told Helen. Maybe she'd guessed – she could read my face. It was after she told me about Clare. My turn now. And the strange thing was a bit of her was shocked – or she was good at pretending – more shocked than I'd been. Though what she did next was *laugh*. Well, who'd have guessed? Her old dad, her policeman dad.

But wasn't it a time-honoured remedy – and only what she'd half-recommended, half-urged? Sitting there in the candlelight, being wined and dined. You wash away one woman with a blur of others. You press away memories as you press down flesh.

(And it was *her* revenge, too, on her mother?)

'So there you are, Helen – now *you* know.'

What shall I say? I let myself be used, get pounced on? But I didn't exactly resist. I was even ready to pounce, myself. All included, no extra charge. The first time I slept with a client I thought: So what happens now, about the fee – I forget it? But what would that make her? So I took the cheque. What did that make me?

A phase? A cure? Hollow revenge? A different kind of hound on a different kind of scent.

Until I felt used up, or emptied, or just plain worse

for wear. Till Helen's look was no longer intrigued, amused, even vaguely conspiring – just a little sad.

Was this how it was? I was just going to the bad? Looking after myself (eating well), but letting myself go. Fucking clients. Swigging now and then out of that bottle in the office that was meant to be just for them.

Corrupt as they come.

I thought her husband might come back at any moment (his name was Terry). The standard scene. A Sunday morning: bursting in. Double revenge. But she said no, no chance of that. Not after last night.

Whatever she'd done.

So I didn't leave till after four in the afternoon. Sneaking away under cover of dark.

She couldn't cook scrambled eggs (you have to take them from the heat when they're still not quite done). Later I found out she couldn't cook much at all. Not her strong point. Her strong points were elsewhere – like in walking into an office, taking a cool look around and knowing how to put it into shape. But they didn't stop there. She had a talent for detection too, so it proved. She'd never known it was there.

Something else that happens too: they get a taste, a glimpse, a hankering. Undercover work. I could do this too.

But with Rita it wasn't just a fancy, it was real. She had the knack, she had the makings. She was good at it. All her life and she'd never known: she could be a detective. These unsuspected people inside us. And why work in a factory making empty cardboard boxes, letting your talents go to waste?

'You need help, you know, George' (while she cleared away the tray). 'That office is a tip. You need sorting out – you need more than just you.'

So in the end I took her on. I took her in. On a strictly professional basis, of course. And I started giving her jobs – assignments – outside the office. Nothing too tricky at first. But there are some jobs that are best done by a woman, or in combination with a woman. And she was good at it, no question, she's never let me down. A real find. One of those women whose fate it is to be told they're worth their weight in gold.

'My weight in gold? That won't help me keep my figure, will it, George?' Running her hands down over her hips.

She's there right now – holding the fort.

Where would I be without you, Rita? I think I'm about to find out.

And I might have given her the Nash job, I nearly might.

53

Marsh said, 'But in fact nothing happened on the journey back. Mr Nash got home safely.'

'Yes,' I said, 'he got home safely.'

If 'safely' wasn't an unfortunate word.

'You watched him drive into Beecham Close at eight thirty-five. You always note precise times?'

'It's an old habit.'

'Even when you'd finished the job?'

'I was still finishing it.'

' "Making sure", you mean – seeing him home?'

'Yes. Suppose, after I'd told Mrs Nash he was coming home, he hadn't.'

'Though where else would he have gone?'

'I don't know.'

He looked at my statement, unsigned, in front of him. 'He drove into Beecham Close at eight thirty-five. He left the airport just after seven. That's still a long time . . .'

But I wasn't going to tell him. Some things are best left unsaid, and they can't arrest you for what stays in your head.

'Traffic,' I said.

He could always check. Traffic Division: M4 and A4 eastbound, between seven and eight.

'Traffic – of course. Eight thirty-five. And Mrs Nash's call was logged at eight forty-six. Eleven minutes. You saw him into Beecham Close. Then you drove away. Then, ten to fifteen minutes later – because of your "intuition", because you thought something bad was going to happen – you turned round.'

'Yes.'

'Why then? Why not when Mr Nash arrived home? Why drive away first? If you were going to – intervene – why not then?'

'I didn't think—'

'But you must have thought something – ten minutes later. "I know what I'm doing," you said to the constable. If you were going to make it your concern.'

The superior officer's stare. When is a cop not a cop? So – I'd failed him? Failed *Marsh*?

'I should have intervened earlier,' I said.

'Were you thinking of him – of Mr Nash – or of her?'

I should have intervened when he came out of that flat, but I let him pass. Thinking he was spared. Sarah was spared. We were all spared.

'Were you thinking of her – were you thinking of Mrs Nash the way you think about all your clients?'

'Can't I see her?' I said again. 'Just for a moment?'

He looked at me as if he had a bad taste in his mouth. The flint coming and going in his eye.

'You know I can't do that,' he said. My statement was still clamped under his hands.

He looked at me for a long time, as if he was standing on some edge – might even have needed my help.

He pushed the statement across to me.

'Okay,' he said, 'I think that'll do. Sign.'

Then he said, 'You know – we got Dyson. We got him in the end. He'll be put away for years.'

54

I PUT THE CAR in gear and drive off. Almost four-thirty. I need to be back in the office by five forty-five, for Mrs Lucas. But I know what I have to do first. Now it's dark.

He got back into the Saab, took his time to start. I crept back to my car, watched him pull out. Pulled out myself and followed him again, as if we were a team.

He'd have driven those last three miles back to Wimbledon knowing it was the last time he'd make that journey (not knowing it was the last journey he'd ever make): that sneaking, skulking but conceded journey. Each homecoming like a little charade. Her not needing to ask where he'd been and not bothering to ask – the absurdity of the question – how his day had been. The mockery, the misery of it. But better an unhappy peace, she'd said. Did she say it to him?

The lights will be on in the prison now, in the cells. At a certain time they all go off.

How would it end? How could it end? He'd wanted that war – out there – to go on for ever. Or wanted the

Croats to get beaten, smashed – so she might ditch this idea of one day returning. Not caring about the killing and maiming. And him in a caring profession. Jealous of another country, 'Croatia', like you might be jealous of another man.

Better an unhappy war . . .

But the Croats had won, and he'd lost.

How would it end? Well, now he knew – or almost knew. That flat in Fulham, like an empty cage. He might have locked himself up in it for good. Somehow he'd burst out.

So – was he free, released?

Always the hope that if it had to end he might become 'himself' again, the real Bob Nash – only that *other* man would suffer. But wasn't that other man (and wasn't this the heart of it?) the real Bob Nash?

The misery, the mockery, every time he returned. But a small price to pay, a small pain to endure. Not like *this*, now. And anyway the pain was only in that direction. It would leave him as soon as he let himself into that Fulham flat. The real pain, he knew it, was Sarah's. So why had she gone on letting him back in, not kicking him out?

Only one reason, only one crushing reason.

So, if it ended, if it had to end, he might even feel that a weight was lifted off him, he could breathe again. He might even feel – saved.

A look about him in those last days, Sarah told me later, of strange composure. (Though that might only have meant there was a secret plan.)

But now he knew. He was still in that flat and wasn't. He was high up somewhere in the night sky, not knowing, either, if he was really going home. He was the real Bob Nash and he wasn't.

Fulham to Wimbledon. I followed him. Hadn't he cottoned on by now? Always this same car behind.

At Fulham Palace Road he turned left towards Putney, and, like a fool, I might even have let out a cheer. Like a fool I was suddenly rejoicing – rejoicing for Sarah's sake, for the moment when she'd hear his car in the drive. Yes, we'd all been saved.

Putney Bridge. The river, black and invisible, below. Putney High Street: the blaze of shops. Superdrug, Body Shop, Marks and Spencer. This safe familiar world.

Past the station, through the traffic lights, the climb up Putney Hill. Then the roundabout at Tibbet's Corner and the turn for Wimbledon.

Less than a mile from Putney Vale.

Yes, he was going back. The long straight drive along Wimbledon Parkside. On the left, Parkside Hospital. No crazy stunts – another hospital, another old haunt where they'd cart him in. But I was watching, without knowing it, the last minutes of his life.

On the right, the Common, dark as a forest. Then the turn into the quiet, well-kept streets where the lights of houses loom like lanterns through the trees.

Now as I head back to Wimbledon myself, I know what I have to do. Another try. Now it's dark, like then.

55

CAN I EVER TELL HER? That he went to the flat first? Not straight home. That I waited outside. Watched, waited.

The number one rule of police work: don't get involved. Don't let it get to you. The beauty of it: it's a police matter, it's got everything to do with you, but at the same time – it's nothing to do with you. You're only the cop on the scene, on the case – how else could you do the job? The beauty of it. That you might go untouched, protected. Your ticket for life: I'm a cop. I'm a cop, let me through.

Bob too, in his world. A necessary detachment, a necessary steel. I'm just the gynaecologist round here. And of course they trusted him – his women. The man for the job. In his hands. They'd tell him intimate things. And sometimes, given the situation and the way they were brought together, it might go – he'd know it – a bit beyond trust.

But don't get involved.

They'd even thank him, too, when he told them bad news. Sitting there with his hands on the X-ray, the lab report. But he didn't have the fall-back that an ex-cop, or a bent cop, has. This need go no further, this can stay right here. We can even destroy the evidence.

Some things are best never known.

I never told Mum: I always knew. She'd never have to know *that* at least. There was Dad breathing – gasping – his last. My own dad, dying anyway, but just for a moment I could have throttled him.

How can I tell her? That even after the thought occurred to me, I sat there waiting outside. As if a hand – someone else's hand – was on my shoulder: stay right there.

Nothing to do with you. And you're not even a cop any more. And no one need know you were here. No one's watching *you*.

And even good cops can be too late.

How can I tell her? That I leapt out, and my heart leapt, when I saw him. 'My heart leapt': words. That less than an hour before she killed him I rejoiced to see him, to know he would soon be hers.

And of course sometimes the news – the X-ray, the report, the evidence – is *good*. The power you have then. The light that crosses their face. It's okay, it's all right, you're being let go.

And what more could I have wished than to see it through, to be sure? Then to have flown away, like Kristina to Switzerland.

Rejoicing: at my own escape.

56

I DRIVE INTO Beecham Close. As if I'm him, I'm Bob Nash on a night two years ago.

Nothing stops me this time, no invisible barrier. And nothing stopped him, though it should have done. The cordons go up after the event.

Dark and quiet. Ten past five, but it might be the dead of night. The lights of windows, beyond the hedges and gates, seem to be backing away.

Is it remembered, noted – by the street at large? This night, this very night, two years ago. Number fourteen. Let's lock our doors, not let anyone in – just in case.

But of course it wasn't like that, it was the other way round. She was waiting for him – dinner was waiting for him – in that kitchen of theirs. You can't lock your door against what's already inside.

Or forgotten? Deliberately wiped from the record? A missing file. No, not here. You must be thinking of somewhere else.

Streets in Dubrovnik. In Croatian villages. Walls, yards, squares. It happened here.

And anyway, in two years, a street changes, people

move in and out. Memory gets scattered. At some point, maybe, a new arrival gets told: Did you know . . . ? But things carry on.

Even number fourteen itself. It's not standing unoccupied, like a house condemned, like a house with a curse. It didn't even take that long – I know this – to sell. A low price, for a quick deal – common enough. But this was a real snip, for a street, a location like this. The estate agent's problem, how it was handled. Though months had gone by. And anyway: let the buyer beware.

But first a house has to be cleared: vacant possession. It wasn't the usual sort of job, it wasn't detective work (I never took a fee). But assignments, after all, come in all shapes and sizes. There's no rule book. The things people ask you to do . . .

I posed, I acted, as her representative. Who cares if she was a convicted murderer? *I* was her agent – forget the estate agent – Mrs Nash's personal agent. Had been and still was (and always will be). I had my instructions: to be given a set of keys.

Yes, there was family. Just the one son, as it happens. In Seattle. He'd shown up to see his father buried and see his mother get life. Then he'd flown back. He was – what's the expression? – washing his hands. Though what would you do? If your mother—

Bad enough if he'd just had to find out that his dad was screwing a Croatian refugee. But then he might never have had to know that at all.

But it was his house now, his to dispose of. With his mother's stuff inside. She had his permission (a lawyer's letter) and I had my instructions. I knew better than to say his name. Michael . . .

So, there was me. And a set of keys. And Nicholls from the estate agents. But he didn't want to inquire too much. He wasn't like Marsh. And there was Heywood, the solicitor – and solicitors and private investigators, well, they're well known for rubbing along.

Not detective work? But it was, it was. And didn't I know anyway – forget the bunch of keys – about secret entry and surveillance? All the skills of a semi-licensed thief.

Her house, her home once, I moved about it like some lodger. We had to meet, by special arrangement, some-where else, but for a brief while I was a guest in her house. I floated through it like a diver in a wreck. The kitchen was as far as I'd got before.

You wouldn't know now, you wouldn't guess. Not a mark on the floor. Though every kitchen, if you think about it, contains about fifty lethal weapons, hanging on hooks, stowed in drawers. Here Bob had bled, the blood had spread. Here Sarah had sat, shaking and under arrest, and here, once, at the table in the corner, Kristina had sat . . .

The innocence of rooms, houses. Their discretion, their hush. A wonderful kitchen, wonderfully equipped. Winter light on copper pans. In the living room, in the dining room, a feeling of assembled, lived-in comfort – or luxury, depending on your scale. The good life, the sweet life. The way lives get furnished, belongings gather round. The innocence of carpets, cushions, mirrors, vases. Who must have lived here?

I felt like I felt when I first went, for Helen's sake, to art galleries. As if I'd somehow intruded, stepped through the wrong door. The squeak of my shoes. No, you can't touch.

And there were things here beyond me too, beyond and not beyond me – I had the keys. Pictures here too. As if mere walls were sad things. Perhaps they are.

And books, lots of books. Upstairs (up the stairs where Bob would have carried Kristina's few pathetic possessions) was a room, at the back, completely lined with books. Sarah's room, of course: her study. Where she worked, did her translation. This was her desk. This was her chair.

I sat there, put my hands on the desk, ran my fingers gently across its surface. In front, a window looking over the garden. Bare trees. The lawn – where that photo was taken. Bob's old jacket. But, all around, there were books. So many books. Books in foreign languages too.

The chair swivelled round. I felt dizzy. I looked at the books and breathed deeply. Ha – as if you could do it without reading, take in their contents, just by breathing. Not my thing, books, man of action, me. A cop, a thief-catcher. On-your-feet stuff.

But when it came to it, it was fifty per cent watching and thinking, fifty per cent in your head.

And would the person who'd used this room, these books, this desk – who must have lived a lot, clearly, in their head – would they, could they, have committed such an action? Picked up a knife—?

Detective work. Intuition.

I breathed in her books. I picked one up. The words blurred. A diver, out of my depth. But you never know what you have inside . . .

It hadn't begun yet – I'd only discovered I could cook. But an old law enforcer (weirder things happen) can take lessons from a murderer.

I moved along the landing. Marsh would have done

this too, had a snoop round the whole house. Not that more evidence was needed. Just for his own satisfaction, to be thorough, for curiosity's sake. A house like this, a home like this — that had pretty well everything?

And this would have been *her* room, Kristina's room — at least up to a certain point. The 'guest room' as they'd planned it, after Michael took off for the States. They'd had work done, a bathroom added on. This new phase in their life, when guests would come and stay.

Well, they'd had a guest.

Kristina would have taken showers here. Here she would have slept. One day — over three years ago now — after she'd dried her eyes, she'd have sat on this bed here, as if in some expensive cell. She came from Croatia. But this is where she was now, where she had to be. Wimbledon.

And this, along the landing in the other direction, would have been Sarah's bedroom — their bedroom.

But I didn't think of him, I didn't think of him at all. I sat on the bed and breathed.

An empty house in winter. It was cold. I still wore my coat. Not detective work? But I hadn't found yet what I was looking for . . .

I had my instructions, my clear instructions. To deal with the house contents. Not a small job.

'Get rid of it all, George. Sell it, chuck it. Get someone to take the lot, any price.'

As if what she wanted was a complete cancelling out.

'Even the private stuff, even the personal stuff?'

'Burn it all. Fucking burn it.'

But I disobeyed. I didn't follow instructions. How could she check? And anyway, one day, some day, she might thank me. Something kept. It was what I was looking for: the personal stuff. In my job it's often what you have to go for. Clues. Evidence. Not just of that other, cancelled-out life – before she took a life. But of that even more remote and extraordinary life: the life before I knew her.

And I found it. Albums, photographs, odds and ends – the things that get set aside, not to be thrown away. Evidence? More than evidence. Visible, precious proof. Including a photo taken in Chislehurst when she was five.

Who knows what's in store?

Several visits. Not a small job but, anyway, I eked it out. Arrangements with removers, valuers, auctioneers. (No one need know whose it once was.) But I carried out boxes myself, cardboard boxes containing special selections, hugging them to my chest. And there's a corner of an old warehouse in Southfields where I've put all her books and several box-files, of papers and small bits and pieces, in store.

'Vacant possession.' It's a strange expression. If you look at the words. It's what I have, I suppose: possession without possession. Possession with nothing to it: I don't think so.

And it's like *she* was, like her face was, in those weeks, fortnights, before she realized I wasn't going to stop. Her face, but nothing in it, *her* face with nothing there. Until, one day—

Several visits. I'd sort of made it mine: number fourteen, my camp, my home-from-home. Neighbours peered. I didn't care. An agent, a representative, with proper instructions.

Then one day I had to lock the door for the last time. I can't go back in there again.

I cruise along slowly, as if I'm on patrol. Or up to no good. If they peered out now and saw me, could they possibly remember, guess?

Number ten, number twelve ... And there it is. Occupied, of course. Lights on. So what are *they* feeling tonight? A shiver, a shudder? A shrug? Or is it just possible they don't even *know*? It could be a different lot now from the ones Nicholls sold it to. Their name was Robinson, but they could have gone. And the whole street might have conspired. Some things are best not known. Like Kristina, in Geneva, stepping off her plane ...

Don't mention it, not a word. Let them find out. Their problem – if it is one. We don't want to rake up that old business again. Carry on as if it never happened. And isn't that just the point? A good street: things like that don't happen here.

When Rachel and I bought our house, our first decent house – Fairacre Road – there was that flicker of a look, I remember, on the faces of neighbours. Behind the smiles and the obvious jokes. You'd think it might be reassuring, a cop on their street. And I was a DI by then. Plain clothes, suit and tie – just like them. You needn't have known. But this was '78. Who loved a cop? And anyway it wasn't *me* so much, George Webb – George and Rachel Webb, and little Helen, number twenty-nine – but all that *stuff* I dealt with, all that stuff that came with me, so to speak, that stuff out there. Not wanted round here.

Fairacre Road!

And, here, it could be a million miles from the Callaghan Estate. It's actually less than ten. But a million. The whole idea.

And we never wanted that – refugee girl either. And weren't we right?

I park the car opposite. They might not even know, even tonight. I should tell them maybe. Knock on the door. I've come to inform you . . . Like we had to do in the Force. Someone has to. No real training for it: handling distress.

It might have happened on *that* night too. Not a key in the lock. A cop car, yes – but just a knock on the door.

I turn off the engine, switch off the lights, sit. A familiar situation. As if I'm on a case, keeping watch – always ready, if needs be, to slip down off the seat, under the steering wheel. It's not comfortable, it's not dignified, but it goes with the job.

But, of course, there's nothing to watch. As if, because it's the same night, something should happen all over again.

I'm just here, on duty, on the spot.

He turned in there. I saw him. I hadn't followed, but I could see him from the end of the road. He turned between those two square brick pillars, against the hedge on either side. Each with a little outdoor light built in, behind glass, like the plates of glass you break in case of fire. Lit up then, like now, to guide him in. I watched his red rear lights slip between the two white ones. Then I turned and drove away.

I sit in the dark. The black taste. I knew it would come.

There's one thing no one in this street is thinking tonight, I'm prepared to bet. Where is Sarah Nash now?

On the grass verge under the street lamp you can almost see the frost beginning to form already, stiffening each little blade. In the morning, another crust of white.

At night, walking the beat, or cruising around in the Panda, I used to get the feeling, like a dream, that I was the only one on watch. As if I'd personally put the world to bed and it wouldn't see another day if it weren't for me. Absurd.

All the houses, fleets of them, forging through the night. And, look, in the morning, all still there. Just because of me.

All the houses. A night watchman, that's me. Lift off the roofs of houses, lift up their lids, and what would you see? What would the aggregate be? More misery and hatred than you could begin to imagine? Or more secret happiness, more goodness and mercy than you could ever have guessed?

But no one can do that, can they? So how do we know? Lift off the roofs of houses, peer inside. Except the police.

Police – open up.

57

ALL MY FAULT. I could have stopped him, stepped in, I had enough chances. At the airport, in the terminal, in the car park. Outside the flat.

'Mr Nash? A word.'

Like a fool, I'd even rejoiced.

I didn't think. I watched him turn into Beecham Close. Eight thirty-five. My job done.

Or not done. Since the job includes a report. There never would be one of those. She'd wanted to know *how* they said goodbye (*if* they said goodbye): I was to have been her eyes. As if her own eyes wouldn't see for herself, now.

But I didn't think.

I watched him drive into number fourteen. Then I drove away. As if my instructions might have been: my husband, dead or alive. As if I was already standing over his grave, mouth full of blackness.

No, Marsh, I didn't think anything, I wasn't thinking at all. While I drove away, in those ten to fifteen minutes, I'd stopped thinking, as if I might have been a dead man too.

I was almost home myself. A man driving home too. Then I stopped. A tyre-squealing halt. There wasn't a junction, no lights on red. Just clear road. I stopped. An intuition, Marsh, let's call it that. As if something had hit me in the chest. The car seemed to turn itself round: a U-turn, more squealing tyres. As if the call had come straight to me. I should have switched on a siren, a flashing light, cop though I wasn't.

But that was already being done: two police cars (more to come) and an ambulance, already on their way.

I drove back into Beecham Close, I might have been the even bigger fool. And rejoiced again? Or sat here – right here – with my head in my hands? Intuition? All would be quiet. Deepest Wimbledon. I'd have come to a halt again, heart hammering. Fool! Fool!

But some things you know. It's not detection, it's not even intuition. You know.

And the two police cars and the ambulance were there before me, like something I'd already seen (my job once, stuff like this). If I'd been five minutes earlier I might have been first to arrive.

I should have stepped in.

'Mr Nash? You don't know me but – I know your wife.'

Or it might have been better, a thousand times better, if I'd watched them fly off together. Phoned to tell her. 'Mrs Nash?' Worse and better. What we'll never know.

Of course it would have been better. He wouldn't have been lying in that pool of blood. And she wouldn't have been sitting there, shaking. And it might have been just me – how many times have I imagined it, rehearsed it? – who came back that night, rang at the door, stepped in.

Into the smell of *coq au vin*.

I lurched to a stop. Leapt out. Rushed past the constable, only just posted outside. I didn't explain, he didn't stop me. I said, 'Police! Police!' Apparently I also said, 'I'm a detective, I know what I'm doing.' The front door was open, I burst through. Inside was the scene of a crime. I knew about crime scenes. The feeling of things going into deep freeze.

But this was different, utterly different. It was warm. There was the smell of cooking, something wonderful cooking, wrapping itself round you like a hug. There was Bob on the floor in a pool of blood. There was a table, in the corner, with a candle. And there was Sarah sitting, shaking, in a chair. Her hair and her face were made up as if for a celebration, a pearl necklace, a clinging black dress. I'd never seen her like this. Ready for a lover. She looked at me amazed, as if she couldn't believe it was me. But she looked amazed anyway, as if everything now could only amaze her, as if all there could be was amazement.

58

AND THE TRUTH IS, he had flown with her. Or he might as well. He was up there with her, I believe it (and Sarah would have seen it), up in the rescuing air. Only his lifeless body down here.

And, up there, what did she know? Did she feel a sudden flutter: a chill, a warmth, an aura? How many ghosts have been reported on aeroplanes? But best not to know. The best place to be: where you won't know. How her brother died, how her parents died. She was going back to find out? Some detective work. All the pools of blood. Forget Wimbledon, forget Beecham Close.

Her plane was already coming down towards Switzerland. The lights of houses, of picture-book chalets scattered over mountain sides. A glint of moonlit snow, the shimmer of a lake.

Did she ever learn? By accident or intent? Or had she closed that part of her life – was that the nub of it? – hardening her face (and heart?): going through to Departures with those minutes still to spare?

And did she go back to Croatia, really? Is she there now?

The lights of a big foreign city below her, rising to meet her. The high life, the good life. A qualified interpreter, a translator, a citizen of the world.

I see her still in Geneva. I see her (it's just a fancy) finding work with the UN. I see her, yes, going back to her old country – new country – but only as a member of some official team. A UN interpreter, an observer. Diplomatic credentials – but her own personal links. Post-war reconstruction and rehabilitation. The investigation of war crimes. Work that will never be complete.

Working for the UN, the shambling, botching peacekeepers. The wise-after-the-event international police.

59

Sarah will finish her translation soon. I don't want her to, nor does she. A lifeline. My project too. Sometimes on my visits we talk about nothing else.

It's like it was in Gladstone's, two years ago, except it's the Visits Room now. And I thought, then, it could never be: we meet to swap notes – there's nothing more urgent in our lives – on this stuff that happened long ago.

It all came to grief at the battle of Sedan. 1870: Eugénie was a mere spring chicken in her forties. Napoleon III got beaten hollow by the Prussians.

Disaster, downfall. Exile to Chislehurst.

Not a military genius, like his uncle – *the* Napoleon – but he led his own armies into battle and once in an earlier war, against the Austrians in Italy (whatever they were doing there), he'd won two big battles: Magenta and Solferino. He could have driven the Austrians clean out of Italy but at Solferino apparently he called a halt, and one reason, the story went, was that he'd simply got sick of blood.

I looked them up for myself. Homework. Magenta, Solferino. Like I looked up Sedan. Like once I looked up Dubrovnik. And I found out the other story.

There was this Swiss businessman with big schemes, looking for backers, who thought he'd go to the very top: the Emperor himself. And since the Emperor wasn't at home but fighting a war in Italy, he went looking for him there. But instead of finding the Emperor he stumbled on the aftermath of the battle of Solferino, and this changed his big schemes, and his life.

He did what he could, there and then, for the wounded and dying. Once back in Switzerland he made it his job to relieve the miseries of war. He founded what became known as the Red Cross, and this led to the Geneva Convention, which led to the League of Nations, then to the UN.

The Red Cross. Everyone knows it's not there to take sides, just to give first aid. A neutral set-up: charity and mercy. And the Geneva Convention isn't a peace recipe, it just says – it's almost absurd – that if wars have to be fought and people have to kill each other then at least they should do it according to certain rules.

Switzerland itself – where I've never been – is famous for being neutral and safe, a place where the rest of the world goes to sort out its troubles. A place of clean air, clinics and lots of snow. And banks and chocolates and wristwatches. A civilized country. The snag, they say, is that it's just a bit boring. A safe, unexciting place.

I've never been, but I think about Kristina who has – and who might still be there.

Who would want the whole world to be like Switzerland? Though isn't that how the world is, wherever there's civilization and peace? The lights of houses through trees, quiet streets where nothing happens. Napoleon and Eugénie, after the battle of Sedan, might have fled to Switzerland:

some villa by a lake. Instead they settled in Chislehurst, on a future golf course.

So what do we really want? Peace? Really? Excitement? Really?

Helen, I think, doesn't understand me any more, not these days. She was there to help me through, to be the Red Cross (but she took sides) when the chips were down. But this, this now, can't be what she would have imagined for me, what she would have wished. This woman in my life. That I'd be going, once a fortnight, two years now, to see – this prisoner. This killer.

She worries about me maybe. It's strange how things have turned out. My fight-picking daughter: the two of us at war. I never understood. Now it's the other way round. It's undercover love, of a kind: it's no secret, but it can't exactly come out into the open.

And I did meet Clare, eventually – when they set up in business at last, the two of them: interior design. How could I not get an invite to their little launch? And the first thing I thought when I met her was: she's the wife and Helen's the husband. You shouldn't think such thoughts, maybe, but that's how it was.

A small office in Notting Hill, small but well kitted-out. I suppose, if it's interior design . . . Wine and things on trays. People I didn't know. You could see it at once: Clare was the hostess, the people-person – a ready smile, an easy sparkle – Helen was the business brain.

A year or more ago now. Maybe I hadn't met Clare till then because (the thought occurred to me) Helen thought I might fancy her. And given that I was free, and even, for a certain period, putting it about . . .

I might have been an embarrassment.

But now, of course, I was fixed. And to Clare, at that little party, I must have been just a curiosity: Helen's dad, an ex-cop (kicked out for some reason), a private detective who'd been involved in that – episode. A murder! And formed this – attachment. The Nash Case.

A curiosity. An oddball.

And I did fancy Clare – so far as it went. A good-looking woman. A quick-eyed, quick-lipped woman who drew her face close to yours. The kind of woman who does the talking and charming while the husband takes a happy back seat, smiling to himself, knowing he's being envied. Though sometimes he's a little anxious too.

There wasn't a husband, of course, but I saw it was like a marriage. I might have said to Helen (but how could you say it?): Congratulations, you pick your women well.

Clare steered me about, refilled my glass, cupped a hand under my elbow, as if I'd come in from the cold, from some far-away land. This mystery guest.

And of course there was no possibility . . . On more than one count. It was entirely safe.

'Helen says you're – quite a cook . . .'

Interior design. Interior designs. They would have 'clients' too. I thought: it's all the same game. You get an office, you cater for needs. My dad's studio, next to the florist's, in Chislehurst. My own little set-up, over the Tanning Centre. Except it's a little different, maybe. A place of last resort.

And I'm a little different. In the end it's a hunt. Two eyes in the dark.

Fabrics and fittings, curtains and colour schemes. The

good life, the sweet life, windows lit at night. What became of my outlaw daughter? My art-loving daughter?

Peace? Excitement? What's civilization for? Matrimonial work: that's my game. It's not always nice but I'm not the Red Cross. And in my time of doing matrimonial work I've seen quite a few couples who've come to grief, who've gone to war, for no other reason, so far as I can see, than that over the years of being safe and steady and settled, something's got lost, something's gone missing, they've got bored.

60

I SIT OUTSIDE, watching. God knows what I expect to see. Houses don't stir. A thousand things might happen in them but they don't raise an eyebrow, not even a flicker. 'The Emperor Napoleon died here.'

But surely they know, the people in there right now – whoever they are. This was where, and this was the night. And this was where, once upon a time, it all began, with the best of intentions, all three of them, Bob, Sarah, Kristina. A fairy-tale, a mini-Switzerland.

Before I came in on the picture.

Curtains drawn. An amber glow. How many times have I sat like this, watching but not seeing, guessing but not knowing. How do we know what's inside?

I might have lived my life and never known it. A blow to the chest. Though what does it have to do with knowing? I hardly knew her. I'd met her three times. A cup of coffee, a drink. Sarah Nash, a client. I didn't know her enough to know what she could do. And yet I did, I knew it, I spun the wheel round, turned the car. I didn't know her, like she didn't know herself.

It's not having or keeping – it's not even knowing.

This one is not like the others who go into the files. The file in the cabinet, the file in the head. Photo, fingerprint, distinguishing marks. In this one's case the file will always have been lost. It's not fair, it's not just, it goes beyond the law, but it works the other way too. Whatever you are, whatever you do, there'll always be this someone for you who won't let *you* disappear.

A going beyond the law. I never knew who I was, either, I never knew myself. I spun the wheel. I sped through Wimbledon, up Wimbledon Hill. I might have been falling through space.

I stopped right here. I charged past the constable. The bobby, the rozzer, the ploddie, the boy in blue. 'Police.' And there I was on the scene of the crime, all eyes on me, as if I was the perpetrator come back to announce, to confess: it was me.

Sarah was sitting in a chair. She looked – in her own home – like she too had shown up from nowhere, from another world. A policewoman was standing beside her. In different circumstances, in a different story, the police-woman's arm might have been around her. And if I hadn't known it before (but I did), I knew it now. If I hadn't felt it before, I felt it now. A stab to the heart.

Bob's body was between us. We looked at each other, amazed. I might have sworn it aloud, there and then, in front of police witnesses. Ends of the earth. Beyond.

61

Rita said, 'But she didn't have to do it, did she?'

Looking at me cagily but keenly at the same time, softly but sharply, as if she was a version of Marsh – Marsh in a pale-pink top – and my office had become a nick. My own office, but Rita had hauled me in for a session.

'Stick a knife in him. Take her revenge – like that.'

Looking at me cagily but with a small glint of triumph. Well, George, you got in right out of your depth there. But you're back on shore now, safe back on shore with me.

Tea, sweet and strong. Not even bothering to ask. Not even bothering to ask if she could step in with her own mug of tea and park herself by my desk. The morning after. She knew about mornings after. Remembering maybe, right then, her own little mission of revenge, or whatever it was. Me waiting outside, looking at the windows of a house. Wish me luck.

'It wasn't revenge, Reet.'

My own office at nine in the morning. Familiar and utterly weird. I'd been up all night. Nothing odd in that – an occupational hazard. But not under investigation myself.

And now under Rita's.

'It wasn't revenge.'

'No?'

This might have been the moment for it all to come out. You can tell Rita, you can tell Rita everything. In your own words, take your time. But I stared into my tea, gripping the mug tight like people do in a state of shock. Why, except for some old, mad sense of duty (duty?) had I even bothered to show up?

I looked up. Rita looked as if she could pounce.

Back again and not back again, George and not George. More like some strange unpredictable animal in a zoo.

George, she might have said, you look a bloody mess.

And suppose on that night, years ago, when she strode up that front path, things had taken a different turn, got out of hand? She'd come back a wild, changed, glaring thing, holding up her spread hands?

'No? Not revenge? So what was it?' she snapped. 'An accident? Self-defence?'

She checked herself, bit her lip, but I pictured it – the whole picture: Sarah in the dock, Rita in the jury – the jury a whole jury of Ritas. No discussion: put the bitch away.

I think she saw me seeing it. She looked at me suddenly as if I was floating away. Her face went soft again – scornful and soft at the same time.

Out of his depth, the fool, and still out there, flailing in the current.

My interrogator, my rescuer.

'If it was revenge,' I said, 'would she have gone about it like that? Involved a detective?'

(Involved!)

'When I phoned her, from the airport, she sounded so
– so—'

Something, at last, uncontrollable in my voice. Rita put down her mug of tea. What she was waiting for – like the waiting tray, with clients. Nurse Rita.

'—so glad.'

My office. The oatmeal carpet. The two-tone filing cabinets, some black, some sealing-wax red. All Rita's work. The vase of flowers. The framed photos on the wall: scenes of Wimbledon a hundred years ago. A horse and cart outside the Rose and Crown. Why this should put clients at their ease I don't know.

Helen had come once and glanced quickly round. I think she sussed Rita straight away.

I caught myself, collected myself.

'So who knows?' I said. 'Who knows how it happened?'

I looked, steadily enough, into Rita's eyes.

'Who knows?' I said.

She might have given a snort. *Who knows?* What kind of language was that for a detective? I was supposed to know, supposed to find out. My job. And – so it appeared – I'd *been* there, I'd been at the bloody scene.

But I did know, of course. And Sarah knew that I knew. And I knew *that*.

A sort of professional snort. But she moved her head, instead, just a shade, from side to side.

In deeper than he bloody knew. As if I'd been done for just as surely as Bob Nash, as if I'd had it coming too.

She picked up her mug.

'Well,' she might have said, 'we'll see. We'll see how the wind blows in a month or so.'

She picked up my mug. 'More tea?' It was almost like a threat. Nurse Rita. A beast of a patient.

She held the mugs as if they'd just been confiscated.

'Well, anyway, you're in no fit state, are you, to do anything round here? You'd better let me take over.'

She couldn't keep it in. 'A piece of work, if you ask me, that Mrs Nash. A nasty piece of work.'

62

Of course there was only one possible outcome, one possible plea. Marsh didn't have to waste his time with a side-issue like me.

'I did it,' she said. 'I picked up the knife and did it.'

Cut and dried. And Marsh, who'd be a 'free man' in four weeks, didn't have to go to town over it – except for that very reason. Your last case, the one you'll never really wrap up.

I see him maybe once a month. We play golf. It's what ex-policemen do. We're not exactly friends but then we couldn't exactly part company, go our separate ways – sitting there on either side of the table, just that small gap between us. Him with his time running down, me like some reject begging re-admission.

I left it up to him, but I made the offer. What to call it – a charitable, a protective impulse?

'We should have a drink some time maybe – when they've let you out. You've got my number. You don't, by any chance, play golf . . . ?'

Up to him. And – over three months later – he called. The impulse on his part? Anyone's guess.

They let you out. You can get away now: a sunshine cruise, a cottage by the sea. All the time in the world. But it doesn't work like that. Something nags, something grates under your skin. You wake up every morning as if something's still unsolved.

He knows, of course. My twice-monthly visits. He even asks, like you ask after someone's ailing wife, 'How is she?' This woman he had the job of putting where she is.

He looks at me sometimes, still, as if I'm the sick one, the sad one, the crazy one. But then – I made the offer, he made the call.

'How is she?'

'She's okay.'

(What do you say: 'She's fine'?)

We watch each other's game. Trail each other up the fairway. I play with a certain edge (early training as a kid), if neither of us is exactly top-league. But sometimes – I think he knows – I let him win. He outranks me, after all, in a manner of speaking. (Though I'd have made Super.) But it's not the golf really – that's the thing about golf, for me, it's not the golf. It's the walk and the talk. It's the way you can talk when you're looking at something else, shielding your eyes to gauge a line, a distance, not staring face to face.

The whack of a decent drive, and the ball will sit and wait for you patiently, far away. The breeze in the silver birches, the scent of clipped grass. These moments when a golf course can seem like perfect safety.

Of course, when the moment seemed right, I offered him a job. An impulse, a serious proposition, I don't know. Of course I thought of the business implications. A partnership – or I'd always be the boss? I thought of my own hours away from the job these days. My visiting days, my drop-offs and collections. And who knows where one day I might have to go? I thought, of course, of Rita.

All the time in the world. But what you find is that you're at a loose end, something gnaws inside.

He thought about it, he seriously thought about it. A sort of shelter. A retired cop with a restless, searching look in his face. And maybe he reckoned there was a second deal, on top of the first. If he took the job, worked with me – for me – then he'd really get me to talk. He'd get the whole picture, the whole story at last.

But he said no, for the reasons I might have predicted, if in his own careful words. It wasn't him really, not his sort of thing. Bugs under the bed. Spying. Catching husbands in the act. A look of sudden correctness, a schoolmaster's look.

So: golf partners only. Keeping up the connection (the offer still technically stands). Sometimes I think I'm his minder, sometimes he must think he's mine. And one day, he still thinks, he'll get the whole picture.

'I did it,' she said. (What else could she say?) 'Something came over me and I did it.'

It's what they all say, in one form or another (I've heard them): the ones it takes by surprise, the ones who had no intention, no idea, no earthly inkling and are simply amazed at what they've done. Something came over me. As if it was them – they don't deny it – but not them either. Someone else came along.

'I did it.' End of case, end of story. Marsh didn't have to give me the third degree. As if I might have said, 'But, actually, she's right — someone else came along. You're looking at him, you're looking at your man.'

As if I might have waited outside, here, that night. The get-away man. Waiting for it to happen, knowing it was happening. At least I didn't do that.

He came back, but he was already a ghost, a dead man. You can't kill a ghost, can you? The blade goes right through.

He parked the Saab on the gravel. It was still there of course, just minutes later, getting in the way of the ambulance, the police cars. He didn't drive it straight into the garage, in the usual routine fashion — a simple matter of activating the automatic door. But this wasn't routine. As if he might have been not intending to stay, this was just some weird visit. Or, better interpretation: she'd been listening out and had already come to the door. She was already standing there.

So, on this of all occasions, was he going to mess around with garage doors? Not go straight to her arms?

But she didn't come to the door. That's been established. And ghosts don't think of garage doors. She'd heard the sound, the crackle of the tyres. But she wanted to wait (I know this) for that other clinching sound: the key in the door. That thing returning husbands do. Just a key in the door but no one turns it like them. A key in a door, the key to a life.

So she waited. Those simple, irreversible moments. Suppose she *had* come to the door? Stood in the light while he stood there in the dark. Who knows?

She's asking these same questions again tonight, asking them for ever, going over each second. She wanted him to find her in the warmth of the kitchen, to breathe the smell of what was cooking, a smell he'd surely recognize.

A raw November night. The tang, outside, of rotting leaves. He got out of the car, stepped across the gravel. His last steps, but he had no idea. They weren't like his own steps anyway. What was he doing here? He'd left himself, left himself for dead, in that flat. As if he was already visiting his past, this life he'd once had. This house, this comfortable, enviable life. This wife he'd loved. She must still be here.

He moved towards the front door. There was a porch arrangement – the porch light was on – with an outer, unlocked door, then the front door proper. He might have stayed there for a while between the two doors, decompressing, adjusting, working his lungs like a diver, understanding that this was his last chance to be himself again. But Sarah says she heard the sound of the outer door – it would make a soft 'clunk' – and then the sound of the key almost immediately. She took that lack of a gap as a good sign, a confirmation. The sound of the key.

She said her heart leapt. Her own words. Her 'heart leapt'. That's what she said. I don't know what she said to Marsh. It's just an expression, of course, words aren't things, things aren't words. She was conscious of her own heart, literally, as if a key had turned in it too. Just an expression, and any doctor – like Bob Nash – will tell you the heart's just a thing for pumping blood and not all the other things it gets made out to be. It can't be broken or lost or unlocked. Or leap.

He opens the front door. He steps through into the hallway. The kitchen is to the left. A smell hits him, surrounds him all at once, as he steps towards the open kitchen door. A familiar and irresistible smell, but he can't, for the life of him, place it, name it, it only makes him aware of how he's not really there. He hears his wife's voice. He steps into the kitchen. Yes, this is his house, this is his wife, but it all seems utterly impossible. She sees it in his eyes. The smile on her face goes out.

The room is like an embrace. The warmth, the smell. There's a candle, lit, on the table in the corner. His wife is wearing a black dress, he half remembers it from some other time.

She's taken off an apron. She'd been chopping something. When she heard the car on the drive she'd wiped her hands and taken off the apron and wondered whether to go to the door – but decided to wait for the key. The smile on her face – but it's gone now – was partly a simple smile of relief. It's been most of two hours since she received a phone call.

What's the smell, what's the smell? It comes from somewhere far off, from long ago. It should be doing its work, in spite of everything. It should be winding its way through his nostrils and his stomach to take hold of that other thing that's close to the stomach. But it's as though there's nothing left of him inside, he's drained away. She sees it.

He'd hoped, maybe, to be saved, brought back to life. The only reason why he's here. A magic wand, a magic potion. What's the *smell*? But he's too far gone, it's too late. She sees it.

And it's not a magic wand his wife's got in her hand.

She sees it. He knows it. He even knows now it's not to be saved that he's come.

Who moves towards who? They move towards each other. Neither holds back. I see it like one of those sequences of film played backwards, so the victim who's been struck down seems to leap towards the blow. A trick. But this is how she told me (told me and not Marsh) it was.

It took two. Something came over him as well.

And, of course, at such a moment, without any practice, without any previous training (another thing Marsh would have to puzzle over), she would have found the spot, the very spot, the only spot that counted. Without even aiming, but without missing, or even striking a rib first. Something takes over. As if her hand was being surely pulled to its mark.

She did it. Took the knife. It happened. She couldn't have known, he couldn't have known. You never know. A five-year-old girl in my father's studio, by a vase of flowers.

63

ALL THE SMILES he must have winkled out in his time . . .

She said it – smiling herself – as if that was what he'd left to be remembered by: stacks of smiles, a lifetime of smiles. It was his business of course, he was in the smile trade, and they weren't real, half of those smiles, just the trick of the moment. His job, his challenge: to get the smile, no matter the mood, the resistance, the reluctance. And then there it would be, fixed in black and white, a glossy finish, as if it were true and for always: a smile.

But with her it really was the genuine and permanent article and nothing to do (though it's how it all began, one summer in Broadstairs) with looking at a camera. He'd made *her* smile, she couldn't deny it. Look, she was even smiling now.

A bench. Would I do it for her? His name, and then, when the time came, hers. It didn't matter, it didn't make any difference – what she knew now.

Of course I'd do it, she had my promise. And I saw to both things, the two tasks, not so long after each other as it turned out, while I was still in the Force.

You can go there now, to Chislehurst Common, and sit down, courtesy of Jane and Frank Webb and their son George, whose name you won't see, who used to be a policeman.

It's lasted well, over ten years now: a good teak bench, the lettering carved in two stages. Though, if and when the time comes, I mean to get it replaced. Exact replica, same spot.

All this I've told Sarah, of course. I've written it down, it makes a story: my homework.

But I've never told Sarah – I don't know why, since it's what really makes the story – that in my dad's life and even at his death there was this other woman, another woman he must have loved, to speak her name even when he was dying.

I've never told Sarah, just as I never told Mum that I'd known all along.

I just told Sarah about the bench.

'Will you do it for me?'

It must have been only a fortnight or so after he died.

'Of course I'll do it.'

'Thank you, George . . .'

And then she told me (I'd never known) how Dad got into cameras in the first place, into the photo trade, into being a beach photographer, snapping all those holiday girls.

It was in the army. The war was over by the time he got posted to Germany, but only just.

'Displaced persons,' she said.

They gave him a camera and told him how to use it. He had to take photos of displaced persons, to go in the

288

records – yes, just like in the police. Displaced persons, no shortage of them.

'That was his job,' she said. 'Displaced persons, hundreds of them. Someone had to do it. You couldn't say: "Smile."'

'Think of all the reasons,' Charlie Rose would say, 'why people buy flowers . . .'

Well, one of them was Dad's funeral. Another was Mum's.

You can have flowers sent into the prison if you use the approved florist.

'Think of all the reasons, and you tell me . . .'

Just one of his lines, the lines he'd trot out for everyone, a needle in the groove. A big hefty man, with a life in flowers.

Another was: 'Second best thing I ever did: open up a flower shop.' And he'd look at you sharply as if you'd just had your cue. But even if you didn't jump to it, he'd say, 'The *first* best thing? You want to know what the *first* best thing was?'

You had to run with it by now – beg not to be left in the dark.

'You're looking at her,' he'd say. 'You're looking at her.'

And he'd cock his head to Katy Rose, his wife.

64

RITA SAID IT COULDN'T go on – this nonsense. She was telling me for my own good. My own good.

She wouldn't mince words, she wouldn't stand on ceremony. And she hadn't: opening my door without a warning, without a knock, marching in like a dawn raid. So I thought yet again of that husband of years back, who I'd never seen, behind a closed door. Rita coming with her final word. As if I was on the receiving end now.

'Grow up, George. Get bloody real.'

Someone had to tell me. It couldn't go on.

But it had gone on now, for a whole year. Since this was almost exactly a year ago: the morning after I first went – the first anniversary – to Putney Vale. I hadn't said, but she knew. In her calendar too. I'd only said I was going out, I'd be out of the office for the rest of the morning. But she could have figured it out anyway. Might have watched me – then too – crossing the street to Jackson's.

And she hadn't said anything either, on the day itself. Held her tongue, waited. Her own hard-put-to-it mark of respect. Maybe.

But now.

And, like a fool, I'd confessed, I'd told her, when I got back. As if she had the dirt on me anyway. As if she'd *been* there, watching – trailed me all the way to Putney Vale, caught me in the act.

It was a first offence, and this was just a caution – a stiff caution – but it had to stop.

'Flowers! For God's sake. Flowers! Not just bloody visits. Flowers – on *his* grave for *her*!'

Though there were flowers in the vase that morning. Office flowers. Yellow chrysanths.

She must have decided on it, calculated: wait till the morning. A showdown, a face-to-face. If time itself, a whole year, hadn't done the work – he needed telling. He needed a damn good shaking out of himself.

Her last chance maybe. And maybe his.

She must have summoned up her nerve, taken a breath, patted her skirt.

And, now I think about it, I know it wasn't just all fire and fury. For my own good. Her face was all ablaze (she looked splendid) but there was this cooler, steadier light in her eye. I think she saw me just becoming sad – just a sad pathetic case. She didn't want that, for my own sake she genuinely didn't want that.

'Snap out of it, George.'

And she must have known it was all or nothing. The bravery! It could all backfire. All her guns again at once. If it didn't work, if I didn't snap out of it, what would be left? Sadness all round.

'Can't you see? A year. How many more years? You don't even know. Don't you see? It's a cold trail.'

That's the phrase she used. A cold trail. It came out of

her hot face. A professional phrase, a detective's phrase. All the successful cases – all the missions accomplished and fees duly received – and, of course, all the cold trails . . .

It's just a phrase but I could see it like a thing. A long empty path, stony and bare.

'Sit down, Rita. Please. You don't have to stand.'

But some things, she said, you had to say standing up. She was saying them. She'd only blame herself if she never said them.

Her hope, and her gamble – though once it had seemed like a safe enough bet: what man wouldn't come to his senses eventually? What man was going to sign himself over to a murderess?

But it wasn't working: the cautioning, the shaking. It wasn't working, she could see it. And maybe it was bad timing after all, not good timing at all, the worst timing. The morning after. Standing and refusing to sit. As if, suddenly, *she* was on the mat and it was me who'd called her in – to give her a talking-to, a dressing down. Her marching orders, even.

All the other way round.

Fireworks, waterworks. The light in her eye becoming a sticky shine. But she was damned (I could see it) if she was going to go in that direction. Damned. She'd been there before, once, long ago – once too often, maybe. Legs firmly planted, head held high.

'Please, Rita – sit down.'

'If you can't listen, George, if you can't be told. It's your bloody life. It's your bed – some bloody bed – well, you lie in it.'

'Rita—'

Now all she could do was close her mouth, look tight-lipped at me, turn around, show me her arse – which at least wasn't a locked-up arse, an arse behind bars. Now all she could do was say to herself that she'd had her say. Much good it had done.

She'd have to walk out, shut the door firmly. No slamming – sometimes you didn't slam. There'd be an awful silence, a pause, on both sides, and she'd have to pray for the telephone to ring – 'GW Investigations, good morning' – so we could click back into our roles again like robots.

And she'd have to hang on to her dignity somehow, adjust her position, get a grip on *herself*. A sad case . . .

Well, he could have pity, if that's what he wanted – if that's what he didn't mind having. I'll give him pity . . . He might have had something else.

A sad case – a case all right. But you can't stay on a case for ever.

I could stay here all night. As if to prevent it, as if to make it unhappen. A different turn of events this time. Look, they're in there together, right now: Bob and Sarah. They're home, they're happy.

The house looks calm, calm and safe. Can houses be acquitted, let off? It wasn't *their* fault. Someone looking out from one of those lit windows might see it all the other way round: I'm the sinister element round here. There's a man out there, in a car, just sitting there, a suspicious-looking character . . .

I should be home in the warm. No job for a man my age, but it gets in the blood. A night watchman.

It's okay – I was just passing, keeping an eye, seeing all's well.

I start the engine. Almost twenty past five. Over three hours to go yet. And I have to see Mrs Lucas at a quarter to six – to show her the photos. Rita will be looking at her watch, waiting for my key in the street door. My God! – but no, Rita isn't the murdering type.

None of us is.

I turn the car and drive away. I came. I know I'll come back in another year. I'll go to his grave in another year. And another . . .

I turn left out of Beecham Close, down the hill. Inside me is a glow. As if I'm the black shell of a house at night, lit up inside.

65

IT'S HARD TO THINK of an emperor in Chislehurst . . .
Of course, he wasn't an emperor then. An ex-emperor, a
fallen emperor, just the husk of an emperor with less than
two years left to live.

'*Napoleon III, Empereur des Français y mourut . . .*'

The emperor of a golf course. Eighteen greens, each
with a flag fluttering over it like a little conquest – except
it wasn't a golf course then, it was a private estate. And
Chislehurst then, like Wimbledon, would have been more
or less a village in the country, not yet conquered by the
suburbs. London on the march. The empire of the suburbs.

All the same, I couldn't help imagining him looking
out from a window of that club house, that home for
fallen emperors, to where we trailed back, that Sunday
morning – one golf ball less between us.

As if he should have been interested in us. As if he
should have been keeping an eye on us.

Nearly forty years ago now.

Of course he wasn't looking out. It's me who's looking
out, at my memory. Dad, me, my dad's loose-talking pal
– Donald? Dots in the distance . . .

But then Napoleon III, when he looked out, would have looked out, mostly, at his memory – since he was only what was left of an emperor, most of his life was done. So that in that green space before him, which he didn't know would become a golf course, he might have pictured everything that had come before. Through the smoke of a cigar, maybe, the smoke and carnage of all those battles: Magenta, Solferino, Sedan.

Big statements weren't ever my dad's thing, but once I heard him say – I think he got it from someone else, someone at that club – that where there were golf courses there was civilization and where there was civilization there were golf courses. A shaky statement anyway – though one most senior-ranking police officers would back up.

What would my mum have thought? Where there were department stores? Park benches?

And Helen? Where there was Art? Interior design?

And Napoleon himself? A green space. Blue smoke.

He used to play around, apparently – Sarah's told me all about him. Other women. He called them his 'distractions'. It wasn't a rock-solid marriage, him and Eugénie. There would have been imperial tiffs. But she played around too – in the other direction – with politics, affairs of state: his department. So people would say it was the Empress who was really in charge. And she led him up some pretty unfortunate paths.

She was Spanish by birth. Strong-minded, ambitious, beautiful. But devoted. He was always a bit of a ditherer – a bit distracted – and, for a leader of armies, a bit short on command.

But she staked her life on his. After the disaster of Sedan she fled in a coach from Paris to the coast – no longer an empress, just a woman on the run. At any point she might have been stopped, hauled out and killed. Then, when she was safe on an English boat – it's a good story – she almost died when a terrible storm blew up in the Channel.

All to reach Chislehurst.

She got there first. He had a trickier escape – being at the mercy of the Prussians. She waited for him. He might never have turned up.

And then when they were both safe in Chislehurst, all hell broke loose, apparently, back in France.

I suppose Sarah's been my history teacher too.

How would they have pronounced it? *'Cheez-le-'urst'*?

She had her health. He was already a seriously sick man. Gallstones. At Sedan, maddened by the pain of gallstones as well as by approaching defeat, he'd spurred his horse toward the thickest enemy fire.

But no such luck. He died in bed in Chislehurst.

'. . . le 9 Janvier 1873.'

So she outlived him by those nearly fifty years. Till 1920. And so she might actually have seen, for all I know, the grounds of their home, their place of exile, turned into a golf course.

Those nearly fifty years. That's the strangest part. The part that draws Sarah, I know. Twenty years of marriage. Seventeen years of empire. Nearly fifty years of afterwards.

Half her life still left. She still liked to play around – in different ways now. A plucky, feisty, not-so-old bird, ready to have a go. Motor cars – those weird new things. Yachting in the Med. It must have seemed like a dream, having once been an empress. Going back to Paris – staying in a hotel.

But it had all turned strange. Their son – the son who might have been an emperor – was killed in the British army, fighting the Zulus. The second big blow of her life: she still had over forty years to go.

But the strangest thing of all maybe is that, all that time, there was no one else. She never remarried. No one to take the Emperor's place.

He was our claim to fame. Our bit of suburban importance. He put Chislehurst on the map. Like tennis has put Wimbledon on the map. Though if everyone knows about Agassi and Sampras, not so many people know about Napoleon III.

And the truth is Chislehurst had another, prior claim to fame – and when I was a kid I thought about it more than I thought about Napoleon III.

The caves. The Chislehurst Caves.

First there'd been a village among the fields, then a suburb, with a high street and a golf course, but before all that there'd been the caves: a whole network of them, miles of them, just a tiny part of which – the rest was sealed off – you could go and visit.

No one knew how they'd first got there. An unsolved mystery, disappearing into the dark. I remember being taken there by Mum and Dad, after we moved from Lewisham. Maybe I was five. Listening to the guide. The echoes, the maze of tunnels, the stories of ghosts. The feeling that you might never get back into the light.

The caves ran everywhere. They must have run under our house. Under the golf course. They were supposed to be prehistoric – the earliest people had taken refuge in them. They were supposed to have been lived in by druids.

Or they were just underground quarries, ancient mines for chalk and flint.

But one undisputed fact was that they'd been used as a natural shelter only years before. In the air raids in the war. The guide explained – but people could remember. Mum and Dad must have remembered. The sealed parts had been opened up. People had huddled where once primitive tribes had huddled. Thousands of people, apparently, more than ten thousand people. It's hard to imagine. Chislehurst had gone underground.

66

THE TANNING CENTRE is doing good trade. As I turn the corner into the Broadway and walk towards my office I see a girl going in almost collide with another coming out. The place stays open till well into the evening (those naked bodies, below me, even if I'm working late), and now it's November and the nights have drawn in, its business seems to pick up, as if there's a reverse effect. Tans in winter, sunshine in the dark. Anything is possible these days.

The shop windows gleam. The lights of Broadway. It's an old joke which people in Wimbledon must have made a thousand times, but it doesn't stop me making it again (to ease things along with clients). I have an office on Broadway. I look out on the lights of Broadway.

The two girls laugh as they step round each other.

Sometimes I see it as I think Sarah must see it, in her mind's eye. Another world, like a dream, weird in its goings-on.

Through the Tanning Centre window, as I reach my street door, I see the rattan chairs, the tomato-red cushions, the potted palm. As if you've already arrived in

Marrakesh. The girl who's just entered looking all wrong in her coat.

I fish out my key and open the street door. It's just a plain black door, slightly set back, between the Tanning Centre and a chemist's — and it looks vaguely unlikely, like a trick door, as if it will lead to just a gap between two walls or to some secret unsuspected passage.

Sarah would have stood here once, wondering. One crisp, bright morning.

There's a brass letter box, a key-hole plate, a brass door knob that doesn't turn and is just for show. In the recess to the side there's a bell-push and entry-phone and a little discreet sign that says 'GW Investigations'.

I open the door. The narrow stairs go straight up with just the briefest strip of floor — you can't call it a hall, a lobby or anything — before the first step. It's not appealing, it can't encourage clients. But then it must be also what they expect: the feeling of something behind-the-scenes and sly, the feeling of being squeezed.

Not the broad way, the narrow way.

I look up. Rita's standing at the top of the stairs. That's not usual for her, to get up and stand there when I arrive, and I have the sudden feeling that in my absence everything's changed places. There's been a revolution. It's Rita's office now. She's about to kick me downstairs.

Or: I'm not the boss any more, the man who works here, just some visiting client (business unknown) and Rita's there to greet me — I know she does it with clients — to soften the effect of these uninviting stairs.

She looks like an air hostess up there, at the door of the plane.

It's almost twenty to six. I've been a while but I'm not

too late for Mrs Lucas. And Rita knows where I've been (not counting Beecham Close). Is she in a mood? Relieved? Glad to see me? Or did she just want to catch my face, read my expression, before I had time to prepare it for her?

I climb. I think of my dreams of Dyson. But it's suddenly obvious why she's standing there. A series of little signals, a tap of her watch, a jerk of her head towards my office. I get the picture. Mrs Lucas has already arrived, early, and Rita's shown her in to my desk – all smiles, no doubt, offering tea and saying I'll be along in just a moment.

And now she says in a crisp and all-explaining voice, 'Mrs Lucas is waiting for you, Mr Webb.'

All the same, she looks at me closely as I take off my coat. Do I look strange? I've no idea how my face reads.

'The file, the photos?' I whisper.

'Right here.' She points.

She takes my coat, my scarf. I straighten my tie. It's like something going on hurriedly in a cupboard. I take the file and envelope. She reaches out suddenly and, lightly, quickly, smooths my hair. I can't remember her doing that before. Do I look a mess? She smiles oddly – as if a smile was the last thing she'd meant. Her pink-wool bosom juts.

'Ready?' she says. And that's odd too, as if I'm about to go on stage.

I walk into my office as if I've been gently pushed.

'Mrs Lucas, I'm sorry to have kept you.' Not the best opening line.

I've met her before, of course: the preliminary meeting. Good-looking, late thirties, well dressed. Well heeled. She's sitting, legs crossed, cradling a cup of tea. No nervousness. If anything, pleased to have the edge on me by being there first, taking a peek at what's on my desk.

'I was early,' she says. A briskish smile.

The hard, I-mean-business type. Information, confirmation . . . But you never know how they'll react when you show them – the proof.

I move round to my seat. She looks at the bundle under my arm.

The room smells of furniture polish. Rita's been tidying up, I can see, while I've been out. But she hasn't drawn the blind on my window. Black glass – Wimbledon might not be there – like unexposed film.

I put the file to one side, put the envelope in front of me and plant my clasped hands firmly on top of it. A little polite cough into my knuckles before I begin.

She leans forward – alert, even a little eager – puts down her cup and saucer. Brown eyes. I see the ring on her finger. How do we choose?

Why should she react to the photos? They're not photos of horrors, atrocities. Just of two people being – nice to each other. They're not like the things you see in the police, the things that have to be noted and photographed. The things juries sometimes have thrust under their noses.

But you have to be ready for anything (Rita will be standing by outside). I keep my hands clasped on the envelope, clear my throat again, and before I say them I hear the words I've said so many times.

'Mrs Lucas, I always say to my clients at this point that it's still possible, should they wish, should they have reconsidered, to go no further. This – evidence – can be destroyed. A simple matter. We're not in court. No one need know.'

It's like reading them their rights.

67

Rita said, 'It'll fade.'

Her final shot, a year ago – standing there in front of my desk, her eyes with that shine in them that might have gone either way. Showers, frost. A cold trail, it'll fade.

A final shot which, when it came to it, was more like an offer of mercy, a reprieve. She only wanted to spare me – didn't I see? Future pain and regret. Future looking-a-fool. Even more than I looked now.

Didn't I see what was ahead – and didn't I see what was standing in front of me right now?

She should have turned, walked out on me, but she seemed to dig her heels deeper into the carpet.

And no, she wasn't going to melt, spill over, use that last cheap trick. (Though it often happens, it's well known, it's often how it begins, the tearful assistant in the boss's office: ask a divorce lawyer, ask a private detective.)

The shine in her eyes was simply Rita's shine, Rita's aura.

Look at me, George. The goods may be past their best, but at least you've seen what you're getting. Think about

it, George. A cold trail, a cold bed. You haven't even see
her naked.

(The things you can read in the shine of an eye.)

No? Not seen her naked? Not when they took her
away – dressed for something different – in a police car.
Not when I first went to see her where she is now?

Not seen her naked?

'Think about it, George. It'll fade.'

But it doesn't fade. It's not true what they say, that it
fades, it cools with the years. It grows, it blooms, the
less time that's left. Eight, nine years . . . How long do
we have? Things get more precious, not less. That's one
thing I've learnt. And what we have here inside us we
might never know, there's no detecting it. That's another
thing I've learnt.

It might never happen, we might never know. A spring
coiled inside us waiting for release.

Eight, nine years . . . But one day I'll go for the last
time, one day I won't be just a visitor or come back alone.

Rita might have left me a year ago. I know she's going
to leave me now.

One day it won't be years but months, not months
but weeks. Not weeks but days. One day it will be just a
case of a simple small step, across a line that can't even be
seen. A simple, huge step. It might even seem like another
edge, like going over another edge.

But I'll be there, I'll be there, sweetheart, to catch you.

How will it be? How many times have I pictured it,
dreamt it, rehearsed it? I know it's foolish. A November
day? Though why should it be November? A foggy murky

November day. Sometimes, I don't know why, I've pictured it like that. I've dreamt I'm held up, fogbound, trapped in nightmare traffic jams. My God, I'll be late – on *this* day.

(I know I'll be hours early.)

Fog. Everything hidden and lost. Would that be right? To slip back into the world when it's only half there. Secretly and undercover at first – the full thing might be too much. Like prisoners who step the other way under a blanket, as if they're naked, through the last stab of light.

A blanket of fog. Here, have this blanket. All the blankets.

A foggy day, everything wrapped in grey.

No. I want it to be like this day, that's already slipped into night. A hard night coming, you can tell already, another hard frost. But tomorrow will be like today, brilliant, blue and still.

I want it to be like today. When I'm there, when I'm waiting, heart thudding, my breath billowing before my eyes, when she comes back, steps out at last into the clear light of day.

picador.com

blog
videos
interviews
extracts